Hating
Valentine's
Day

W9-AZH-803

Allison Rushby

Hating Valentine's Day

**RED
DRESS
INK**™

If you purchased this book without a cover you should be aware
that this book is stolen property. It was reported as "unsold and
destroyed" to the publisher, and neither the author nor the
publisher has received any payment for this "stripped book."

HATING VALENTINE'S DAY

A Red Dress Ink novel

ISBN 0-373-89566-6

© 2005 by Allison Rushby.

All rights reserved. The reproduction, transmission or utilization
of this work in whole or in part in any form by any electronic, mechanical
or other means, now known or hereafter invented, including xerography,
photocopying and recording, or in any information storage or retrieval
system, is forbidden without written permission. For permission please
contact Red Dress Ink, Editorial Office, 225 Duncan Mill Road,
Don Mills, Ontario, Canada M3B 3K9.

All characters in this book have no existence outside the imagination of
the author and have no relation whatsoever to anyone bearing the same
name or names. They are not even distantly inspired by any individual
known or unknown to the author, and all incidents are pure invention.
Any resemblance to actual persons, living or dead, is entirely coincidental.

® and TM are trademarks. Trademarks indicated with ® are registered in
the United States Patent and Trademark Office, the Canadian Trade Marks
Office and/or other countries.

www.RedDressInk.com

Printed in U.S.A.

ALLISON RUSHBY

Having failed at becoming a ballerina with pierced ears (her childhood dream), Allison Rushby instead began a writing career as a journalism student at the University of Queensland in Brisbane, Australia. Within a few months she had slunk sideways into studying Russian. By the end of her degree she had learned two very important things: that she didn't want to be a journalist, and that here are hundreds of types of vodka and they're all pretty good.

A number of years spent freelancing for numerous wedding magazines almost made her crazy. After much whining about how hard it would be, she began her first novel. That is, her husband (then boyfriend) told her to shut up, sit down and get typing (there may, or may not, have been threats of severing digits with rusty scalpels if she didn't but it's okay, he's a doctor).

These days Allison divides her days between motherhood and writing full-time, mostly with her cat, Violet, on her lap. Oh, and she keeps up her education by sampling new kinds of vodka on a regular basis.

Hate Valentine's Day with a passion? Feel free to have a vent about it at www.allisonrushby.com.

**Also by Allison Rushby
and available from Red Dress Ink:**

It's Not You It's Me

ACKNOWLEDGMENTS

I'd like to thank Jane Dystel and Miriam Goderich for their help in bringing the book to its full potential; Sam Bell for seeing what was underneath the rubble; the literate guinea pigs who read the manuscript in various stages; Ivy for putting up with the long sits on the couch, the laptop radiation and for only kicking me in the ribs when she was truly uncomfortable or we needed more cookies; Violet for keeping my toes warm while we were all on the couch; and David for the walks, when the long sits on the couch got just that bit too long.

FriDAY 5 February—
nine DAYS to go...

I draw a bright red fake zit on the end of the bride's nose and, satisfied, sit back to admire my handiwork. Sally, who happens to be walking by at the time, stops behind me and places a hand on my shoulder. 'Liv, sweetheart, if I've told you once, I've told you a thousand times. You're supposed to be taking them off, not putting them on.'

'Yes, boss.' I sigh and, without turning around, pick up the computer's pen once more and run it over the palette lying on the desk. I keep right on drawing on the picture that's up on the screen—the bride in her hotel room surrounded by a bevy of bridesmaids. This time I add a pair of horns over the bride's tiara and fangs over her newly whitened teeth. Still behind me, Sally leans over and takes the pen out of my hand. Within seconds, little red dots appear on the bride's eyes. I look up and laugh.

Sally goes over to lean up against the steel counter that runs the length of one of the studio walls.

'Couldn't help myself. She was a particularly silly cow, remember?'

I don't remember.

'I give it three years, max,' Sally says, coming back over to take one last look. I glance up to see three fingers, then, 'Coffee?' she says brightly, taking off for the kitchen, her lavender sandals making little clip-clop noises on the polished floorboards and her glossy, perfectly highlighted blonde hair waving behind her.

'Yes, thanks,' I say, watching as she makes her way around the tiny galley-style kitchen, filling the pot with coffee and putting a few biscuits on a plate. I try one last time to place the couple before I give up. 'I don't know why you make these bets with yourself. Thirty years, three years, three months…you never find out if you're right or not.'

Sally stops what she's doing and looks at me. 'And why shouldn't I make those bets? I do it with my own relationships. May as well gamble on everyone else while I'm at it.' She inspects the lip of the mug she's got in her hand, then rubs it with one finger. Remnants of her favourite lipgloss, most likely. 'I probably *am* right, you know. I've always been spot-on with all my husbands. Three and a half years with Simon, two with Tom, seven months with Luke…'

I try not to laugh out loud at that. *All My Husbands*—it sounds like a good name for a daytime soap. And with Sally's exes there'd never be a lack of characters to bribe/maim/kill off/lapse into a coma only to return in the fifteenth season with amnesia.

I get up and have a stretch before going over to retrieve my coffee from the bench. The two of us carry our mugs over to the sitting area and I take the yellow armchair while Sally stretches out, putting her feet up on the red couch. She offers me the plate of biscuits, one already sticking out of her mouth, and groans as she munches away. 'See what you've got me doing? I can't have a fag, so I'll eat half a packet of biscuits instead.'

I take a biscuit. 'You can have a fag.'

'Only if I beg. And only *outside*.'

'Hey, it's your rule! I'm only supposed to be enforcing it, remember?' A few weeks ago Sally had decided she was giving up the tar sticks of death (her words) for good. She'd decided the best way to go about it was to give me, one of the only non-smokers she knew, any packet she bought. Then, if she wanted a cigarette, she'd have to give me good reason why. I'd handed out approximately ten so far, mostly after she'd fielded phone calls from her third ex-husband regarding their divorce settlement. Ten seemed an awfully small number seeing as before this she'd been a pack-a-day smoker. I was starting to wonder where she was keeping her stash.

'I don't feel like begging. Not on a Friday afternoon. Change of topic. You geared up for next week? Been taking your guarana?'

I groan through the biscuit that's in *my* mouth now. I don't need reminding that it's Valentine's Day next Sunday. And not just because of my failed love-life. In the wedding photography business, Valentine's Day means *big* business. Especially since for the last two years the day has fallen on a Friday and a Saturday. This year it's on a Sunday. The weekend again. Weekends, of course, are always the busiest days of the week for wedding photographers. But when the fourteenth of February falls on a weekend? Let's just say Sally Bliss Photography has been booked out a year and a half in advance.

Sally laughs at me. 'Look at your face! I can never believe the change in you around Valentine's Day— you're such a grumpy-arse. Stop frowning or you'll line for good. Take it from me, there are just some miracles L'Oréal can't perform when you get to my age, however much you're "worth it".'

I stop frowning.

'That's better.' Sally puts down her coffee. 'Anyway, Valentine's Day—just smile, think of the money and remember our unofficial motto…'

We both put cheesy grins on and lift our hands to our faces as if holding invisible cameras. *Click, click.* 'Those who can't, photograph,' we sing-song in unison. And we're definitely two girls who *can't,* I think as I lower my hands again. Sally can't stay married, I can't…well, I can't be bothered.

There's silence as we both return to our caffeine intake greedily. I think we're both feeling a lack of energy. As Sally mentioned, it's Friday afternoon and I've got that drained feeling that people all over the city are sharing.

'Oh,' Sally says, making me look up from my mug. 'Don't forget about Monday. Mrs Batty–Smith's funeral.' And with that we both look over at Mrs Batty-Smith's desk in the corner and stare. 'We'll have to order a wreath,' she adds, before pausing to bite her bottom lip. 'Are there any grey flowers?'

'I don't think so.'

'I'll order something later.' She glances at her watch. 'Bugger. I've got to get going.' She takes one last sip of her coffee and pushes herself up off the couch.

'Engagement shoot?'

Sally nods, running her hands down her black capri pants to smooth out the creases. 'I won't be back this afternoon, so if you could be a darling and close up…' She winks at me. 'I've got a big date tonight.'

'Have you just? I thought you were taking a break from men? Waiting till a decent one came along?'

'Well, I was…'

'For a week?'

'I gave up smoking! I need some kind of a hobby to keep me busy.' She grabs her diary off the coffee table and has a quick flip through. 'Fabulous. The park at the end of the world again. Just what I need.' She sighs as she stuffs it in her bag and heads for the door.

I give her a sympathetic look as I get up and take my coffee over to the computer. The park at the end of the world is the bane of our lives. Sally includes an engagement shoot session in all the higher-priced wedding photography packages, and the couple get to choose the location. Bliss's studio is a few minutes out of the city, but somehow just about every couple manages to choose the park at the end of the world as the location for their engagement shoot.

'Have fun,' I say as the door slams behind my employer. She gives me a wave through the glass and mouths Ta ta.

I sit back down at my desk and undo the zit, horns, fangs and little red eye-dots on the computer screen. Just as I'm about to make a start on the bride's flabby underarm (by personal request), I catch a glimpse of yellow and look up to see Sally speed off in her Ferrari. Smoking.

So that's where she's been keeping them, I think. And, speaking of broken promises, I can't believe she's going on a date tonight! Just two weeks ago, when divorce number three finally came through and Sally was crying poor, she told me in her most sincere voice that she was taking a leaf out of my book and was going to try being single for once. Finally she was swinging around to my way of thinking—men were just too much trouble. Much easier to take up the ice-cream education style of dating that I'd adopted (sitting in front of the TV with a new 500ml flavour to sustain you for the evening—a litre if it had been a particularly hard day). Either way, Sally's single girl life hadn't lasted long. Less than a week, if you figured in when the guy had actually asked her out.

I turn my attention back to the flabby arm, which really isn't flabby at all, and edge out the tiniest sliver from underneath. Not too much, not too little. Just enough. Well, maybe a tiny bit more, I think, sitting back in my chair to take a look. I would if it was me.

As hard as I'm trying to concentrate as I move the pen back and forth over the palette, I can't help but keep catching sight of Mrs Batty-Smith's desk out of the corner of my eye. The desk Sally and I had both been staring at before. Still de-flabbing, I think about Monday and how strange it will be to go to her funeral. Strange because I know so little about her.

What I *do* know about Mrs Batty-Smith has been pieced together over time, gathered from the other wedding photographers around the city. Everyone knows one thing for sure—Mrs Batty-Smith was *the* wedding photographer to book in the sixties, when she was about my age. She wasn't Mrs Batty-Smith then, however. Back then she was Miss Smith and she was the best, commanding the highest fees anywhere in the country, photographing all the top weddings.

Celebrities, politicians, you name it—she photographed the day.

It's the more personal information that everyone's hazy on. I've been told that her husband left her at the height of her career, that this caused her to fall apart a touch and it was all downhill from there. Ten years or so after that she stopped photographing altogether. She never remarried, I know that much for sure, and she spent the rest of her days doing the books for all the wedding photographers around town.

My eyes drift away from the computer screen and I sit and stare at her desk. She was a funny old thing, Mrs Batty-Smith, crotchety as all get out, though she'd talk for ever about her eighteen cats. If you tried to get onto any other topic she'd just clam up. So, that's what we talked about on the Wednesdays she spent at the studio—her cats. I can recite all their names in the order she got them: Betsy, Shu-shu, Mitsy, Sunshine, Pokey, Hortense… The list goes on. Oh, and Mrs Batty-Smith always, *always* wore grey. I never saw her in any other colour. Grey stockings, grey cardi, grey dress, grey hair— leading to Sally's comment about the grey flowers.

She was, I have to say, a tad clichéd. Still, as awful and as grey and as clichéd as she sounds, there was something about Mrs Batty-Smith—something I'd connected with. I'd never been able to put my finger on it, but there was something there, beneath the grey clothes and surly ways…

Work. *Work*. Think about work.

With a one-more-time, here-we-go-again huff, I turn my attention back to my bride. I finish off the non-flabby arm, blend a few lines underneath her eyes and delete the mother-of-the-bride's packet of cigarettes which I spot her waving around in the background, as if she's participating in a product placement exercise. I give myself a pat on the back for that one. Fag withholding from the boss is probably in my job description, but fag deletion from photographs—now *that's* service.

The minutes creep by. I take a phone call from a prospective client and set up a meeting in two weeks' time. I phone another client to tell her that her wedding album's ready to be picked up. A few *more* minutes creep slowly by.

With nothing better to do, I start on the next photo that needs work. As I do, I start to remember the couple—he was French; she was a pain in the arse. In this picture, the groom is watching the bridesmaids fix the bride's bustle. I blend more lines, erase more flab, draw a little word bubble out of the groom's mouth that says, '*Oui*, my darling, you are right. Your *derrière* does look big in that.'

Hey, how did that get in there?

I give myself a mental slap on the wrist, remove the bubble and keep going. I manage to finish the corrections off on this picture without procrastinating again, but when I load up the next file I know it's just not going to happen. I've got the attention span of a goldfish with a new rock today, and am torturing myself needlessly—what I'm doing isn't anything that can't wait until next week.

I check the clock again. Four-thirty. I may as well knock off early, seeing as I have to swing past Rachel's. I give her a quick call to check if she's home already (even though, with her great-find cruisy new job as an English-as-a-second-language teacher at an international college, I'm pretty sure she skived off home at about two minutes past three). She picks up, just like I knew she would, and tells me to come on over.

Off the phone, I start gathering my things together and shutting up shop. When I'm done, I pull an album out of the holding cupboard. Rachel and Ryan's album from their wedding three weeks ago. Sally photographed it. I put the box on the coffee table and sit down on the couch to have one last flip through.

As everyone's do—well, I think they do. Either that, or I'm particularly vain—my eyes scan the first photo and move straight on to myself. And there I am. In a bridesmaid's outfit once again. Well, that's not quite true. In this photo I'm in a white brushed-cotton dressing gown, full make-up on and hair upswept. A 'getting ready at the hotel' photo. I lean in and take a closer look. Spectacular cheekbones I've got there, if I do say so myself. If only they were like that in real life…

I turn a few more pages before I stop again at one of the 'we're all set to leave for the church' photos. There's Rachel, looking absolutely stunningly gorgeous in her ivory gown. And me, in between the other three bridesmaids, looking...well, kind of sickly, is the phrase that comes to mind. In a lilac satin dress. A lilac number that is quite like something that I have in four other colours in my wardrobe—burgundy, navy, hot pink and pale blue.

Anyway, now Rachel's married off, I'm hoping she's going to stop with the 'insert man here' dinners. Rachel loves to entertain, and watches Nigella and Jamie like religion. Both these things would be more than fine by me and my entrée, main and dessert stomachs if it weren't for the ring-in males she invites along to these occasions.

Take, for example, last year's Rachel-hosted Valentine's Day dinner. The guy I'd been paired up with for the night asked me out at the end of the evening. We decided to go out for dinner a week later, and set a time to meet at an area where there were a number of restaurants, agreeing on a Greek place he'd been to before and enjoyed. When we met up, he confessed he'd forgotten to book, but, thinking we might get lucky anyway, we tried to get a table for two. The place was packed and the waiters looked at us like we were crazy for even asking. I remember one of them just laughed. Right in our faces! We ended up going from door to door down the restaurant strip in the hope of finally getting something to eat.

After restaurant number eight, I started to see the funny side of all of this and told him maybe we should change our names from Liv and Terry to Mary and Joseph. Actually, I thought this was so funny I could barely stop laughing and had to lean against a bus stop sign for a minute or two to catch my breath, intermittently calling out, 'There's no room at the restaurant.' I caught it, however, when I saw the look on his face. Recovering a touch, I looked at him very seriously and said in my best Deborah Kerr *An Affair to Remember* voice, 'Maybe we should book now and meet at the top of the road in six months' time. At five o'clock.'

He turned around with a huff and said, 'I don't think there's going to be a next time, Olivia.' And then he took off. Just like that! I stood there for a few minutes, wondering if he was going to come back. (He didn't.)

Maybe I went too far when I asked him where he'd parked his donkey… I don't know. I thought it was funny!

In the end I picked up some KFC on my way home (with real Coke instead of Diet, and extra seasoning sprinkled on the chips to get over the shock of being dumped *before* dinner).

Oh, well.

I look back down at the album and start flipping

over the pages again until, finally, I reach the end.
Then I close the ivory fabric-lined cover, put it back
in its box and get up off the couch.

It's beautiful outside, sunny with a completely blue
sky, and hot in the kind of way I know will be nice
while I'm coming down from the air-conditioning
I've been in for hours, but won't be so nice when I'm
sitting in traffic. There's no air-conditioning in my
yellow Ferrari. There's no yellow Ferrari either. Just a
smallish, not too oldish, but not brand-newish either,
dark green Honda hatchback that I stick my key into,
open up and get in. I put the box on the passenger
seat and set off for Rachel's house.

Y Y Y Y

'Let me see! Let me see!' Rachel says as soon as she opens the front door.

I give her the box, which she takes from me eagerly. 'Go easy, tiger, you'll hurt yourself...'

She laughs. 'Coffee?'

'Why ever not?' I follow her inside the townhouse, closing the door behind me. As we make our way through to the kitchen I wonder for a second whether I should have said yes to coffee. I've practically caffeinated myself up to the eyeballs today in order to keep going. But I guess one more can't do too much damage. Well, it might give me the odd palpitation here and there, but I'm far too young for a full-blown heart attack.

I hope.

I take a seat at the kitchen table and watch as Rachel tears around the kitchen trying to arrange mugs, coffee, sugar, milk and some good-looking blueberry muffins in the microwave all at once so she can get to the album.

'Sit down,' I say when I start to feel exhausted just watching her. 'I'll make the coffee.'

She doesn't argue, but comes straight over, plonks herself down at the table, opens the box and pulls the album out, feeling the fabric. 'Oh, it's lovely.'

By the time I bring the coffee and muffins over and take my seat again, Rachel's only on the second photo. I realise, at this rate, we could be here till Christmas.

Slowly, meticulously, taking in the detail of every photograph, she turns the pages. When she gets to a close-up of the four bridesmaids, she finally looks up at me, back down again, and up one more time. 'Nice cheekbones.'

I shrug. 'Hey, a girl's got to do what a girl's got to do.'

'Yes, well. You seem to have done a whole lot.' Rachel keeps turning until she reaches the end of the album. 'I love this one,' she says, turning back the pages and pointing to one photo in particular.

I take a look. It's my favourite. An intimate shot of Rachel and Ryan talking, their heads together, that Sally caught when they thought no one was looking. It really is a beautiful photo. Those sort of moments are Sally's specialty, and the good reason she gets paid the amount of money she does. We both sit in silence for a few moments before Rachel closes the album.

'So...' she says.

I glance up from my coffee mug and picked-at muffin, wary.

'There was something I had to ask you,' Rachel starts, then pauses for a moment, looking confused. 'Oh, now I remember what it is. Valentine's Day's coming and…'

I give Rachel the evil eye and a strange look comes over her face.

'What was that?' she asks.

'What?'

'Did you just…growl?'

'Um.' I don't think so. Still, anything's possible—she did say the V and the D words.

'Right. Right…' She pauses, gives me another look—this time an assessing one. 'You know, if you're growling about Valentine's Day, I'm not having a dinner party this year. I'm not trying to set you up any more. I've run out of men. No, what I was going to ask, before you so *rudely* interrupted—' she gives me a pointed look with this '—was whether you thought this would be a good present for Ryan.'

She brushes a few muffin crumbs off her fingers, fishes a catalogue out of the basket of bits and pieces sitting on the table and starts flipping through it, looking for something. Finally, she finds it, spins it around so I can see it and points something out.

'Or is it too, you know, silly…?'

I take a look. It's a sleepwear catalogue. I pick it up in order to have a better look at what she's pointing out. It's a pair of pyjamas that read GROUCHY in big letters down the side.

She checks my expression carefully. 'You don't think it's a bit lame? I've already got some "Good Morning" ones.'

'No.' They really are cute, as pyjamas go. 'But I guess the question to ask is whether or not Ryan's grouchy in the morning.'

Rachel snorts at this. 'Very.' There's a pause as we eye each other off. 'Now, was that so hard?'

'Um.' I look at the table, my coffee, the floor, the ceiling, not wanting to let Rachel win. 'Oh, look at the time,' I add. Table, coffee, floor, ceiling.

'You know what would be really nice?' Rachel says when I finally meet her eyes.

I stop. Aha! I knew it! She *has* picked a guy up for me from somewhere and arranged a dinner. And what would be nice is if I come along, chow down, think he's fantastic, book the celebrant before the main course and marry him on the front lawn after dessert so we can double date with Rachel and Ryan for evermore.

Still, I take the bait. 'What would be really nice?'

'It would be really nice if you actually looked at your watch when you say "Look at the time".'

'Oh.'

She nods, looking very self-satisfied.

Rachel: 2 Liv: 0

We chat for a while after this, and I check out the latest honeymoon photos from the Maldives. When I look at the time for real, I'm surprised to find it's almost six o'clock.

'I'd better get going,' I say, standing up and starting to collect my things. I didn't know it was so late. Ryan will probably be home soon.

'Oh, I keep forgetting to tell you,' Rachel says.

'Mmm?' I keep searching for my car keys in my handbag.

'I'm going away on a conference on the thirteenth. That's why I can't have the dinner. I should be back the next day, early.'

'OK.'

'Thanks for bringing the album round.' Rachel pats the box.

'Any time, babe,' I say, swinging my bag over my shoulder and heading for the door.

Following me, Rachel laughs. 'I was kind of hoping this would be the only time.' She leans on the doorframe as I step down outside, and it's only when I look back at her that I realise the expression on her face doesn't match her laugh. I pause, not wanting to say anything, but giving her the time to bring something up if she wants to.

She doesn't.

'Well, I'm off,' I say, taking another step towards the car.

Rachel hesitates for a moment and wrinkles her forehead in thought.

Oh, no. I freeze and wait for the worst…

'You really think Ryan would like those pyjamas?' she says. 'I'm still not sure…'

As I start reversing out of the driveway I spot Ryan's car coming up the street. He pulls over to the kerb when he sees me and waits while I back the rest of the way out. My car on the road, I wave at him, then at Rachel, and head for home.

Ryan.

Driving down their street, I eye him carefully in the rear-vision mirror, my stomach doing those all too familiar flip-flops about him even now. About his cheating, that is. Or, to clarify, his almost cheating.

It was over a year into their relationship when it happened. I'd been in the city, shooting a couple's engagement portrait at a restaurant. Having finished, I'd rounded the corner to leave and there he was on one of the red leather banquettes. With a woman who wasn't Rachel.

Seeing him, I'd frozen on the spot, unable to move, not caring if he spotted me.

I must have stayed there, my mouth hanging open, for ages. I kept thinking over and over again that I must be seeing it wrong, that it couldn't be him. But I didn't have it wrong. It was all too plain just what was going on across the room. Whoever she was, he was touching her, and *boy* was she touching him. My heart dropped right down onto the parquetry floor of the restaurant for Rachel.

When I managed to unfreeze, I picked up my heart and went to the ladies', where I tried to calm down and decide what to do. After an emotional merry-go-round and a whole lot of pacing between the hand-dryers, I came up with a plan. I decided not to confront Ryan then and there. I didn't want to cause a scene. Instead, I'd approach him the next day and tell him that I'd been at the restaurant.

So that's what I did.

The next day, quite calmly, I went to his office in the city and described to him what I'd seen the night before. I also told him that if he didn't tell Rachel what was going on, I'd tell her myself. I gave him twenty-four hours.

He told her.

After it was all over, she came over to my place. And after we'd talked it through, I asked her what she was going to do.

She said that her first reaction had been just to kick him out. End it all. Like they said, once a cheater, always a cheater. But then, Rachel added, she'd thought about it and he hadn't actually cheated, had he? He'd come close, but had caved at the last minute and told her everything because he felt terrible. Because he felt guilty about what he was doing to her and to their relationship. She wasn't sure what to do.

Of course, I had to keep my mouth well and truly closed when Rachel said all of this. Still, I thought, at least Ryan had had the decency not to tell her about my part in his confession. It wasn't just that I was glad that he'd spared me getting involved, it was that he'd left Rachel something. A grain of something to believe in—that he was, underneath it all, a half-decent guy.

Rachel went around and around in circles all night with her dilemma—once a cheater, always a cheater—but then he hadn't actually cheated, had he? The next night, she did it again. Around and around and around.

And I learned things in those two nights. Things about Rachel and Ryan and relationships in general that I hadn't even thought about before. I'd never questioned Rachel and Ryan's relationship. They just were. It was only a week or so into their seeing each other when she started telling me he was 'It', 'The One', 'my soul mate'. All the lines. And I'd believed her. But after Ryan had strayed, I started to wonder if their whole relationship had been some kind of mirage I'd simply wanted to believe in. Did things like 'soul mates' and 'It' and 'The One' actually exist? I didn't think so, considering I'd once thought I'd met 'The One' and he left me. Plus, my parents hadn't exactly set the best example for me to follow. But Rachel and Ryan had given me hope. Until this. Rachel's predicament certainly strengthened my resolve to stay single. I didn't want to end up in the kind of situation she'd found herself in. To trust someone wholeheartedly again thinking they'd never hurt me and then, right when you least expected it…

Accordingly, I stopped thinking about the guy I'd had my eye on at the time—a new photographer across town. At the next bridal convention I avoided him. The suffering Rachel was going through I didn't need.

On the third day Rachel stayed with me, Ryan called for about the one hundred and seventeenth time, and Rachel accidentally answered her mobile. He begged her to meet him for a coffee.

They announced their engagement only a few weeks later.

Soon afterwards, turning the tables, Ryan came to visit *me* at work. He wanted, he said, to explain the whole situation. I told him I didn't want to know, that it was between Rachel and himself. But he insisted on telling me. All of it. He kept saying over and over again how much of a mistake it had been, how it had only been that once, how sorry he was, that he knew he'd hurt Rachel and felt awful. And that it would never, ever happen again because it would kill him if he saw a repeat of the expression on Rachel's face when he'd told her what had been going on.

I didn't believe him. I couldn't. All I could think about as he told me this was how it had looked, that scene in the restaurant. Him touching her. Her touching him. How Rachel and Ryan's relationship had been my great white hope and now it was gone. So, no, I didn't believe him. But with all my heart I hoped he was telling the truth.

For Rachel's sake.

Y Y Y Y

Saturday 6 February—
eight more sleeps...

'Morning!' I yawn, stretching as I come into the lounge room. I expect to open my eyes and see Justine on the phone—I'd heard it ring just a few minutes before—but being in my pyjamas with troll-like morning hair, of course there's someone other than my flatmate in the room.

Drew.

'Ah,' I say, mid-stretch, definitely awake now.

'Hi,' he says, looking up from the newspapers scattered around his place at the dining room table. 'What time of day do you call this to be getting out of bed?'

I check the clock on the kitchen wall. It's seven-thirty. 'Normal-person time?' I think about going and getting changed as we have a visitor, but then decide I can't be bothered. I go over to pull out a chair and sit down with an automatic slump. 'Don't tell me you've been doing that awful running thing again.'

'Sure have.'

'You guys are sick. You must have been up at—what, six?'

'Five-thirty.'

I shudder.

'Lifestyle or news?' Drew holds up two sections of the paper for me to choose from.

I have another quick think—should I say news and seem worthy and good, or ask for the lifestyle section, the section I actually want? 'Lifestyle.' I reach over and take the paper from him.

Drew meets my eyes as I take it. 'You win. I'll just have to turn my brain to mush later.'

I laugh. It's nice to know he's not worthy and good either.

We settle into our sections in companionable silence. I'm halfway through an article about why marriage is good for you (sure, I'll just put that on my 'to do' list for today…), when I smell it. Him. How is it that guys always smell so good after exercise—well, the deodorant-wearing ones, anyway—and I just smell… well, funky?

Behind my paper, my eyes start to wander a little. He's been over here a lot recently. Drew, that is. Quite a lot. I quizzed Justine about his presence a week or so ago, but she swore there was nothing going on between them. She said they'd dated once or twice before they'd realised it was all completely ridiculous and they'd be better off as friends and running partners. I was surprised to hear this—Justine wasn't usually the kind of girl who kept her leftovers for lunch the next day. Still, it's all fine by me. Drew seems really nice, he decorates the apartment nicely (he's not exactly bad-looking) and once he even did the washing up. Justine's obviously right—the boy is a keeper.

In front of me Drew's paper moves slightly sideways. 'Hello again,' he says as his eyes meet mine again.

'Oh. Um, I was just wondering where Justine is?'

But there's no need for an answer because Justine comes into the room now and gives me a wave. She *is* on the phone, just as I'd thought—pacing around the apartment on the cordless. She can never sit still while she's on the phone. She says the movement helps her think.

'Who's she talking to?' I ask Drew, putting my paper down.

Drew puts his down as well. 'Er, I think it's your dad's girlfriend.'

Justine comes over, holding the phone out, but before she passes it to me she clamps one hand firmly over the mouthpiece. 'Um, here's the thing…' she begins and I know well enough to brace myself for whatever's coming. There's usually a 'thing' or two where Justine's concerned. 'I've booked tickets. For a ball. The Cupid's Choice Ball, you know? The one where they computer-match you with a date? Anyway, it's next Saturday, and I know you can't come because of work, but your dad and Eileen kind of think you should go anyway, and…'

I hold my hand out for the phone with a final withering look and she trails off.

'Hi, Eileen. How's it going?' I say wearily. We spend a minute or two exchanging social pleasantries. Eileen asks about work. I ask how she is, how Dad is, how the cat is, how the ant problem in the kitchen's faring, etc. Then she gets down to business…

'This ball Justine's going to sounds like fun, doesn't it? Maybe she'll meet a nice boy there?'

Sigh. I think about next weekend as I form a reply in my head. Saturday and Sunday are really going to take it out of me—days with two weddings are bad enough, but ones with three weddings are a killer. Of course, as Sally mentioned just this afternoon, the money's spectacular, *and* it's all going to a good cause—what she calls the 'That Bitch Who Set Up On Her Own and Took All My Business' fund. Because that's what I'm going to do. My Big Plan. In a year or so I'm going to set up my own studio.

'I can't go, Eileen. I've got three weddings to shoot that day. But say thanks to Dad for getting you to nudge me along, won't you?'

Eileen coughs. 'No, no. He didn't. He, um… Oh, look. Here's your father. He wants to say hello.' She passes the phone over.

'Nice one, Dad. If you can't set me up, you'll get Eileen to do your dirty work, hey?'

'I was doing nothing of the sort! I've tried before and failed. Look at that fiasco with Bob's boy, Clarence. Now, why would I try again?'

Good question, I think, remembering last year's failed date with Clarence. Clarence, the guy who makes glass eyes for a living, just like his father, his grandfather and his great-grandfather before him. It was all he talked about. At the end of the evening *I* could probably have made a glass eye.

'I really don't know, Dad. Why *would* you try again?' As I say the words, my mind works its way back to another of his all-time greats—funnily enough, another Valentine's Day special.

A retired primary school teacher, Dad now provides daycare for three little girls from the neighbourhood. He does the whole deal around every holiday. At Christmas they play Secret Santa and decorate a Christmas tree and make popcorn strings and paper chains to hang around the living room. At Easter they hard-boil eggs, colour them with food dye, wear bunny ears… You get my drift—it's little-girl heaven. Dad heaven too. My dad's always been a bit of a little girl man…

No, not in that kind of way.

What I mean is he's always been the kind of guy who doesn't mind wearing silver glitter fairy wings, having his face painted like a pussycat and sitting down to pretend tea from a china teaset in the back yard. He's having the time of his life doing this child-minding thing. The kids are ecstatic. Their parents are ecstatic. My dad's ecstatic (he gets to play all day). Whatever makes them all happy, I say. And it's nice to see him happy, because for a long time after my mother left us he wasn't.

The kids he'd been minding last year all being four-year-old girls who were *very* into pink, they'd gone all out for Valentine's Day. They'd made each other cards and baked pink patty cakes with pink icing to give to their parents. It was a cochineal love-in over there. Anyway, at that time, a distant second cousin of mine happened to be staying at Dad's. He'd come to check out the job prospects in the area and my dad was putting him up for a few days. We hadn't seen him for years, but as soon as he got there, Dad was on the phone trying to lure me over to the house, because apparently this second cousin had become 'very good-looking'. It didn't seem to matter to Dad that said second cousin and I were related and, if married and mated, would most likely have children with two heads and six fingers. No. I was to get over there pronto.

After the fourth phone call in two days I couldn't bear his nagging any more and I went. To be fair, the second cousin *was* very good-looking now he didn't have a pizza face. But the way Dad left us alone in the kitchen to 'finish off the Valentine's Day patty-cakes' was a touch obvious. Then there was the way I brought up Dad's little plan as soon as he'd left the room, mentioning, in passing, the two-headed, six-fingered children.

That didn't seem to go down very well. The second cousin choked on the patty-cake he was eating, some pink icing actually *came out of his nose*, and Dad had to come rushing in to pour him a glass of water. When he'd done that, he had the gall to ask me in a loud whisper how I thought we were getting on. Eileen didn't make things much better either, shouting, 'Leave the poor girl alone!' down the hall.

I appreciated the gesture, but I'm expecting to get strange looks and wide clearance by all the single males at our annual picnic in the park family reunions from now on. Poor disillusioned Dad. He thinks a guy—any guy, really—is the solution to all my problems, and that when I find one I'll be able to live happily ever after. It's funny that what he sees as the solution to all my problems I see as the cause of all my problems. Frankly, the last thing I need is another guy screwing up my life and my head.

I sigh again. And it is way too early on a Saturday morning to have sighed thrice already. I knew I should have got in earlier. I'd told myself to get onto the problem a good fortnight ago—before it *was* a problem. Right. That's it, then. Time to say my piece. I compose myself for a second, then hold the phone out at arm's length.

'Is everyone listening?' I say loudly.

Beside me, Justine jumps. Across the table, Drew sits up in his seat. A noise bleats out from the phone.

'This year, you are all going to leave me alone. I know what you're all doing, but I'm OK. I'm not thinking about…anything. I'm busy. I'm working. I don't need a date. There won't be any set-ups. There won't be any fortuitous meetings. There won't be any friends of friends of friends who just happen to be in the same place at the same time as me. So, um, yes…that's the announcement of the day. Thank you for listening. We'll now return to our scheduled programming.'

Beside me, Justine snorts. Across the table, Drew looks confused. Another noise bleats out from the phone. I bring it back to my ear. 'You hear that, Dad?'

'Er…ah—how's work, then?'

I knew it. I knew he was up to something. It's my dad's favourite pastime, playing matchmaker. But I let him off the hook and talk about work instead. I explain about the line-up that Sally and I have next weekend, and he asks a few questions before he moves into father mode.

'Now, don't you overwork yourself, or you'll fall ill,' he says. 'Maybe you should start drinking those little greebie drinks Eileen's got me on.'

'Greebie drinks?' I say, starting to pull fluff off the tablecloth absent-mindedly.

'There's some kind of creature in them. I don't

know. Here she is. She'll tell you about it.' He passes me back over to Eileen.

'What's he talking about?' I ask her.

She clicks her tongue impatiently and I can tell she's giving Dad what he fondly calls 'one of her looks'. 'He's talking about those lactobacillus drinks. He needs them with his diet. I know for a fact he's been sneaking packets of pork rinds at the pub.'

I hear a protest from my dad in the background.

'Now, what were we talking about before? That's it. The ball...'

I stop de-fluffing the tablecloth. Will they never learn? And I have now officially run out of my daily quota of sighs. 'Um, I've got to go, Eileen. Sorry. Something's, um, burning on the stove.'

Drew looks over at the empty stove and then back at me as I say this. He laughs.

Eileen pauses. 'I've never seen you cook anything on that stove,' she says dubiously.

'It's film,' I shrug. What anyone would be doing with film on a stove is beyond me, but she's quite right—I don't think I've ever cooked anything much on the stove besides two-minute noodles, so it's not a very believable excuse.

'Oh, right. You'd better go, then. Be a dear and put me back on with Justine, will you?'

Obviously it was the right thing to say. 'OK. Bye, Eileen,' I say, and hand the phone over to Justine, who's been sitting down next to me and listening the whole time.

'Hi, again, Eileen.' She takes the phone off me and gets up to start pacing once more.

I look over at Drew.

'Parents, huh?' he says, with a lift of his eyebrows.

I can't help laughing then. I must have sounded like a complete teenager with my 'Yes, Dad; No, Dad; Fake excuse got-to-go, Eileen.'

Justine starts giggling over in the corner of the room, making Drew and I look over.

With a shrug, I turn back. At least someone can laugh about my life. 'Coffee, tea?' I get up from the table and head into the kitchen.

Drew follows me. 'What are you having?'

'Coffee. Definitely, definitely, definitely coffee. Strong coffee. Maybe two cups.'

'Sounds good.'

I put the jug on, then grab two mugs and two coffee bags. Drew takes a seat on the bench.

I'm pottering around, sorting out sugar and milk and chatting to Drew, when Justine has another giggle. 'No, she's not seeing anyone and keeping it a secret from you, Eileen…' she says, pointing to the phone with a 'your sort-of-stepmother's such a card' grin.

'Oh, God,' I say, looking over at Drew and shaking my head. 'You know, I do have a limit. I wouldn't want you to think I'm a complete doormat.'

'What's the limit?'

The jug boils and I go over and grab it. 'If either of them ask me if I'm a lesbian, that's it. They're off my Christmas card list for good.'

'Fair enough,' he says, as I pass him his mug. 'You've got to draw the line somewhere.'

I lean against the opposite bench and take a sip of my coffee. It's only then that it really hits home. Justine, Rachel and now my dad and even my sort-of-stepmother. I pause with that. God, but I'm sick of saying 'sort-of-stepmother'. I've been having to say it for over ten years now, ever since Eileen came onto the scene.

Somehow, though, I don't think anything's going to change on the sort-of-stepmother front, because my dad is—how should I put it?—a little *scared* of remarrying. A little *worried*. Personally, I think he's frightened that if he marries Eileen she'll leave him, like my mother did. The thing is, she wouldn't. I know this. Eileen knows this. It's Dad we're both waiting on.

Now, what was I thinking about? Oh, yes. Justine, Rachel, my dad and Eileen have all said in one way or another today that they're not man-hunting for me any more. That they've given up even before I made my little speech…

'Oh, I wanted to ask you something,' Drew says, bringing me back from my daydream. 'Can I come in to your studio one day next week for a chat? I need you to take me through some of the wedding packages.'

I try to swallow the coffee in my mouth before I choke. 'You're getting married?' That was quick.

He laughs. 'No, I'm being someone's best man. It's just that I told him and his fiancée that I know a good wedding photographer…'

'And who would that be?' I try to look offended for a moment. 'You shouldn't talk about the competition in front of me like that. Very rude.'

'Sorry.' He grins and his eyes light up. For the first time I notice the tiny flecks of green in them. God, he really does smell good. Is that sick, or what?

I take a second or two to think through my schedule before I reply. 'Um, come in any day except for Monday. I'll be out and about a bit that day, but any other time should be fine.'

'Maybe Tuesday, around lunchtime?'

'Sure, that shouldn't be a problem.'

Off the phone now, Justine strolls on over to the kitchen.

'About time,' I say with a roll of my eyes.

She snorts. 'I'll swap you sort-of-stepmothers any day.'

'And I'll raise you one,' Drew pipes up. 'Though I've only got a real stepmother.'

We both turn, wide-eyed.

'Well, la-dee-da!' Justine says. 'Aren't we grand? Only a *real* stepmother!' She pulls herself up onto the bench beside Drew. 'Hey, we're going out for breakfast,' she says to me. 'Want to come?'

I shake my head. 'I can't. I've got an, um…' I glance at Drew for a second before I turn back to Justine '…appointment.'

Justine gets what I'm talking about instantly. 'Oh, right. Tania.'

'I've got a couple of hours, but I just want to have a bath and curl up on the couch with my book for a bit. I'm supposed to be conserving energy for next weekend.' And I know conserving energy for something seven days away sounds like a pitiful excuse, but I'm going to need to fill my reserves. Last year I didn't and as soon as I slowed down I caught the flu to end all flus.

Justine snorts once more for good measure. 'Curl up with that thing?' She jerks her head in the direction of the dining table, where my collected works of Dickens is resting. 'You'll need a forklift to get *that* onto the couch with you.'

'I'll manage, I'm sure. I don't do all those biceps curls at the gym for nothing.'

'Oh, come on—come out with us,' Justine wheedles. 'Come on, come on…'

I push myself off the bench and stick my now empty mug in the sink. 'Haven't you seen the ads? No means no.' I point at my flatmate. 'And now I'm going to have that bath. Have fun, though, kids,' I say as I head for my bedroom. 'And don't spend all your pocket money at once.'

Y Y Y Y

I add some pretty luxurious-smelling vanilla and mandarin bath oil that Eileen gave me for Christmas to the bath water ('It'll help you relax, dear.'). But even after a full ten minutes of floating and staring at the ceiling I can't stop my brain from ticking over.

Something isn't right.

And it all revolves around what I was thinking about before, in the kitchen. About everyone having given up on me. First Rachel, without any man up her sleeve or her usual Valentine's Day dinner party. Then my dad, with his 'I've tried before and failed—now, why would I try again?' line. And Justine, all too readily understanding that I couldn't come to her latest wacky singles event.

There was always one on the go—dinners for six, dinners for eight—singles paintball (Please! I'd drawn the line there…). Last year Justine had pushed me into attending a terrible, last-minute speed-dating exercise which had cost me eighty dollars to find out that only one of the guys there would be half bearable. Naturally, he wasn't the guy that gave me a big red tick on his form. That guy was a thirty-nine-year-old computer programmer with a pet rat named Stevie.

Lucky, lucky me.

Frankly, why they've become united in the desperate search to find me a partner over the last few years, I have no idea. No, hang on, that's an outright lie. I know exactly why—they're all scared. Scared I'm in a dating slump after the break-up to end all break-ups. But isn't that normal? And, anyway, what's the point of getting back out there so quickly? What are the odds, after all, that I'll find someone like Mike again? I just don't understand those three. Then again, they all cried during *Titanic* while I laughed hysterically, choking on my popcorn and trying not to clap when Leo finally drowned. (I think we all know it would never have worked out between that pair—it simply wasn't a landworthy relationship...) So maybe I'll never understand a lot of things about them and this is just another point to add to my long list of noncomprehension. And it is a *long* list, believe me.

OK. So I know I sound ungrateful. I know everyone's only trying to do the right thing by me—and, yes, I love them to death for it. Any other time of the year I can take their 'helpfulness' on the chin, but around Valentine's Day? Sorry. Tania, my therapist, thinks my reaction to the whole *Titanic* thing is 'telling'. I'm not quite sure what she means by this, but I don't think it's entirely complimentary.

Another Tania-ism pops into my head at this. Tania also thinks I should try to look at the positive side of things instead of just the negative, but there *are* no positives where Valentine's Day is concerned. And I've tried to think of one, I really have! (The woman costs me a fortune and will put another dent in my credit card at my appointment today—something I'm definitely not looking forward to…)

'I hate Valentine's Day,' I groan at the ceiling, and I mean what I say.

Hmm. The mandarin and vanilla stress-relief scent mustn't have kicked in yet.

Yes, yes, I realise I sound like a Valentine's Day Scrooge, with all my 'Bah, humbug'. But, really, someone should rename the day and call it what it's become—S.A.D. Singles Awareness Day. Anyway, that's how I feel.

Sort of.

Because I guess you could say I've thought about it a little bit more than this over the years…

THE TOP FIVE REASONS I HATE VALENTINE'S DAY (IN NO PARTICLUAR ORDER)

1. Because it's so fake and ridiculous

Right. OK. Look at Christmas. Christmas started out as a celebration of the birth of Christ.

Now, for most people it's a commercial hell, where the closest thing you'll get to a religious experience is nabbing the last 'Tickle Me' Elmo at Toys R Us. Valentine's Day is shot too. It's a complete commercial fake. The thing is, no one will come out and say it. Why?

Because everyone's too scared.

If you break the silence and admit the truth about Valentine's Day you either look like a cheapskate who can't be bothered to buy their partner a present, or a bitter single person who doesn't have anyone to share the day with.

So everyone fakes it for the day.

Why we should all celebrate the one saint at the one time is beyond me, anyway. There are plenty of saints to go around. One for everybody. There are saints for architects (St Barbara) and authors (St Francis de Sales), bakers (St Elizabeth of Hungary) and bankers (St Matthew). For the mentally ill among us (St Dympna) and skiers (St Bernard). There's even one for cab drivers (St Fiacre), and no one likes them. Personally, I think we should just go with our respective Saints and do something festive on that day instead. Plus, if people knew more about St Valentine, they'd *want* to switch.

I did a bit of research a few years back, for Bliss's Valentine's Day wedding packages. What I found out blew me away. For a start, Valentine's Day has its origins in the Roman festival Lupercalia, where goats and dogs were sacrificed and women were lashed in the streets with goatskin thongs. Apparently being lashed in the streets with goatskin thongs was supposed to ensure fertility and easy child delivery.

Sure.

There's no disputing it in my mind. Valentine's Day is fake and ridiculous and, as far as I can see, says nothing about 'real' love. The kind of love that means you can clean up your partner's vomit and not be sick yourself.

2. Because it's bad for relationships

It's simple, really. Guys hate Valentine's Day.

When it comes to Valentine's Day, guys are smart. They know what's going on and that's why, for them, it's a day of fear. Guys have somehow evolved to the point where they are now able to cut through the emotional bullshit of the day to the truth—that Valentine's Day is all about doing the 'right thing' so no one yells at you. To keep out of trouble they buy the over-priced flowers, the heart-shaped goodies and the weekends away. Everyone's happy. And the day over, they can breathe a sigh of relief.

But what I'd like to know is how many fights/break-ups/divorces occur because of Valentine's Day compared to other days of the year? The men sit at home and wait in fear in case they've done the wrong thing. The women who don't receive flowers at work rush home snarling. There's so much pressure on relationships on Valentine's Day it's practically unbearable. People all over the world are pushed into proposing when they're not quite ready. I know this for a fact because I see them a few months down the line (they're the guys who hit the office mid-March with the scared, wild-horse-like eyes that flick all over the room searching for exit points).

Valentine's Day. It simply brings out all the ugly relationship problems that manage to lie fallow the rest of the year.

3. Because, for me, it makes work a nightmare

A wedding photographer who hates Valentine's Day. I know it's stupid. Strangely enough, I absolutely adore my job for the rest of the year. It's great being involved in one of the biggest days in someone's life. Every once in a while I'll be out on a shoot when I realise this and look around me for a moment. It's then that it usually hits me that what I'm doing is all that's going to be left for these people after the day is over, and, while I'm not exactly saving the world or anything, I'm making a difference in a little way at least. It's a great job. Everyone looks their best. Everyone has a good time. After all, everyone loves a wedding (well, they tend to get a bit cranky at the dry ones…).

But, while I love my job the rest of the year, around Valentine's Day I lose faith in it a little. The weddings I shoot on those days are that little bit soppier. A touch more cutesy. And there are always, *always,* gold Cupids, or cherubs, or something blah along those lines. I don't like Cupids or cherubs. Especially the gold ones. Fat, stunted, shiny little things that they are…

4. Because it's the one day of the year you're not allowed to be single

Any other day of the year it's not unusual for me to receive the odd comment from my married friends along the lines of 'You're lucky you're still living the single life.' But not around Valentine's Day. Oh, no. On Valentine's Day, living *la vida sola* is strictly *verboten*.

Poor, poor Liv. While other people receive tiny pastel-coloured sugar hearts that read 'Be Mine' and 'Let's Be Friends', I don't even get ones that say 'Be Someone Else's, *Please*' and 'Let's *Just* Be Friends'.

On Valentine's Day people assume all kinds of things about me because I don't have Noah's paired-off stamp of approval. They assume I don't like men. Not true. I do. They assume that I can't be bothered to date. Not true. I can. I've been on hundreds of dates. Well, maybe not hundreds, but lots. There was even a stage where I became a dating fiend. Someone pointed out to me that I was perhaps being a bit picky who I went out with. I'm not proud, so, for about a six-month period (on the rebound, I might add), I went nuts dating anything and everything, just to test the waters and see if they were right.

I called it crazy dating.

It didn't work out.

I dated a guy who chain-drank four martinis and then offered me a lift home on his motorbike. I dated a guy who told me he smoked cigars because it 'looked cool'. I dated a guy who, between our mains and desserts, told me he could see me in his future. I wanted to ask if he saw me in his *immediate* future, waving him goodbye as he left the restaurant in a taxi, but I didn't. I made a go of it. I tried. And I tried. And I tried.

I did learn something from it all, however.

What it comes down to is that men and I—we just don't seem to get along.

I'm hopeless when it comes to the whole dating game. With me, what you see is what you get. And I think maybe it's better that way for all of us—the guys I date *and* me. I mean, this way they get the real Liv up front, and if they don't like what they see—well, it saves us both wasting our time.

Now, happy singledom seems to be the obvious choice. After the umpteenth scare-off during my crazy dating frenzy, I was tired. I was bored. So I made the conscious decision that I was going to stay single for a while. I came to the conclusion that it was stupid, waiting and hoping and putting my life on hold for something that might never happen. I had to get on with living. Be happy how I was. I went on the occasional date after that, but after a while I couldn't even be bothered doing that. It's been almost a year now since I've been out with a guy at all.

I don't think they mind.

Rachel, however, has told me many a time that my 'love and relationships are things that happen to other people' theory is all too convenient, 'I don't want to put myself out there again' rubbish. Whenever she says this, she also brings up Mike. Mike who I saw for just over a year and a half. Before he left me, that is. But Mike, in my opinion, must have been a fluke.

These days, not having a guy in my life means I've got a lot more 'me' time. At the moment I'm on a bettering myself binge. I've started going to Spanish classes, dragging my butt to the gym three times a week (it's the bit that needs to go the most) and reading more. As Justine pointed out before, I'm halfway through the collected works of Dickens at the moment.

I'm proud to say I'm really enjoying the single life. So much so that I realised lately that it would have to take someone pretty special for me to be ready to give all this up and date again.

Someone pretty *darn* special.

5. Because I was dumped by the love of my life on Valentine's Day two years ago and I can't, won't, and don't want to get over it

Damn. I hate getting to number five. For some reason, I always think it puts my other four, very salient and well-thought-out points in a bad light.

Taking one large, last whiff of the vanilla and mandarin, I slide down in the bath until my head is under the water and I blow some bubbles. If I was a cartoon character, I'm guessing they'd say: 'Please, please, please God, this year give me a break and let me just slip under the Valentine's Day radar quietly.'

Y Y Y Y

The people I pass by at the sidewalk cafés look happy. And so they should. It's a gorgeous blue-skied day, the heat hasn't hit yet and they're surrounded by their friends and good food they haven't had to cook themselves.

I long to join them. I long to have donned my jeans, singlet shirt and cap this morning and to have strolled down the road looking forward to an organic blueberry muffin and a large skinny latte. OK, so I really mean a white chocolate-chip muffin and a large hot mocha with extra chocolate sauce, but the longing's just the same. For a moment or two I let myself pretend that in just a second I'll wave to one of the groups, go over, sit down, place my order and shoot the breeze until eleven. Maybe even midday.

But I don't.

Instead, I keep walking. I realise now it was a mistake to make an appointment with Tania on a Saturday. I usually see her on a weekday afternoon, when the coffees are takeaway and everyone is in a rush to get back to the office. Those days are fine. Saturdays, however, are a downer. I feel my mood sink lower and lower until it reaches subterranean levels. I probably should have skipped that bath this morning and headed on out with Justine and Drew. Well, too late. Maybe I'll just have to cheer myself up later with a slice of baked cheesecake.

I walk past the cafés and up to the office buildings that adjoin them. When I get to the most boring-looking redbrick one, I push open the glass door and head for the lifts. On the third floor, I exit and walk all the way down the corridor to the office with the non-descript door. The office where all the glass has been covered from the inside with wooden venetian blinds. I worked out a while back that this is so you can't see into the waiting room. All the other waiting rooms on this floor you can see straight into. On my right, I pass by an office filled with kids with shiny braces on their teeth. On my left, quite a few people sit with crutches by their sides. But not in the office I'm headed for.

As I push open the door I know exactly what I'll see, and I'm not disappointed. This is a psychologist's office, and as I take a seat next to the magazines I re-alise why they put the venetian blinds up. It's people's minds that are sick in here, and they're embarrassed about it. I'm sure they all call Tania a 'therapist', like I do. I'm also sure that the rest of the people waiting with me this morning all trudge off to their general practitioner once a month, collect their script for their low-dose anti-depressant and pop their pill each night—just like me. Yep, 'therapist' sounds a whole lot nicer than 'psychologist', any way you look at it.

Not that anyone here is actually crazy, mind you. Really, it's just a sad waiting room full of sad-looking people. They're not crazy, they're not nutcases—because this is a nice, up-market area. They're just people like me whose lives haven't quite worked out how they figured. I often wonder what's going on in the little worlds of the people who wait with me each week, and today isn't any different. I glance over at the woman seated across from me. Maybe her husband left her. Maybe her child died. Maybe she can't get pregnant. Or maybe she's just genetically predisposed to being miserable. Who knows?

'Liv?' I look up to see Tania picking out my folder from her secretary's in tray. 'Would you like to come in now?'

I follow her into her office, where she closes the thick wooden door behind us and sits down.

'Now,' she says, flipping through her notes, 'let's finish off what we were having a chat about last week, shall we?'

I have to get her to remind me what we were talking about. I mean, I know generally, because all we ever really seem to talk about are what I like to call

the M&Ms—Mike and my mother. But specifically
I'm lost, until Tania gives me a hint. The funny thing
is, I think to myself before I start on about them again,
most days I'd really prefer to talk about the kind of
chocolate that doesn't melt in your hand.

Y Y Y Y

An hour and a quarter later and I'm asking the most important question in the world. 'What's the baked cheesecake today?'

I'm in luck. Today it's berry—my favourite. Phew! For a moment I'd got a bit worried when the waitress had thought it was lime… I order a slice with ice-cream as well as cream, because I need the calcium. And I know I should be home, doing all the things I won't be able to do next weekend—cleaning the shower, cleaning the toilet, scrubbing the sink—but stuff it. After the session I've just had with Tania, cheesecake is the only thing that's going to get me *through* till next weekend.

Well, at least next week I've got the week off. No Tania. No M&Ms (not the therapy kind, anyway).

Waiting for my cheesecake and coffee, I look around me. The tables are dotted with couples. I used to be a couple. Just like them, I used to go out for coffee and a shared piece of cheesecake on a Saturday. I wonder absent-mindedly if I should get up and warn them. Warn all the females to get up and leave now, before they *need* the cheesecake like I do.

The thing is, though, even if I did go over there, to each and every table, those women would only look at me as if I'd lost my mind. Just the same as I would have looked if someone had done the same thing to me when I was dating Mike. Because, of course, I never thought what happened to me would happen. I never saw it coming. Not on the first day. Not even on the last day. It was the kind of thing that happened to *other* people. The kind of people who ring into day-time talk radio stations.

Mike and I clicked straight away. From the very first second. Even though he was still getting over the split from his wife, the warning bells didn't sound in my head. And why should they have? It wasn't as if he missed his wife—Amanda—for a start. She was long gone, and he seemed to think this was a good thing. That they were all better off this way. Well, except for Toby, I guess. The thing was, Mike had been desperate to be a dad, but it hadn't been Amanda's scene, really. She loved the whole pregnancy bit—the shopping, the fuss—but when her nine months were up, she wasn't so keen on the actual baby—the mess, the screaming. She should really have been presented with Toby when he was about five. Which is what he is now. I can feel my face fall as I think about him.

I miss Toby. He was—still is, I suppose—such a sweetie.

Anyway, when Toby was just a baby Amanda had decided the whole happy families experience was too much and took off. Or, that is, she took off for a year and a half and then decided to come back. Which was when my life had kind of turned from talk radio to Jerry Springer.

'Cheesecake and a skinny latte?' The waitress standing beside me places a plate and glass down on the table. I nod and she retreats, taking my table number away.

I realise what's happened and am just about to get up when she comes back.

'Sorry, I forgot…' She places the single napkin-wrapped cake fork down on the table. 'Can I get you anything else?'

I look down at the single set of cutlery. The gigantic slice of cheesecake. With a huge scoop of ice-cream as well as an ample dollop of cream.

Something else? I try to rearrange my facial expression. Just how depressed do I look?

Y Y Y Y

MONDAY 8 February—
Six Days and counting...

As I drive the car out of the garage on Monday morning, I realise it hasn't emerged since I put it in there Friday night. I've pretty much kept to my promise of conserving energy for the week ahead.

I turn left out of the driveway onto the street and head for the studio, counting the times I've left the apartment this weekend. I only have to use one hand. And four fingers at that. Once to go to my appointment with Tania, once for my trip to the gym, once to pick up some Sunday-morning croissants and the paper, and once last night, when I went to my Spanish class at the local high school—all within walking distance.

I should have plenty of energy stored up from a weekend spent on my back reading my Dickens collection and eating Clinkers (not the yellow ones—I hate the yellow ones). In fact, I expended so little energy this past weekend that it kind of reminds me of the time, during the Tamagotchi rage, that I overfed

Sally's pet on virtual ice-cream to boost its energy levels and it died.

Now, there's something to think about…

But better to think of that than the other thing that's been in the back of my mind these last couple of days—Mrs Batty-Smith's funeral. I check the time on the dash clock—8:52. The funeral starts in an hour, and I have to say I'm not looking forward to it. Not surprising, really. What kind of a sicko looks forward to a funeral?

I pull into the car park at the studio at one minute to nine to see Sally hovering around the open door. When she spots me, she surreptitiously stubs out her cigarette and puts up a finger. Not the one that gets the most exercise out and about in the Ferrari. This time it's her index finger, in a 'just a minute' gesture. She ducks inside and comes back out with her handbag, giving the door a good slam behind her. I notice she's wearing a dark grey linen dress for the funeral—a colour far removed from her usual wardrobe of blinding yellows, screaming pinks and way-out limes.

I unlock the passenger door and she opens it and sticks her head in. 'I thought we'd better just go. It's probably like a wedding—it'd look bad to come racing in behind the coffin, wouldn't it?'

I nod. 'Most likely.'

'Is it OK if we take your car? Mine's a bit flashy for a funeral.'

Yep, just a touch, I agree with her silently. 'Do you know where we're going?' I have a quick feel around on the back seat of my car for the street directory.

Sally snorts. 'The crematorium at the end of the world. You mean you don't know it?'

'Sorry. I don't get asked to do a lot of engagement shoots there.'

We spend a few minutes locating the place—this crematorium really is at the end of the world; it's going to take us the full hour just to get there—and head off.

'How did the two weddings on Saturday go?' I ask Sally when we're safely on the freeway. I'd been extremely lucky to get a weekend off at this time of year. Poor Sally, meanwhile, had been booked out with couples who wanted Sally Bliss and only Sally Bliss and were prepared to pay a premium.

'Boring.' She yawns. 'White. Roses. Sugared almonds. Beef or chicken. Chocolate mousse. Fruit cake that everyone picked the icing off. Need I say more?'

'No.' I've been there, done that, a million times over. 'What about the date, then?'

'Oh, that. We went out for "just drinks" on Friday.'

'Of course.' Sally always books them in for 'just drinks' on the first date, and if it works out she moves them straight on to dinner. If it doesn't, she casually mentions she's got plans and makes a run for it like a rat up a drainpipe.

'*And* dinner, as it turns out. *And* lunch out on his yacht on Sunday. Hey, can I have a fag?'

'Didn't you just have one?'

'Pretty please?'

I wait, hoping she'll give up.

'Pretty please with a cherry on top?'

'Oh, all right.' I wait as she lights up and blows her first puff of smoke out of the window. 'So?'

'Well, I ditched him Sunday night…'

'What?' I look over and then, just as quickly, down at her lap.

'Yes, I'm wearing undies. I'm going to a *funeral!*'

'Just checking.' I smile as I change lanes. When Sally is suddenly manless she often falls back on her old friend exhibitionism for entertainment. The no-undies-and-very-short-skirt-in-a-Ferrari trick is a great favourite of hers. Also of the workers at various toll booths around the city who she hands her change up to, even when it's exact.) Her other piece of performance art is applying her cocoa butter body lotion in the well-lit, curtainless living room of her twenty-fourth floor apartment.

'If we hadn't been out on that damn boat I would have ditched him right after lunch.'

'What happened?' I glance at her briefly.

'I saw him in direct sunlight.'

'I don't know what that means, but at least he isn't a vampire.'

'It would have been a more exciting option,' Sally says, pausing to blow another lungful of smoke out of the window. 'Anyway, the point is, my date had hair plugs. I'll have to keep out of those dimly lit bars in future—I'd met him twice and hadn't realised. From now on it's daylight, or carrying one of those tiny torches in my handbag so I can do a quick spot-check. I can't bear hair plugs. I can't bear vanity in a man, full-stop.' Sally wriggles around in her seat so her body's facing me. 'A piece of wisdom for you from your resident elder—never date a man who's going to wrestle with you for mirror space, darling. It'll only end in tears. Remember that.'

'I'll try,' I say, trying not to laugh at the seriousness of her voice. As I change lanes again I think about Sally's latest dumping and wonder at how alike Sally and Justine are, in that they can get over relationship hiccups and just keep going. And you have to admit that in Sally's case three divorces are fairly significant hiccups—more like choking or suffocation or a quick smoker's hack, really… But they do keep going. And with seeming effortlessness too. I wish I was like that. That I could treat my exes like speed bumps that are just obstacles to mount (in want of a better word) and speed off. But I can't. My tissue consumption at my Tania sessions is still high. I'm Brontë-ish when it comes to break-ups, and am, unfortunately, the kind of girl you'd find on the moors yelling 'Heathcliff!' and getting the bottom of my dress double-dose-of-Napisan dirty…

Pathetic, really.

But that's how it is. Still, when I hear Sally and Justine talk about their lives the way they do, sometimes I wish I didn't play my life quite so like a game of chess—planning, looking ahead, thinking that somehow, if I concentrate and think about my moves before I make them, I'll win in the end. It's a method that obviously doesn't work. Look at the whole Mike situation.

'Oh, no,' Sally says.

'What?' I glance over.

'I know that look.'

'What look?'

'The Mike look.'

Shit. 'It's that obvious?'

Sally nods. 'That time of year again, I guess.'

Like I mentioned, Mike and I broke up on Valentine's Day. And it wasn't exactly mutual.

'I was just thinking I wish I was more like you. I wish I could say "Yeah, it didn't work out" and move on without glancing back.' I look over at Sally to see what she's going to say, but just as she's about to start she pauses. 'What?'

'Sweetheart, you don't want to be more like me. You really don't.'

I shrug. 'Look, I know I'm pathetic. I know everyone thinks I'm a sad case because it's taking me so long to get over him.'

Sally shakes her head. 'No one thinks that.'

'Well, OK, maybe not in those exact terms, but they don't understand why I'm not straining at the leash, dying to get "out there" again. They're so damn cheerful about it all. It's like living with a cheer squad. Gimme an L, gimme an I, gimme a V. What does it spell? *Liv!* And what do they want me to do? *Date, Liv, date!*'

Sally laughs. 'I can see your dad with pom-poms and a pleated skirt. Look, you know they mean well. They just don't remember how much it can hurt. They haven't been playing with fire recently, while you remember having your poor little marshmallow heart toasted all too well. You know what I think?'

'What?' I turn my head to look at her.

'I think it's all just a case of bumping into Mr Wonderful when the time's right. You'll be over Mike in a flash when that happens. Even Mr Only-Slightly-Wonderful would do. So long as he doesn't have hair plugs.'

'Believe me, Mr Wonderful doesn't have hair plugs.'

'Look, I'll let you in on a secret,' Sally says, lowering her voice. 'The first one you really love is the hardest to get over.'

I glance over at her again. 'How long did it take you to get over Simon?' Simon was Sally's first husband and her longest marriage.

'Geez, I don't know…' Sally thinks back, then meets my eyes with a glint in her own. 'Six days at least!'

I can't help but laugh.

Sally blows her last puff of smoke out of the window before stubbing her cigarette butt out on a tissue from her handbag. 'Enough about me. What did you get up to over the weekend, chickadee? Any Valentine's Day fun on the horizon?'

Sally knows about Rachel, my dad and Justine's annual efforts all too well. 'There were some rumblings about a ball, but nothing concrete.'

'No ticket? No dress? Nothing? Is your dad sick?' Sally knows that by this time of year I'll have generally been roped into something or other to 'keep her mind off the day', as I'm sure they say behind my back.

'I know! I was pretty surprised too. They seem to have formed some kind of a pact to leave me alone this year. I'm not asking any questions. I need the break.'

'Good for you. Don't rock the boat. You're right, anyway. It is a piece of crap day—I don't know what the three of them see in it. All that chocolate.' Sally pats her absolutely flat three-times-a-week personally trained stomach muscles. 'I'm eating enough of the damn stuff as it is, giving up the smokes. And all I ever seem to get for Valentine's Day is filthy lingerie and gigantic boxes of soft centres. I hate soft centres.'

'You poor thing.'

Sally gives me a look. 'Oh, poo to you. You know, dearie, maybe if you dated even once in a while you'd understand—you'd get your filthy lingerie and boxes of soft centres too.'

'I can buy myself filthy lingerie and boxes of soft centres—which, by the way, I don't like either, thanks.'

'Sure, sure. Hooray for Women's Lib. Black crotchless undies and strawberry soft-centre cellulite here we come. I just hope that's what Mr Wonderful is looking for in a woman.'

I snort. 'I'll ask him when I finally meet him.'

After another fifteen minutes or so of solid freeway driving, I'm starting to wonder if this crematorium even exists. Plus, Sally's proving to be a handful.

'Hey, are you reading that street directory or is it just decorating your lap?'

'I am too reading it.' She looks up at the sign looming ahead, down at the street directory, and then back up again. 'This one! This one!' She points at the exit we're passing. I screech off the freeway at the very last second.

'Thanks for that.'

'No worries. Now, first right, second left, and follow the smell of charred bodies.'

'Sal!' I give her a look.

'Of course I'm going to behave!' She closes the

street directory with a flourish. 'Oh, and we'll fast-track
it out of there after the funeral, if that's OK. I've got a
lot of work to do.'

A few minutes later we pull into the crematorium
parking lot and I park the car.

'Look at that. Right on time.' Sally glances at her
watch.

I check the dash clock before I turn the engine off
and pull the keys out of the ignition. We *are* right on
time. 9:55. We've arrived with five minutes to burn.

Oops. Better not say that inside.

Sally and I get out of the car and walk quickly across
the car park up to the vaulted front door of the crematorium. There's a board with the names of six different parties and directions to the respective chapels
where the services are being held. The Batty–Smith
service is in the Chapel of Tranquility. In other words,
down the path and turn right at the toilets.

How eloquent. Just where you'd want your final
send-off.

When we get to the chapel itself, another board tells
us this is, indeed, the Batty–Smith service, starting at
ten a.m. As there's no one milling around, we both poke
our heads around the still-open thick polished wooden
doors to check whether they've already begun.

They haven't. Everyone's sitting down, the coffin's
placed up at the front, but it's obvious the service
hasn't started yet from the way there are several peo-

ple standing in the aisle. Sally gives me a 'phew, we made it' look and we stand upright again.

'Ready?' she says, and I nod.

We enter the chapel and find ourselves two seats halfway down the aisle—or, in this case, up at the back. There are only—I count them—twelve other people in here, and we could probably all fit into the front row if we squished. Everyone turns around to see the new arrivals.

As Sally and I sit down, we acknowledge the people we know with a quick smile. Pip, Susan, Matt, Karen, Bill, Miranda, Sam 1 (female), Sam 2 (male), Trudy and Chris. All wedding photographers. All Mrs Batty-Smith's employers.

There are only two people in the chapel I don't know. The two people in the front row. Relations, I guess. A woman around Mrs Batty-Smith's age and a younger woman. Who they are, I have no idea.

When the clock at the front of the chapel has clicked over to 10:05, and everyone's sitting down, someone gets up and moves forward. It's one of the two women from the front row—the younger one. Mrs Batty-Smith's daughter, I'm guessing, by her age. I'd always vaguely known she had a daughter, Veronica, but I'd never even seen a photo of her, let alone met her, though I'd asked Mrs Batty-Smith about her a number of times. I look at her closely, interested. She looks—well, completely normal—probably about fifty, wearing a navy suit.

The atmosphere in the chapel changes as everyone waits to hear what the woman is going to say. She coughs a little before she begins.

'Hello. I'm Veronica Batty-Smith. Edna's daughter. I'd like to thank you all for coming today, especially her employers. As we all know, my mother lived for her work and was very good at what she did. Now, if you could all turn to…'

And that's it. A hymn. Followed by a reading. And when the coffin is pulled inside on some kind of conveyer belt and the little red velvet curtains swish closed around it I am still none the wiser about Mrs Batty-Smith. *Edna* Batty-Smith.

I sit, confused. I thought at these cremation things they usually have a photo up at the front and an order of service that says something about the person's life and family. That it's all supposed to be a bit more personal.

I guess not.

The red curtains remain fully closed and people start filing out of the chapel. I keep sitting, staring at where the coffin was, until Sally nudges me with one elbow.

'Gawd. That was cheery. I don't know about you, but I feel as if I should skip out singing a rousing rendition of "Ding-Dong the Witch is Dead". I'm going to make a concerted effort to be nicer to people from now on. At least the ones who'll be arranging my funeral.' It isn't until she's stood up and smoothed her dress out that she looks at me. 'Hey, I think we're supposed to go outside now. You know—talk to people. Mingle.'

'Oh, right. Sorry.' I glance up at her blankly.

'Are you OK?' Sally leans down to inspect me a bit more closely. 'You don't look too good.'

I shrug slightly. 'It's just that it's a bit sad, isn't it? We didn't know anything about her, really. I didn't even know what her daughter looked like until today.'

Sally sits down again and pats me on the arm. 'It's not like we didn't ask. Mrs Batty-Smith was a touch eccentric, that's all. She didn't want anyone to know. She was happier that way.'

I know this is true. I asked Mrs Batty-Smith about her daughter numerous times. Asked about her friends, the rest of her family, what she'd done over Christmas, when her birthday was. But I only ever heard about her cats.

'It *is* sad.' Sally pats my arm one last time. 'But it was obviously the only way she could cope with things. She didn't want anyone's friendship. I think she looked at it as pity, even though it wasn't. Now, come on. We'll go outside. Get some fresh air. You look like you could do with some.'

And with that we head for the door—the last ones out of the chapel.

Outside, Veronica is talking to people as they exit.

'Hi, Sally Bliss and Liv Hetherington,' Sally introduces us. 'Your mother worked for us. We're very sorry for your loss.'

Veronica nods as if she recognises the names. 'Thank you. It's good of you to come.'

There's a long pause.

'She spoke about you often,' Sally lies.

Veronica smiles at Sally's line, which sounds like it's been extracted from a specials bin box—101 Things to Say at Funerals. 'I'm sure that's not true, but it's very nice of you to say so. I didn't really see my mother all that often. In the end she'd alienated herself from just about everyone, you see. Even her twin—my aunt.' With this she nods at the elderly woman who'd been sitting with her in the front row and who's now outside chatting to people.

'Oh,' Sally says, at a loss for words. Something I don't think I've ever seen before.

'You said Bliss, didn't you? As in Sally Bliss Photography?'

Sally and I both nod.

'She liked working with you two the best. No men there, you see. Not a great one for the menfolk, my mother, as I'm sure you noticed.'

There's another pause. And as neither of us knows quite what to make of this, but need to say something, I blurt out the first thing that comes into my mind (always trouble). 'She spoke about her cats a lot.'

'Now, that I *can* believe,' Veronica says, raising her eyebrows. 'Do you have a cat?' She turns to Sally first, then me.

'No,' we say in unison, and I don't know about Sally, but I'm thinking it's pretty strange that she's asking. Some kind of pop psychology thing, perhaps?

'It's just that Betsy and Shu-shu still don't have a home. The other cats are a lot younger, so people took them first, but Betsy and Shu-shu are about twelve. They're sisters. From the same litter. They've been de-sexed, of course.'

'Um,' Sally says.

Veronica takes a step forward, closer towards us, and moves in for the kill. 'They're very quiet. No health problems. They don't even eat much. They just like to sit in the sun all day…'

'Sorry.' Sally butts in here. 'But I've got a one-year-old German Shepherd. They probably wouldn't be a great mix.'

Liar! My mouth falls open as I know quite well Sally doesn't have any kind of a dog, let alone a German Shepherd. But Veronica buys it—she visibly cringes, and I can almost see the mental picture she's conjuring up of Sally being able to cut down on the Pal on her shopping list for a day or two if she takes both the cats. I look at the ground.

Think of an excuse, Liv. Think of an excuse.

'I don't know what else to do,' Veronica continues. 'They're old, and their coats are a bit tatty, and…' The rest she leaves unsaid, but we all know what she means.

Kitty death row.

When I look up again, everyone's staring at me. 'Um, well, I…' I can't think up an excuse fast enough, so I tell the truth. 'I don't really want a cat, thanks.'

'Right…well…' Veronica looks around then at the people still outside, kind of desperately, and it becomes quite clear that no one wants Betsy and Shushu. All of a sudden, guilt stabs me square in the chest like a knife.

'Right,' Veronica says again. This time with a sigh.

I look back inside, past the still open chapel doors to the red velvet curtains. The knife twists.

I turn to Veronica and open my mouth slowly, knowing I'm going to regret this, 'Look, if no one else wants them I'll take one.' And I know then that that's it. My cat-free mini-break, with no hassles, no smelly kitty-litter to constantly empty, is over, but I figure it's the least I can do for Mrs Batty-Smith.

Veronica's face lights up at this, and she grabs one of my arms. 'You're an angel. Now, what am I going to do about the other one?'

Yep. Just when I'm feeling as if I've been let off the hook, the second knife of guilt is thrown straight at me. And this one's poisoned. How can I take just one of the cats? God, they've just lost their owner. They're sisters who've never been separated, for Christ's sake. And, hell, at twelve years old they should both be receiving a letter from the Queen pretty soon, congratulating them on their old age. How many more years can they last?

Finally, I cave. 'OK, OK, I'll take them both,' I say. Sally snorts.

Veronica, of course, is ecstatic. This time she grabs both my arms and pronounces me to be a treasure. When she's calmed down, she takes my details and then, wisely, pushes off before I can change my mind. 'I'll call you,' she says as she leaves.

I'm sure you will, I think uncharitably.

'Sucker,' Sally says with a laugh when Veronica is out of earshot.

We spend the next half an hour talking to the other photographers. And I must still look miserable as Sally and I cross the parking lot to the car, because she gives me a dig in the ribs with one elbow.

'Seems you and Mrs Batty-Smith had more in common than you imagined.'

'How's that?' I ask, guessing I'm not going to want to hear the answer.

'No men, a cat collection… If you're not careful, you'll end up with eighteen four-legged friends, a permanent bun on your head and a wardrobe full of fashion stories in grey.'

I groan.

Sally flips her hair. 'But then you'll also get to live to eighty-five, eat three Snickers bars a day washed down with two litres of Coke, and have your name on a plaque in a rock garden. So cheer up.'

I stop in my tracks when she says this.

'What?' In front of me, Sally stops as well.

'Scarily enough, that's what I had for breakfast.'

'Three Snickers bars and two litres of Coke?' Her eyes widen.

'Well, one Snickers and a can of Diet Coke. Still, it makes you think.'

Sally pauses. 'Yeah, I know. I always thought it was a bit weird. An eighty-something-year-old addicted to Snickers and Coke. Still, cheaper than crack, I guess.'

I don't answer.

'Liv? Liv? Hello? Sorry, what were you saying? Makes you think what?'

I pause. 'I don't know...' I say slowly, then glance over at the car and think of the long drive home. 'Except that maybe I should make a quick trip to the ladies' before we head off.' I toss Sally the car keys. 'I'll be back in a sec.'

Y Y Y Y

That's strange, I think to myself as I cross the parking lot. I'd forgotten about Mrs Batty-Smith's Snickers and Coke addiction. And having them for breakfast, together, on the morning of her funeral… Well, it's a bit of a coincidence, isn't it? Especially seeing as I usually manage to throw down at least a cup of coffee and a piece of toast. This morning, however, I slept in and had to hurry to work to pick up Sally. On my way out of the apartment I simply grabbed a can of Diet Coke from the fridge and one of Justine's Snickers bars from the freezer (she says they taste better and last longer that way), and ran.

I walk quickly towards the main set of buildings, the sweat starting to bead on my forehead. It must be thirty degrees already, and I feel horrible and sticky in my charcoal-coloured sombre suit. In fact, I feel a bit sick, I think, and I remember I forgot to take my medication last night—often this can make me feel a bit queasy. On my right, the sun reflects off a windscreen and blinds me with a pink flash, making me squint and start to walk a bit faster.

Finally I make it to the ladies'. I'm surprised to find it's reasonably swish, with a little powder room to tidy yourself in, complete with mirrors and a few toiletries, and then a separate room for the toilets themselves. I cross through the mirrored powder room, catching sight of myself as I go. Ugh. Not looking pretty. But in the bathroom proper I smile as the coolness of the tiles hits me. It's beautiful in here. I could lie down right now and stay here all day quite comfortably. For a second I look at the floor and think about it. But I can't. Sally's waiting for me out in the car, so I move over to the handbasins and satisfy myself by turning on the water, running the flow over the insides of my wrists and then bending down to splash a few handfuls onto my hot face.

It's as I stand back up again that the wooziness hits me and I have to lean one hand on the benchtop to steady myself.

I really should have got up in time to eat a real breakfast, I chastise myself, remembering again the Snickers bar and the can of Diet Coke. I close my eyes for just a second. When I open them again I glance up at myself in the mirror, and, behind me, something catches my attention.

Mrs Batty-Smith.

My heart stops, then starts again far, far too suddenly.

I look again. The person, the thing standing behind me, looks exactly like Mrs Batty-Smith. No, wait…

It *is* Mrs Batty-Smith. Dead Mrs Batty-Smith. Cremated Mrs Batty-Smith. Grey and dusty and…luminous Mrs Batty-Smith.

My pulse skyrocketing now, I reach out my other hand to the bench to steady myself further, thinking I'm going to be sick. I lean over the basin and retch. Nothing happens.

And when I gather the courage to look into the mirror again Mrs Batty-Smith is gone.

I put my head back down and suck a big lungful of air into my lungs. I need to breathe. My head is spinning, confused, but at least the nausea has stopped. What's going on, I have no idea. I can't believe it. I've just seen a dead person. A dead person! I'm stunned. Nothing like this has ever happened to me before—I've never 'seen' things. Well, that's not quite true, I suppose. At times I do have some awfully vivid dreams that Tania and I have spoken about at length. She thinks they're stress-related and 'meaningful', and I guess she's right. Either way, sometimes they're so vivid Justine has to wake me up from them and I find myself lying in a pool of my own sweat. But they're never like this. And never during the day.

I splash some more water on my face and after a while start to feel a little more normal. Slowly, I push my hands off the benchtop and stand up. That's better. My head still isn't quite what it could be, perhaps, but other than that I feel…well, average. And by the time I've finished going through my vital signs, like the hypochondriac that I am, I've almost forgotten about Mrs Batty-Smith.

Except that she hasn't forgotten about me, I realise, as I turn around and my eyes immediately lock together with hers.

Because she's still here. Up at the end of the room. Near the hand-dryers. Mrs Batty-Smith, with a whole bunch of cameras strung around her neck, weighing her down.

My mouth opens and I try to scream, but nothing comes out. I take a step backward. Then another. And another. Not watching where I'm going, I hit the wall that separates the toilets from the powder room with my shoulder. It hurts. My eyes suddenly sting like mad and I can't blink, can't look away from Mrs Batty-Smith's gaze.

And, oh, my God, it's definitely, definitely her. There's no mistaking it. Grey clothes, like always—grey stockings, grey cardi, grey dress, grey hair in a bun, and the same old ravine-like wrinkles across her forehead. I can see them clear as day from here, from across the room. The kind of wrinkles you get from a lifetime of frowning at people. The only difference is the cameras. The cameras around her neck. There are so many of them they're making her stoop. Wait. One other thing I notice. Her eyes. That's why I can't stop staring. Because her eyes—they're different. Almost hypnotic. They used to be a soft greyish blue, a colour that gave her away—told you that she wasn't hard through and through like she pretended to be. But now...now they're just grey. Grey and lifeless. Cold and hard.

We stand looking at each other from opposite ends of the small room, saying nothing. And I know, staring at her, that there's something wrong here—apart from the fact that we cremated Mrs Batty-Smith just half an hour ago and now she's taking a final bow in the crematorium ladies'. No, there's something really wrong, and it's in those eyes. This isn't a social call. This is no lippy-borrowing trip to the loo. There won't be any girly 'have-you-got-a-tampon-darl?' moments here. Mrs Batty-Smith's eyes mean business, and they're boring right into me.

This is her funeral and she'll haunt if she wants to.

I shake my head and force myself to look away. OK, Liv, time to wake up, I think to myself, coming to my senses. After all, that's what's happened here. I've fainted, haven't I? And any moment now someone will walk in here and find me and shake me and I'll wake up. Yes. That's what will happen. I look over at the door hopefully.

It doesn't happen.

Fine, then. Maybe I can wake myself up? I reach

down and pinch my arm—that's what you're supposed to do, isn't it? Pinch? I pinch good and hard.
But when I look up again Mrs Batty-Smith is still
there. Staring.

My eyes dart around the room quickly, trying to
figure out what to do, how I'm going to wake up. I
want out of here. Now. I attempt to push myself away
from the wall, but I can't seem to move. I'm stuck.
Think, think, think, I repeat over and over to myself,
my breath starting to come in shorter and shorter
bursts and not reaching my lungs at all. I've got to
wake up. Got to get out of here. My gaze slides back
warily to the grey shape, and, keeping one eye on Mrs
Batty-Smith's form, I attempt to collate all the tips I've
learnt from the horror movies I've seen over the years.
I can only come up with a few. Try and stay awake (all
the Freddy Krueger movies—but I guess I've already
stuffed that one up by fainting); remain a virgin (various teenage horror flicks—oops, too late there); and
sometimes being super-nice and smart-talking to a
ghost will buy you time (*Ghostbusters*).

Right. *Ghostbusters*, then. *Ghostbusters* is the way to go.

At the other end of the room there's a movement,
and my eyes flick back up to look directly at Mrs
Batty-Smith. She's moved forward a touch, which
makes me want to take a sprightly step back, or sideways, or anywhere, really, but I can't. I'm still stuck
against the wall.

'Um, um,' I stutter, before I remember—*Ghostbusters*. 'Um, can I get you a drink or something?' As this comes out of my mouth, I realise how ridiculous the words are. We're in a bathroom, for God's sake. And I'm talking to a ghost. A figment of my imagination. 'Or a piece of toilet paper?'

By the look that crosses Mrs Batty-Smith's face, I guess she doesn't want either a drink or any toilet paper. But at least I'm thrown a crumb—I know she can hear me because the look I get isn't just any look. It's *the* look. The famous Batty-Smith narrowing of the eyes.

I used to see it quite a bit at the studio, that withering look that would tell you exactly how stupid she thought the comment that had just come out of your mouth was. Generally, she was right. People, including myself, tended to get verbal diarrhoea around Mrs Batty-Smith. She'd watch you with that look while you got more and more uncomfortable until you said anything—the first thing that came into your mind. About your favourite aunt's special shepherd's pie, how those little nodding dogs you put in cars are supposedly making a comeback, or that in Switzerland it's against the law to mow your front lawn while dressed in an Elvis outfit. It was like some kind of disease. So now I make a conscious decision not to say anything else. Instead of speaking, I look straight at her and meet her gaze.

Big mistake.

She starts moving towards me then—shuffling, really, still stooping, weighed down by the cameras. Scared, I press myself into the wall. But as she gets closer, with her last few steps, she veers off towards the basins. She leans against the benchtop with a *humph*, facing me, the cameras crashing around, banging against each other and the basins, some kind of grey dust-like substance coming off her.

I keep very, very still for a while, looking at Mrs Batty-Smith looking at me. After a few minutes I start to feel a touch braver. My heart-rate begins to slow to under three hundred beats per minute. And knowing it's probably not a good idea, but also knowing I'll do *anything* to pull out of this, I try something. And it works. I'm able to take a few steps forward, closer to Mrs Batty-Smith.

She watches me carefully.

With my next step, as my foot goes out, the worrying thought runs through my mind that maybe I'm not unconscious at all. That maybe this is…real. Actually, truly real, and that Mrs Batty-Smith's ghost *is* haunting the crematorium. Haunting me. I decide to take one more step, closer to Mrs Batty-Smith again, and I get a rush of adrenaline as my foot hits the floor. Finally, I stop.

'What are you doing here?' I ask.

Nothing.

I look away again, not able to keep staring at those

eyes for very long. Those awful, awful eyes. This time my gaze rests on the cameras around her neck. I try and work out how many there are, but keep losing count halfway. Fifteen, eighteen, twenty...

'Do you know what they are for?' a voice rasps.

I exhale quickly and shake my head. Got to leave. Got to get out of here.

'Do you know?' she asks again. 'Do you know my story?'

'Not really. Not properly. Only bits and pieces.'

'Tell me what you know. All of it. Now.'

So, standing there, only a few steps away from her, I tell her what I know. About her career ending. Her husband leaving her. When I finish, I instantly wish I'd had the sense to lie. I've got no idea how she's going to take this. And really I don't know for sure whether anything I've said is true. I watch closely for her reaction to my comments.

'Word gets around with you lot, doesn't it?' she snorts, nodding her head outside in the direction of the photographers who are still chatting in front of the chapel. I know that this isn't her usual snort of derision, which I heard many a time sitting at my desk in the studio. Something tells me it might be OK to follow this snort up a little further.

'So he, um, did leave you? It's true?'

Suddenly the grey eyes don't seem as hard as before. 'Oh, he left me all right. Left me for some red-haired telephonist floozy. No brains and all legs. But she did the right thing. Whatever she was told. Gave up work, for a start.'

'And you stopped photographing?'

'Rubbish.' She draws herself up to attention with this. 'That was years later. Years!'

There's a pause as I try to work a few things out. But I can't. I don't have enough information to go on. 'I don't understand,' I say hesitantly. 'What happened that made you stop photographing?'

She looks straight at me when I ask this. 'I hated weddings,' she says. 'Hated couples. Hated it all. That's why I stopped. Couldn't bear it. Pah,' she ends, with a shake of one fist, and sends dust flying once more.

I almost take a step back again. The way she said 'hated'. It was with real venom, actual, real hate. But something makes me stand my ground. I feel like I need to know, need to understand after all these years of not knowing. 'But why?'

'Because of men,' she spits. 'Lying pigs. Swine, all of them. Couldn't bear to be around weddings. All that false love. False hope.'

'Right,' I say, the bits and pieces that I do know about Mrs Batty-Smith starting to fit together perfectly. I mean, if you felt like that about weddings, you could hardly hang around them all day. Doing the books would look like an enjoyable pastime if you felt like that about relationships and marriage.

Veronica's words from before pop into my mind now—how she mentioned that her mother liked working at Sally's studio the most because there weren't any men around. That makes a lot of sense after what I've just heard. Still, while things are starting to fit together now I have more information, how Mrs Batty-Smith got to be the way she is, with these views, doesn't.

I work up some more courage to ask what I want to ask. 'And you felt this way because of your husband? Because he left you?'

'Him? Pah.' Another wave of the hand. 'Fool.'

'But you never remarried?'

'A man?' Mrs Batty-Smith looks at me like I'm insane.

'Well, yes.'

'Wasn't possible. Men didn't like me.'

Funny, I think. That's my line. And it's one I find hard to believe coming from Mrs Batty-Smith. I've seen pictures of Mrs Batty-Smith when she was younger. She was stunning. Tall and coiffed and up-to-the-fashion-minute, dressed in the shortest European-length skirts, the most daring patterned and fishnet tights, in order to show off her legs. (Even in her late forties she had a pair that I would kill for now, in my late twenties.) The kind of woman who looked like she should have a full dance card in one hand and a very dry martini in the other at all times.

'But men must have been queuing to take you out.'

'Ha! That's how much you know about those days. Didn't like my clothes, my job, my money and especially my attitude, did they?'

Oh. I start to get it now, including what Mrs Batty-Smith said earlier about the red-haired telephonist floozy doing what she was told. Back then, Mrs Batty-Smith's job—how much she worked, how much she earned—had been a problem. A big problem. 'But you must have dated, surely?'

Mrs Batty-Smith snorts again. 'One date here and there. Hardly what you would call successful. Too strong-willed. Too involved with my work to have time for anyone else.' She pauses for a second or two. 'There was someone…'

I catch her eye, wanting to know more. Asking to be told more. I take another small step forward.

'But I got rid of him, didn't I?' she spits, and I take two steps back in surprise. 'Yes. Quick-smart. Too hard. I'd had it with men. Fools. What were they good for? Nothing! They just got in the way, stopped me from doing things my way.'

I want to ask why—why she got rid of the guy, why it was too hard when she obviously had a soft spot for him—but when I see the expression on her face I think twice. 'And then what?' I ask instead.

'And then nothing. After him I stopped seeing men. Looked after myself and the business. And Veronica.'

Glancing down at my now crossed arms, I fill in the details for myself. She stopped seeing men, slowly dropped photography as she became more and more bitter, did the books for all the wedding photographers around town and started collecting cats.

'Yes. Then I stopped,' she says, directly into my right ear.

Instantly, my stomach contents rise up to my throat. In the space of a few seconds Mrs Batty-Smith has moved over to stand beside me. Right beside me. So close I can see the wisps of stray hair that have come out of her bun. So close I can count the frown lines on her forehead. So close I can see how the cameras are pulling around her neck, swaying because of her movement. Her dust is settling on my suit. I start panting in fright.

'Stopped *just like you will.*' With her final four words she pokes me in the chest with one finger and I stumble back to the wall, startled by the feeling. I hadn't thought she'd be able to do that. A ghost. Touch people. It felt so real.

'Wha…what do you mean?'

She looks at me with those cold eyes again, her neck craned uncomfortably up against the weight around it, and I know that at this moment she hates me. Really hates me.

'You stupid, silly little girl,' she hisses. 'Don't you know why I'm here? Don't you know what I'm trying to tell you?'

I press into the wall once again, more scared than I've ever been before in my life. 'No,' I say. 'I don't know. *I don't know!*' I yell at her.

She steps forward, closer, the cameras bumping. 'I'm here to warn you. Because you are just like me.'

I laugh at this. A short, frightened laugh. 'What? I'm nothing like you. Look at us. Look at us when you were alive. I've got a job. I've got a life.'

Mrs Batty-Smith pauses when I say this, a mocking smile on her face. 'Not for long.'

When I hear this, I turn cold. So very cold. I look down and I have goosebumps all over my arms. I was boiling before, and now my feet and hands are freezing. I cross my arms for warmth and safety. What does she mean, not for long? I'm going to die? I move my gaze slowly back up to meet hers.

'I don't… I don't understand,' I say weakly, thinking I just want to wake up. I want to wake up and have this all go away. This isn't real. I *am* unconscious. I've hit my head on the sink as I've fainted and fallen, and my thoughts have turned nasty, just like my night-time dreams. All I have to do is wake up for it all to go away.

But I don't wake up. Mrs Batty-Smith moves closer still. Right up to me. Her ashen face in mine. One of the cameras pushes into my stomach.

'Because I was offered all kinds of love in my life and turned it away I must roam the world for ever. I pushed love aside time after time, and now I have to stand by and watch what I might have had. I must suffer, as I made myself suffer in life, because of my own selfishness. Because it was safer not to give of myself.'

Shaking, I try to follow what she's saying—something about how because she pushed away everyone's love she's being punished for it now. This much I understand. But what's it got to do with me? I was always nice to her. I *tried*. I'm even taking two of her cats, for God's sake. The old ones that no one else wants. What else could I have done?

Mrs Batty-Smith reaches out an arm to touch mine and I start shaking even more fiercely. 'You are not going to die. You have a choice. You do not have to be like me. You can change. There is still time for you to change.'

The news sinks in that I'm not going to die, like I thought she was suggesting before, but right now I don't feel all that relieved. I shake my head, trying to come to grips with what's going on. 'Change? Why? What for? I'm not like you. I'm not. I don't understand. I have a job and friends and—'

'You will be visited by three spirits,' Mrs Batty-Smith interrupts me.

What? I stop babbling. Three spirits? For some reason my mind returns to home and I remember the story I was reading only a few weeks ago from my Dickens collection—*A Christmas Carol*. There are three spirits in that book too. And their names aren't

Jim, Jack and Johnny. These were scary ghosts—the ghosts of Christmas Past, Christmas Present and Christmas Yet to Come. But wait a second. It's not Christmas. It's not even close to Christmas.

'Without these spirits, you will not change.'

I tune back in. 'But I don't want to change. I—'

'Olivia,' she breathes. 'You must change.'

And with this she moves backwards a step or two, and then starts shuffling towards the powder room, slowly, her load making her movements awkward.

'You *must* change.'

'No, I…'

Mrs Batty-Smith puts her hand up and I stop talking. When I'm silent again, she turns and keeps going. I want to stay here, to let her go, but I can't. Something drags me along with her. I'm swivelled on the spot and turned ninety degrees to face the doorway, still being pulled.

Suddenly I want to stop.

Because, and I'm not sure why, when I see inside the powder room I get the distinct feeling I don't want to go in there. I put both my hands up, holding onto the doorframe, and try to stop moving forward with all my might.

I'm not strong enough.

In the middle of the room Mrs Batty-Smith turns and moves her head to meet my eyes, waiting for me to follow. My hands are ripped from the doorframe and I'm forced to take a step forward. And in that one short moment everything changes.

Now there are people everywhere. Surrounding me. Women. Grey women. Ghostly, dusty figures like Mrs Batty-Smith, but younger and in sparkly grey evening outfits. There must be thirty or forty women crammed in here, circling me. They're standing, talking in groups—like a normal party. One of them walks past holding a tray of canapés. When she sees me, she stops and offers me one. I go to take one off the tray, worried about what will happen if I don't, but when I pick it up, it turns to dust. The woman doesn't seem to notice.

'You know…' she leans in towards me conspiratorially. 'I should have answered that man's ad that I liked in the personals. The one that caught me eye.'

I wipe the dust from my fingers on the hem of my jacket and notice that I'm shaking again.

Another woman turns, hearing this, and takes a canapé off the tray. I notice it doesn't turn to dust. She nods first to the woman holding the tray, then to me. 'I always wanted to join a singles dinner club, but all my workmates told me it was a ridiculous idea.' That said, she turns away and starts talking to her group of friends again.

I look around for Mrs Batty-Smith, but she's gone.

While I'm trying to catch a glimpse of her in the crowd, another woman walks over and selects a canapé from the tray. She eats it, studying me as she nibbles. 'I should have accepted that dinner invitation from my co-worker,' she says, and then taps a woman on the shoulder, the one who's just turned back to her friends.

But it's not just that woman who turns around.

They all turn. Every single one of the women stops talking, turns and looks at me.

'I should have,' they say together. 'I should have, I should have, I should have…'

They start to chant, getting louder and louder. 'I should have, I should have, I should have, *I should have…*'

I cover my ears as their voices rise, but it's not enough. They get louder still and I take a step backwards, moving towards the toilets. I stumble through the doorway, almost falling as my feet hit the slippery tiles. The women's words are piercing my eardrums. I keep stumbling, turning halfway as I enter the room, and hit my knee hard on the edge of a basin. I grab it to steady myself, both hands gripping the porcelain so tight I think it will break.

The chanting keeps going. Louder and louder and louder. When I don't think it can get any louder, it does. Time and time again. I reach down and quickly turn on the tap, hoping to drown out the sound and close my eyes.

The noise stops.

I wait for what seems like for ever and then, very,

very slowly, I open my eyes. There's nothing there. Only me. And the mirror. And the toilet stalls.

I turn around equally slowly. No Mrs Batty-Smith. No women. Again, just me.

I move over and peek into the powder room. Nothing.

I take a few hesitant steps into the room itself and lower myself into one of the chairs, sitting for a minute or two until I feel slightly more normal. And then I get up and walk out, shakily, to the car.

As I cross the bitumen Sally winds the passenger side window down and yells across the parking lot for everyone to hear, 'God almighty, girlfriend! You could have told me it was number twos. I'm baking in here!'

Y Y Y Y

TUESDAY 9 February—
five short days left...

I'm late leaving home for work on Tuesday morning, because I make myself drink five large glasses of water. I remember to take my medication and force-feed myself a proper breakfast of a poached egg on toast, strawberries and yoghurt, and green tea. Then I pee three times and, in between each trip to the bathroom, spend a good fifteen minutes hunting down cool natural fibres in my wardrobe.

I hate being late. But I am not going to have a repeat of yesterday's dehydrated delusion in the crematorium ladies'. No siree.

My little hallucination completely freaked me out all afternoon and well into the evening. So much so, I drank a litre of water as soon as Sally and I arrived back at the studio from the funeral, ate a healthy dinner of steamed veggies and brown rice and made sure I took a multivitamin. Two, in fact. And later that night I indulged in more herbal treats—valerian, to be precise—because I wasn't able to sleep. The thing was, I couldn't stop thinking about Mrs Batty-Smith. And Tania—she'd said this kind of dream could mean things. That I could be trying to tell myself something. Mrs Batty-Smith kept telling me that she was there to warn me. That I had to change.

But change what?

Why I should change, I didn't understand at all. And, staring at the ceiling for hours as I tried to fall asleep, I still couldn't figure it out. I liked my life. I was happy. Everything was fine. *Is* fine.

Isn't it?

At two thirty-seven a.m I got up, fetched myself a glass of water and gave myself a good talking to. I was being ridiculous. There was no ghost. Ghosts didn't exist. But Snickers bars, Diet Coke and forgotten medication *did*, and if I looked after myself a little more I'd probably fare a lot better on the seeing things scene. So, I decided, that was it. Easy. No more junk food before midday.

Standing in the lounge room, searching for my car keys, I shake my head, bringing myself back to the real world. Work. I have to get to work.

But then I pause. Because I catch a glimpse of it again—the tiny bruise on my arm that I can't seem to stop looking at. Reaching out to grab my keys from the basket near the phone, I'm unable to help myself. For the hundredth time this morning I bring my arm up closer. There's definitely a bruise. Right where I pinched myself during my Batty-Smith encounter. I look away quickly and let my arm drop. I'm not going to think about it. I should be thinking about work.

As I lug my equipment downstairs, my mind races, thinking about anything and everything. Anything and everything *but*. I try being positive about the world, Tania-style, and as my camera case bashes against my right leg with each step I take I give myself a quick pat on the back for having the foresight to bring everything with me from the studio in the first place, thus saving a few minutes. It weighs a ton and it's a pain bringing it all home after what's already been a long day, but the times I actually do, it's worth it. This way I can head straight off to my first booking for the day—an engagement shoot—without having to go to the studio first.

I open up the garage, load everything into the boot of the car and rest my handbag on top so I can check my diary for the couple's names. Kirsty and Shaun, that's it. And, thankfully, this time the shoot's not at the park at the end of the world. It's at the park I used to live across the road from, so I know exactly where it is and how to get there.

It's a good twenty-minute journey, even using my insider knowledge. I turn the radio up loud and sing along as I go, trying to keep my mind occupied. Late as I am, as I pass my old apartment I turn the radio down, slow the car and take a look up at it. I can't help but think of Mike as I sit there and stare, because Mike and that apartment—well, they used to go to together like, I don't know... I catch myself about to think 'horse and carriage' and move the car on before I can take the thought any further. Mike still lives around here as far as I know. With his son and... *her.*

I reach forward and turn the radio up again, not wanting to think about anything this morning. Not yesterday. Not Mike. I should be concentrating on work. I'm only going to think about work. As I pull into the dirt car park, I pray that the Kirsty and Shaun are running late too.

They're early.

I take a deep breath, tell myself to get on with it, then open the car door and go over to them. I remember them now, though their names hadn't really rung any bells before. And they're not bad, this couple, even if they are getting married on Valentine's Day. Maybe because they have a better reason than most. From what I recall, they told me his birthday was on the thirteenth of February and hers was on the fifteenth. Because of this, they thought they'd get married on the day in between and make it their own little three-day festival every year. The cost doesn't seem to worry them because Kirsty's dad is a rather eminent cardiac surgeon, still has the guilts from running off with one of her mother's friends when Kirsty was a teenager, and is paying for the whole bit. Thus, they decided to go all out. Including the digital album and all their photos on CD ROM. They haven't asked exactly what it's going to cost, but there are going to be plenty of 0s appearing on Daddy's Amex bill next month, that's for sure.

'Hi, Kirsty; hi, Shaun,' I say as I run the last few steps over. 'Hope I haven't kept you waiting.'

They both shake their heads, getting up off the wooden bench they were sitting on.

'We've only been here for about five minutes,' Kirsty says. 'Was the traffic bad? We live just around the corner, so we walked.'

I pause, wondering whether to lie or not. I mean, bad traffic—it's the usual excuse, isn't it? In the end, my smile gives me away. 'The traffic was fine. It was breakfast that made me late. Sorry. I really needed it this morning.' I take a quick glance around the park. 'I'll just go and get the equipment out of the car. Anywhere in particular you'd like the photos?'

'Any ideas?' Shaun asks.

'Well, along the timber fence is nice, and I've taken a few underneath the tree over there. Those shots always seem to work out really well. Some people like the swings…' I watch the two of them carefully as I say this and note the quick glance they give each other '…but personally, I feel it's a bit tacky.'

'Thank God for that,' Kirsty says. 'I hate that kind of stuff.'

'Good. Great, even. I think we're going to get along just fine.'

I remember then that she was the girl who looked at me as if I was crazy when I mentioned lingerie shots. 'I'm not going to go floozing all over the bed in my underwear looking like a beached whale,' I think she told me. Yes. My kind of girl.

'Anyway, you guys have a think about what you'd like,' I say, and with that I turn and do another quick run back to the car. As I busy myself arranging things in the boot, the breeze changes direction and carries their banter across the park. I have to smile as I listen to it. They're funny, these two. Every so often I stumble across a couple like this. The thing is, at some weddings I find myself wondering as I watch the bride. How does she know he's the right guy? How can she really promise him 'for ever'? And just as I'm thinking no one could ever make 'happily ever after' work, I'm always met with a pair that aren't so fairy tale. A pair I can almost believe in.

When I get back, they've decided.

'The tree, we think,' Kirsty says, and Shaun nods.

'And an excellent choice it is.' I start off across the grass and Kirsty and Shaun follow me. Halfway there, an idea comes to me. I explain it to them. And then I take my boots off.

'Um, Liv, are you sure about this?' Kirsty says, holding my camera as Shaun gives me a leg-up so I can reach the first branch of the tree.

'Umph.' I make a truly graceless noise as I push myself up, grab the next branch above and swivel around. Perfect. The fork in the tree is a made-to-measure sitting spot, and there's even a branch placed strategically so that I'll be able to rest the camera on it. Settled, I get back to Kirsty's question. 'Sure about the angle, or sure about me being up here?' I ask.

'Sure about being up there,' she says, passing me the camera.

'Ask me again after I fall out, OK?'

'It's the least I can do. So, where do you want us?'

I take a look around. 'How about sitting on that patch of grass right there? In the clover?' I glance at the sun. 'We'll try and get this over and done with quickly, before it gets too hot, OK?'

The pair position themselves. 'Um, leaning back like this?' Kirsty asks.

'That's good.' I nod, getting back down to business. Kirsty's looking up at me, knees bent, leaning back on her hands, which she's placed behind her. I bring the camera up. 'Now, Shaun, if you can just do the same thing…that's great. You're naturals.'

Kirsty laughs. 'I can assure you I'm not a natural. Cameras and I don't get on very well as a rule.'

'Ah, but you haven't met my camera yet. Ursula. A girl's best friend.'

'Your camera has a name?' Shaun looks at me, then

over at Kirsty in surprise, and laughs as well. I snap off a few shots.

'Yep. Kirsty, if you can just lean in a bit more? Into Shaun's shoulder. That's it. Right. Now, I've got a little trick for you. I want you to look away from the camera then, when I tell you to, look up and smile, OK? Look away. Now, at me, on the count of three and smile. One, two…three.' I snap away.

'Why look away?' Kirsty asks then.

I pause for a moment and rest the camera on my lap. 'It's a modelling trick. Gets rid of the fake smile. If you just keep smiling at the camera it begins to look really forced.'

We start up again and do the one-two-three trick a few more times until I'm satisfied I've captured a few good shots at least. One thing I know for sure—Kirsty's beautiful red-gold hair is going to come up a treat. The sun's just moved through the tree perfectly, leaving some dappled light on the ground, and that combined with the green patch of grass under the tree, spotted with white clover, looks fantastic. I'm going to have to move fast, though, to get the last few shots. I glance around to my left, then to my right, and then up the tree.

'Oh, no. No higher.' Shaun sees what I'm looking at.

I grin. 'Just one branch.'

'You're nuts,' Kirsty says. 'Are you covered for this?'

I think about this for a moment. 'The camera is.'

Before they can argue further, I sling it around my neck, push myself up and turn carefully, clinging to the branch above. It's then, right at the critical moment, that I see him.

Mike…

And Toby. On the swings.

I stay right where I am and stare at them both.

Mike.

I get the exact same nauseous feeling I had yesterday in the bathroom. Now I wish I hadn't eaten breakfast after all. I grip on even tighter to the branch in front of me and will my poached egg to stay down, watching as Mike pushes Toby higher and higher and Toby squeals with delight—the noise carrying right across the park. My eyes quickly scan the grounds, looking for a third person. But there's no one in sight. I wonder where *she* is—Amanda. At work, I guess.

I'm still watching the two of them, staring at them, when something catches my eye off to the right. A flash of something pink. I turn my head quickly, trying to see what it is and completely forget where I am (up a tree) and what I'm doing (balancing precariously), and one of my feet slides out from under me.

'Shit!'

'Liv!' Kirsty yells out as I right myself and sit back down. I glance back over at Mike and Toby.

They're both looking over in our direction. Mike at Kirsty and Shaun and then, as they look at me, he

starts to follow their gaze up the tree. But Toby—
Toby's been staring directly at me the whole time.

I hold my breath as I watch him and wait for Mike
to spot me.

But then, with perfect timing, Toby turns back
around and squeals to be pushed again. Mike's attention returns to the swings. He hasn't seen me.

'Liv, are you OK?' Kirsty tries again.

I look down at her. 'Sorry, sorry. I'm fine.' I push myself up to the next branch and sit myself down. Work.
Work. Think about *work*. 'Right. Let's go. The leaning
thing again. And turn away, one, two…three and smile.
That's it. And again. One, two…three and smile. Now
look at each other. Great. Perfect. And again. Once
more. OK, I lied. Once more…'

A few minutes later I decide I have all the shots I
need. 'All finished.' I look down at them.

'Good,' Kirsty says. 'Because I don't think my neck
is going to take much more modelling.'

Shaun comes over to give me a hand down out of
the tree. I glance at Mike again, to see if he's watching, but he and Toby have moved over to the see-saw
now, further away.

When I'm back on solid ground, I sit on the grass
with Shaun and Kirsty for a few minutes and run
them through what's going to happen on Sunday,
their wedding day, one more time. Then, when we're
done, I try not to be too obvious about slinking back

to the car using the happy couple as a shield against Mike and Toby. After I've waved them off, and put all my equipment in the boot, I get in the car, wriggle down in my seat and stare a bit longer at the guys I used to call the 'terrible twosome'. As I watch, I wonder again where Amanda is, and the whole time I ache, ache, ache to go over and see Toby, who's got so big I can hardly believe my eyes…

But Mike. Mike I'm not so sure about.

And then, a few minutes later, I become sure. I tear my eyes away, start the car and speed off in a cloud of dust before I can change my mind.

Y Y Y Y

I pull my car into its spot at the studio and Sally comes rushing out through the front door to greet me. 'And about time too,' she says, hands on hips, as I open the car door and swing my legs out.

'What? What have I done? Am I late for something?' I freeze, knowing I don't have any appointments down in my diary, but with a sudden fear that I forgot to write one down.

'I'm desperate for a fag. *Desperate.*'

'Oh, is that all?' I breathe a sigh of relief and reach behind me onto the passenger seat for my handbag.

'Is that all?' she says loudly.

'Yes—*is that all?*' I look up again. 'Why don't you steal one from your stash in the car if you need one so badly?' I realise as the words come out of my mouth they're too harsh. Sally's just being her usual over-the-top self.

'The car's at the garage. What's up, buttercup?'

As I open the door and get out I sigh one of those big fatalistic Russian novel 'life's shit and then you die' sighs. 'I just saw Mike and Toby. In the park across the road from my old apartment.'

'Oh, dear. Now I get it.' Sally closes the car door and then leans up against it. 'And Ms Indecisive?'

'No, she wasn't around.'

'Did you talk to him?'

'No.' I shake my head.

'Did he see you?'

I shake my head again. 'I don't think so. I guess I just thought it was better if I didn't go over…'

Sally nods.

There's a long silence.

I bite my lip. 'You think I should have gone over?'

She looks up the street, away from me, for a second. 'No, I think you were right,' she says slowly. 'Sometimes it's better not to know. There's no point forcing yourself when you don't want to, is there?'

I shake my head, realising Sally's right. I *didn't* want to go over, and, as much as I wanted to see Toby, I know that at this point in time I still can't face talking to Mike in one of those jolly five-minute supermarket 'I didn't expect to see you here' encounters. I smile a small smile, knowing that for once I've done the right thing by myself. 'You're so wise, Yoda.'

She laughs. 'It's called learning by experience. And if there's one thing I have it's relationship experience.' There's a pause. 'So, um, are you going to be all right?'

'Haven't I been for the past two years?'

'Um…'

'Oh, shut up.'

'OK!' Sally looks like this is a good idea. 'About those fags, then…'

I cave and pick my handbag up off the ground, fishing around inside for the packet. I open it up to see there are two left. 'Here.' I pass the packet over to her. 'Knock yourself out.'

'Two! All my Christmases have come at once!'

It doesn't take Sally long to light up—about three seconds, actually. Then she takes a very long drag, closing her eyes, and, finally, exhales. 'Oh, boy. That's better.' Her eyes flick open then. 'Bugger.'

'What?'

'There's someone inside. Waiting for you. I totally forgot.'

'For me?' My mind works through my appointments again. There shouldn't be anyone here for me.

'Andrew? No—Drew. That's it.' Her eyebrows rise. 'A bit dishy too. Where'd you find him?'

Oh. Drew. I'd forgotten about our appointment. 'Um, Justine found him.'

'That'd be right. The competition. I should have known.' She nods her head in the direction of the studio. 'I set him up with some albums to look at. He's only been here ten minutes or so.'

'Thanks,' I say, heading inside. Through the window Drew sees me coming and stands up.

'Hi,' I say as I open the front door and then let it close behind me. Immediately the air-conditioning hits my face. 'Oh, that's beautiful.' I drop my bag to the floor. 'Much better.'

'I know.' Drew comes over. 'If I worked here, I'd never go home in summer.'

'You'd take that back fast enough if you worked with Her Highness.' I look out at Sally, who's watching us. She waves at us encouragingly, like we're two shy sixteen-year-olds on a first date.

Drew and I look at each other and laugh.

'Sorry if my timing's bad,' he says then. 'Do you want me to go?'

'No.' I shake my head. 'Of course not. It's fine.' I motion towards the lounge area. 'Come and sit back down and we'll have a chat about the packages we offer.'

Just as we're getting settled, the door opens and Sally comes back into the office.

Drew stands up again.

'Oh!' She stops halfway across the room and stares at him. 'A gentleman! I declare, I do so like a gentleman.' She does her best Scarlett O'Hara fluttering of the eyelashes impersonation and I wonder if I should offer her a mint julep.

'Sally…' I start, giving her a warning look, then stand up as well. 'Have you met properly? Um, Drew, this is Sally Bliss, my boss. Sally, this is Drew Thomas, a friend of Justine's. He's probably told you, he's best-manning for a friend and wants me to take him through a few packages.'

'Nice to meet you *properly*, Drew.' Sally comes over to shake his hand. She heads off for her computer then, passing me and giving me a look that says, quite blatantly, 'Husband number four, do you think?'. I give her a look back and a quick 'keep your claws out of him you hussy' shake of the head. Drew's too nice— she'd eat him alive and line up his friends for dessert.

'OK.' Sally out of the way, I sit back down again and Drew follows suit. 'You've had a look through the albums?'

Drew nods. 'Yeah, they're great. I think they'd really like this sort of thing.' He points to one of the more informal albums, which he then picks up and starts flicking through one more time.

Out of the corner of my eye I see Sally get up again. She starts to saunter over towards the kitchen. 'Coffee, Drew? Liv?'

'No thanks, Sally,' Drew says, looking up from the album.

'Not for me.' I watch as Sally minces her way across the room, showing off her behind to best effect. She just can't help herself. Thankfully, Drew's attention is focused back on the album. But right when I'm about to turn my eyes heavenwards at her strutting, Sally turns and gives me a quick 'are you going to be OK, kiddo?' glance. I nod, knowing she's referring to me seeing Mike before. She may have a better butt than I'll ever have, twelve years down what should be the sag track, but I can't hate her for it—I don't know where I'd be without her.

I get up and locate another album and take it over, sitting beside Drew this time. We flick through together and I explain what the packages do and don't include, and finally walk him through our pricing system. 'Of course I'll cut you a bit of a better deal than that,' I add.

'Will you just?' Sally calls out from the kitchen.

'Yes!' I say to the wall.

When I turn back, Drew has a worried expression on his face. He stands up and starts for the kitchen. 'No, it's OK. I didn't mean…'

Sally pops her head around the corner. 'I was only kidding.'

I stand up as well. 'She's always kidding,' I say to Drew with a roll of my eyes.

He looks from one of us to the other.

'You're confusing him, poor boy.' Sally shakes her head at me before she disappears again.

'*I'm* confusing him!'

'No, I…' Drew starts, his head still moving from one side to the other, Wimbledon fashion.

'It's all right.' I laugh at his now truly confused state. I take the costing papers I've given him from his hand and put them together with the ones he's left on the table. Then I grab one of our clear plastic advertising folders and pack everything inside it. 'She really is joking. We'll be able to do anything from ten to fifteen per cent off, depending on the package they choose. Don't worry about it. It's less than she tips her Ferrari's mechanic.'

Sally pops her head around the wall for the second time. 'I have to tip him to keep him on side. A girl needs a good servicing from time to time, you know.'

'Sally!'

'What?' She tries to look innocent, but isn't all that successful at pulling the expression off, her facial muscles being unfamiliar with the position. 'Fine.' She disappears again. 'There's just no good conversation to be had these days.'

I turn to Drew. 'If *double entendres* about her car's servicing is good conversation, civilisation as we know it is in trouble.'

He laughs and looks at his watch. 'Have you got time for some lunch?'

'Yes, she does.' Sally comes back into the room for good this time, with a mug of her favourite strawberry and mango tea. So that's what she's been up to in there.

Before I say yes, I think about my schedule. I've got an engagement shoot this afternoon, but not until four-thirty. Frankly, a distraction sounds like a good idea. It might help me to stop thinking about Mike. And about the other thing that I'm not supposed to be thinking about at all, but somehow keeps popping into my head at the oddest times—Mrs Batty-Smith. 'OK. That'd be nice.'

Drew turns to Sally. 'Lunch?'

She shakes her head. 'Thanks, but I can't. Stacks of work.'

'Want me to bring you something back?' I ask her.

'No, I'll be right. I've got some red curry leftovers in the fridge from last night.'

'OK, then.' I shuffle Drew out towards the door. 'I'll be back in an hour or so.'

'Take your time!' Sally sings out, and gives me a wink that makes me herd Drew out through the door even faster. You just can't let a single guy in that studio, I think as I close the door firmly behind us. It's like lambs to the slaughter.

Y Y Y Y

As Drew and I start off down the road, he asks me if I know anywhere good to eat and I suggest the nearby café Sally and I usually go to. We chat as we stroll down towards the row of shops. On entering, I spot the specials board and notice the baked berry cheesecake that Sally and I shared on our last trip is on again.

There's just something about baked berry cheese-cake…

We decide to take a seat inside in the air-conditioning as the day's another scorcher. 'Turkey, cranberry, avocado and camembert focaccia for me, I think,' Drew says, looking at the menu. 'And a mineral water. A large one.'

Perusing the menu myself, I decide to up my food intake quota a tad more now my stomach is feeling fine again. 'I'll have the Vietnamese prawn rolls. And an orange juice.'

When we've ordered, we both sit back in our chairs.

'So,' Drew says, looking straight at me.

'So,' I say back.

He leans forward then, arms resting on the table. And suddenly I don't quite know where to look.

'You know, I can't believe you and Justine live together.'

'Why? Lots of people have flatmates.'

Drew shakes his head. 'Let me rephrase that. I can't believe you and Justine live together and haven't killed each other yet.'

'Ah. Well, I have to admit we have our *The Odd Couple* moments.'

'I can imagine.'

'What's that supposed to mean?' I give him a strange look.

'Sorry!' Drew says. 'I didn't mean anything by it. I've just been thinking about it the last couple of days, that's all.'

There's a pause in the conversation as the waiter delivers our drinks, taking them off the tray one at a time to set them in front of us. Watching him, I wonder absent-mindedly why Drew's been thinking about Justine and me, and just what he's been thinking about.

'So, how's work going?' he asks when the waiter leaves, changing the topic. 'Busy today? You mentioned you had something on this afternoon...'

I forget about Justine then, and fill Drew in on what's going on in my work life. I'm telling him all about the absolutely hideous wedding I'm shooting first thing Saturday when our meals come. 'I don't know why I'm telling you all this,' I say with a wave of my hand as the waiter places our meals before us. 'It must be boring. I'm surprised you haven't fallen asleep over there.'

Drew shakes his head. 'No, it's interesting. It certainly sounds more exciting than my line of work at times.'

I ask Drew about his architecture then, questioning him about what kind of area he hopes to end up in.

He puts his focaccia down when I ask this, and wipes his hands on his napkin. 'I want to specialise in designing museums.'

I watch him, noting how his eyes light up as he starts to speak about it. 'A worthy cause,' I say.

Drew nods, and we chat about it for a while longer, until he turns the subject back to me again.

'And you're going to set up on your own next year, Justine says?'

I nod as well.

Drew asks some more about this, and I relax and tell him what he wants to know as we devour our meals and finish off our drinks. But after a while, as Drew talks, I remember what he said before—that he'd been thinking about Justine and my differences over the last couple of days—and my curiosity gets the better of me. I hesitate for a moment, wondering whether I should bring it up again.

'It's OK. You can tell me,' he says. 'Do I have a big piece of avocado in my teeth or something?'

I laugh. 'No, I was just wondering about what you said before—that you'd been thinking about Justine and my differences. What did you mean?'

'Nothing.' He waves one hand. 'Really, I didn't mean anything by it.'

'Too late! You've got to tell me now.'

Drew takes his time finishing off his mineral water. 'Well…' He looks cagey.

'Come on. You can't start to say something like that then back out. I hate it when people do that!'

'All right.' But then he stops. 'I guess… I don't know. It's just that you know what Justine's like…'

'What's she like?'

Drew stops, looks at the ceiling, then back down at the table, frowning. 'This is going to sound weird, but she's rather like one of those tiny super-bouncy rubber balls bounced too hard in a squash court.'

I nod slowly. That is, in fact, quite an accurate description of Justine. 'I'll buy that. And I am…?'

'Well, you just seem really…er…settled. You know, like you've carved out an existence for yourself and you're sticking to it. I think it's interesting that you two get on so well, that's all.'

I laugh. 'Is this the diplomatic way of calling me a homebody?

'No! I…'

'Sure. Don't worry about it. My family and friends tell me pretty much the same thing on the hour every hour. Anyway, like I said, Justine and I have our moments.'

Drew's eyebrows go up. 'You argue?'

'No, no.' I shake my head. 'Nothing like that.'

'Then what?'

I give him another strange look.

'Sorry, I'm being too nosy, aren't I?'

I shrug. 'It's not that we argue. I suppose you could just say we agree to disagree on some points, and that's probably why we get on like we do. Most of the time, anyway.'

Drew opens his mouth, then closes it again, his eyes giving away the fact that he's not sure whether or not he should continue.

And, while I realise I could end the conversation right here and now, I want to know why he's asking these questions. I want to know if he's going somewhere with this. And, of course, I also want to know what he's been thinking about me.

'What it comes down to,' I say slowly, choosing my words with care, 'is that Justine is a really social person. And I'm not. That's where we differ.'

'What do you mean, you're not social? You deal with hundreds of people for work each year.'

I eye him steadfastly across the table. 'I mean with men.'

'Ah.' He stops, and I know from his expression that

he *is* going somewhere with this.'Well, you don't have to agree with each other on the subject. What's the problem?'

'She thinks I should date more.' Not that I could date less, I think to myself. But I don't have to reveal everything to Drew, do I?

'Should you date more?' he asks me, his eyes twinkling.

I choke on the final piece of spring roll that's in my mouth.'What is it with you?' I ask when I manage to swallow, and Drew at least has the good grace to look a bit sheepish.'What's Justine told you about me?' My eyes narrow.

'Nothing.'

My eyes narrow further.

'Much.'

'Is she trying to set us up?'

'Oh, definitely.' Drew nods without hesitation.

'And you have to report back right after lunch, yes?'

He nods, as if it's a given.'But of course.'

I laugh at his truthfulness.

'No, not really. Justine knows I have to see you about the photos this week, but I didn't tell her I was coming in today. So, back to the subject at hand.' Drew leans forward again. 'Why don't you? Date, I mean.' His expression turns serious.'Is it a religious thing?'

Now I really laugh.'No! It's just…' My mind clicks back over to Mike and the smile suddenly drops from my face. 'I don't know. I suppose Justine dates because men like her. Men like Justine *a lot*. She feeds their egos or something. Whereas I'm… Oh, I give up. There's no other way to say it. Men just don't like me.'

'What? Rubbish.' Drew laughs. 'Who told you that?'

I snort and look away. 'No one told me that,' I say flippantly. 'I figured it out for myself. Trial and error. Mostly error. Don't ask me why it is. I've no idea.'

When our eyes meet again, Drew is giving me an unbelieving stare. This time I can tell what he's thinking, funnily enough—just the same thing Tania did. So I spell it out for him. 'Don't think it's a self-esteem thing, because it's not. It's just the cold hard truth. Men don't… OK, so it's not that they don't like me. It's that, um…they don't *take* to me.'

I glance out the café window as I say this, starting to wonder if he's going to ask about the sex thing. Probably. If Justine has told him I haven't dated for well over a year, as a guy, it'll be one of the first things that crosses his mind. Men can never believe it—that I've gone almost a year without sex. As for women, if they find out they never even bat an eyelid. They've all seen *that* page in the back of *Cosmo*. A cheque made out for $69.95, a pack or two of batteries (or three, if you're that way inclined) and everybody's happy.

A car drives past in the bright sunlight and distracts me from what I'm thinking. There's a flash again. Another pink flash. That's weird. Another one—just like

I'd seen in the park. Maybe I should get my eyes checked? With this thought, Mrs Batty-Smith creeps back into my mind again. Just my eyes? Maybe I should get a proper check-up at the doctor's as well. Blood pressure, blood test, the lot. When I turn my attention back to Drew, he's laughing.

'I can't believe you just said that.'

'What?' I say, forgetting the pink flash and thinking back to what we've just been discussing. Shit. Did I say something about the vibrator out loud?

'Men. You think they don't take to you?'

Phew I shake my head. 'It's true. I am *not* their scene.'

'Well, that's understandable.' Drew doesn't even pause to take a breath.

'What? Why?'

He smiles. 'You mean you really don't know why? I thought you were joking. The reason you don't get on with some of them—I'd say it's because you scare them, Liv. You're intimidating.'

'Gee, thanks. Why don't you tell me what you really think?'

'No, I didn't mean it like that…'

'Is that right?' I butt in, as the waiter takes our plates. 'I'm an intimidating homebody? It's an interesting combination. And what *do* you mean? There's another meaning to "you're intimidating"? A nice one? God, I can't believe I'm sitting here discussing my love life with you. I haven't even had anything alcoholic to drink. It's embarrassing.'

Drew shakes his head. 'Don't be embarrassed.'

'Oh, OK. Now I feel better,' I say sarcastically.

Drew gives me a look that makes me shut up. 'I never said you were a homebody. And about the intimidating comment—what I meant is that some guys, they're scared by a woman with drive, who knows what she wants and goes out and gets it. They're intimidated by that kind of attitude, especially if they don't have it themselves.'

'And you?' I look him straight in the eye, thinking two can play at this game.

He doesn't flinch. 'It doesn't bother me. I think it's sexy when women are self-confident. Not arrogant, mind you. Just comfortable being who they are, knowing what they want and asking for it straight out—no games.' His eyes meet mine. 'Like you.'

'I…' I start, but then choke once more. When I finally glance up at Drew again he's still watching me. His eyes are twinkling like before.

'Oh, don't be so coy.' He laughs and, after watching him open-mouthed for a second or two, I can't help but laugh as well. 'You see, I know what I want,' Drew continues. 'I think it's good if other people do too. Doesn't matter if they're men or women.'

'And what do you want?' I try and gain a bit of conversation control back here.

He leans back in his seat. 'That I'll just have to leave for our next lunch.'

Our next lunch. My mind goes blank when he says this. I can't think of anything to say. Drew wants to have lunch again. With me. For some reason, I'm surprised. I look at the time then—one-fifty p.m. 'I've really got to be getting back...' I say.

'We *will* leave it for another day, then.'

'Um, sure.' I nod. 'I, um, love a good interrogation,' I add, when my brain kicks back in. And so much for that cheesecake. Oh, well.

'What is it?' Drew says, following my eyes to the refrigerated cabinet across the room.

I laugh. 'Absolutely nothing. I'm just being a pig. Last time Sally and I ate here we had the baked berry cheesecake. It was out of this world. I thought I'd have time for a piece today. You know—do my bit in keeping up the café's quality control.' I go to reach for my wallet, but Drew shakes his head.

'My treat. I owe you for fitting me in this week when you're so busy.'

'That's OK. You're sure?' I'm still holding my wallet.

'Of course I'm sure.'

We both get up and Drew goes over to the counter to pay while I inspect the free postcards by the door.

'There you go,' he says when he comes over. He hands me a white polystyrene box. I look down at it.

'Two pieces of cheesecake. For you and Sally.'

'Oh! I—' I begin, but Drew butts in.

'I really don't want to hear any of those "just a salad, thanks, I'm on a diet" girl lines.'

This stops me in my tracks. Just a salad, thanks? They're words my lips wouldn't know how to form. 'OK. It's not what I was going to say, but thanks. For the cheesecake, I mean. Sally will love you for ever.'

We walk back to the studio slowly in the heat, stopping by a dark blue Jeep parked on the left of my car in the studio car park, which must be Drew's.

'So, Justine tells me you're not coming to this Cupid's Choice thing? The ball on Saturday?' Drew asks, jingling his car keys.

I shake my head. 'I can't. I've got three weddings on that day and three on Sunday. I don't think I'll be home till after nine.'

'You're probably not missing much.' He pulls something out of his back pocket—a piece of paper. He opens it up. 'I got this just before I left work.'

'What is it?'

'My date. Michelle. She runs a website about breeding poodles, or something, and likes romantic walks along the beach in the moonlight. It's pretty bad.'

I laugh. 'Good luck.'

'Well, thanks for this, anyway.' Drew holds up the folder I've given him.

'That's OK. Thanks for lunch. And the cheesecake. It was nice.'

He moves to get something else out of his wallet. As he's fishing around, I start to run a mental check-list of things I have to do this afternoon. I can't help myself. I'm always zoning out and running checklists like this through my head when I've got a big week-end coming up. Shot lists, hotels, reception venues…

Finally, Drew finds what he's looking for and hands something over to me—his business card. 'So you can call me,' he says.

I look at it, confused. I'm still half thinking about this weekend and all things wedding, and don't catch on quite as quickly as I should. 'What for?' I say bluntly. 'I thought your friends were going to make an appointment?'

For the first time today Drew looks as if I've caught him on the back foot. 'Er, I just…thought you might like to call. Or not. It doesn't matter.'

Oh, shit.

Double shit.

Triple shit.

I'm such an idiot. He thinks that I haven't had a good time this afternoon. 'Sorry, sorry. I didn't mean that. I—I was thinking about work,' I stutter. 'And I…'

There's a pause as our eyes meet and we size each other up. I start to think about what the card means before Mike enters my head again, as always, and I have to look away as my chest tightens and I feel the backs of my eyes start to fill with tears. God, sometimes I really hate myself. When I turn towards him again Drew is still waiting for an explanation. 'It's just…' I start. 'I don't know if I'm ready for…'

Drew shakes his head. 'No, no, you don't have to explain. It, er, doesn't have to be like that.' He reaches down to press the card into my hand. 'Just take the card, and if you want to call, you can call. For any reason. There's no pressure. It's just a piece of cardboard with a phone number on it, that's all.'

I listen to what he's saying and slowly my eyes start to feel normal again. I close my fingers around the card and he leaves his hand on mine for a moment before he pulls away. He turns towards his car then, busying himself opening the door. When he's inside, he starts the engine and lowers the driver's side window. 'You're right,' he says. 'Lunch was nice.'

I nod, not saying anything.

'Bye, Liv,' Drew says, holding my gaze for a second before he starts to back the car out of the car park.

I watch the car travel down the road and stop at the lights. It's a good few minutes before they turn green and Drew's car turns left and is out of sight.

My eyes frozen, I keep staring up the road, thinking. Mainly about Drew. About Drew and me.

But also recalling something that Mrs Batty-Smith said yesterday—about men. What was it? I frown,

breaking my promise not to think about the event, trying to get the words right.

'*Lying pigs. Swine, all of them… All that false love.
False hope.*'

And I look at where Drew's car was and think to
myself that she's wrong. Drew doesn't seem like that.
Drew doesn't seem like that at all.

But then, just as fast, some other words pop into
my mind.

Neither did Mike, at the start. Remember?

Y Y Y

When I reach the front door of the studio, it's locked, and the Closed sign is hanging inside the small lead-light window. I fish the key out of my handbag and open up, the air-conditioning hitting me once again. Sally must have only popped out for a minute or two, I think, before I spot the note on the kitchen bench. I'm right. She's gone to the corner shop to buy some more milk.

I put my handbag on the bench and go to place my keys back inside, but stop when I spot Drew's card sitting on the bottom—next to the lipstick I never remember to reapply and the fluff-gathering tampon I'll probably never use. I'd let it fall in there, finding its way to the bottom, but now I pluck the card out with two fingers, look at it for a moment, then tuck it carefully into the side of my wallet.

Right, Liv. Work.

I cross the room, sit down at the computer and start the work I have to finish before I head out to my engagement shoot this afternoon. Today I have to complete an engagement portrait I'd started on last week. More de-flabbing. More zit-disintegration.

I finish my work on the photo the couple have chosen (good news, they've both got great skin) and then start ringing around the couples whose weddings I'm going to photograph on Saturday and Sunday, just to check they don't have any last questions. When that's done, I print out the shot lists for the weddings as well—all the photos the couple have said they definitely want on the day.

It's surprising how different each wedding is. Kirsty and Shaun's will be quite informal. They want me to run around taking a photojournalistic approach to the day, capturing moments here and there. Another couple on the same day, however, want something completely different. Theirs will be a very formal wedding and they want a very formal photographic approach. The photo with Mum and Dad; the photo with Mum and Dad and the grandparents; the photo with Mum and Dad and the grandparents and the siblings; the photo with Mum and Dad and the grandparents and the siblings and the neighbour's three-legged guinea pig and so on. I bring up all the shot lists and have a quick run through them one last time.

It's a good hour and a half before Sally arrives back.

'That was some trip to the corner shop.' I look up.

'Oh, bugger. The milk.'

'You mean you didn't get any?' I check her hands and see three large bags from the gorgeous little clothes boutique down the road, but no dairy products whatsoever. Sally looks back at the door.

'Don't worry about it,' I say. 'I'll pick some up later.'

'You're a doll.' She blows me a kiss before going over to rest her shop-sore bones on the couch. She closes her eyes and sighs loudly. Just as I'm about to turn back to my computer, she opens one eye. 'Not so fast, young lady.'

'Mmm?' I say.

'This Drew. What's the deal?'

I shrug. 'Like I told you, Justine found him. They've become quite chummy.'

Sally sighs again. 'Bugger Justine. What's his caper with *you*?'

I catch sight of my handbag and think of the card inside. I shrug slightly.

'Ooohhh, you sly dog. Well, good luck. He's not bad. Not bad at all.'

'No hair plugs,' I point out.

'I noticed. Believe me, I noticed. And is he a NG?'

I roll my eyes. Sally has decreed that I am only allowed to date NGs rated eight or higher (that's Sally-speak for Nice Guys). She thinks it's the only way I'm ever going to get back on the dating bandwagon (a wagon I'd frankly rather see roll right on by).

'You know what I think about the NG scale…' If

I've told her once, I've told her a thousand times—the NG scale is useless. In my opinion it's the NGs you've got to watch out for. At least you know you have to be careful with the TSs (Total Shits) from the start. It's the NGs that suck you in and spit you out again. Hard. Which is why I'm prepared to let that wagon roll by. With Drew on it. Like I'd remembered before, Mike had seemed nice at the start. More than nice.

'I'll take that as a yes. Rating, please?'

I sigh a Sally-weary sigh. 'Um, eight, I guess. Maybe a nine if he hadn't followed Justine home.'

'Nine! We haven't had a nine for…for ever! Oh, damn!' The phone rings and Sally rushes over to pick it up. It's a new client. They book in to talk to us both a fortnight from today. When she puts the phone down again, she nods at it. 'I forgot to tell you—both Justine and Rachel called almost the minute you left.'

'Oh. Anyone else?'

'Yes. Justine and Rachel.'

Huh?

'I think it went Justine, Rachel, Justine, Rachel, Rachel,' she counts off on her fingers. 'What's wrong with those girls?'

I shake my head. 'It'd take all day.'

Justine, Rachel, Justine, Rachel, Rachel. A little much, really. But that's two for Justine and three for Rachel, so as I pick up the phone I decide Rachel's more desperate to get in contact with me and call her first. I try her home number to start with—she couldn't possibly be calling that many times from work.

Rachel picks up. 'Taking a sickie?' I ask.

'Who's the hot date?'

I look up from the phone. 'Sally!'

She doesn't turn, but waves a hand over her head.

'There's no hot date.' I sigh, wondering how much I should, or want to, tell. 'It was just a groom. He was hungry, so we had a, um, working lunch.'

'Oh.'

'You don't have to sound so disappointed.' I laugh at Rachel's tone. 'Are you taking a sickie or not?

'No. They've taken all the kids to see an exhibition at the art gallery. We drew straws to see who'd go and I got lucky. Actually, I was calling about dinner. Here. Tonight. I know it's short notice, but I didn't think you'd be doing anything…'

'Gee, thanks. I guess I'll have to cancel that première and send the Valentino gown back.'

Rachel sighs. 'You know I didn't mean it like that. I just knew you'd be taking it easy before this weekend. It's no big affair—just a casual, relaxed dinner at ours. And before you ask, no, I'm not setting you up.'

'Did I suggest in any way that you were? Dinner would be lovely. What time and what can I bring?' We finalise the arrangements and then I make my second call—to Justine at work. 'It's me,' I say when she picks up.

'Who's the hot date?'

If only my friends weren't so predictable. I repeat the working–lunch–with–a–hungry–groom story.

'Oh.' I get the same reply I had from Rachel. But Justine recovers faster. 'Oh, well. Hey, you've got to come out tomorrow night. That's what I called for. It's Drew's birthday.'

Drew's birthday? He didn't mention that. 'Oh. OK. Great.'

'And Drew says you have to come because he's never seen you outside of the apartment. He's starting to think you're on home release from jail or something. He said next time he's over he's going to check out your ankles for those little tags.'

My eyebrows raise themselves with this. 'Is that right?'

'Can you make it? I think we're just going to grab something to eat and meet up with a few of his friends at some club or other.'

'Um.' I think about work first, as per usual. I don't think I've got anything on, but I reach for my diary and flip through the pages quickly. 'Yep. I'd love to come. Leave me a note about it. I'm going to Rachel's for dinner. And before you ask, no, she's not setting me up. She promised.'

Justine laughs. 'Sure. We'll see.'

'Yeah, yeah. Very funny. I'll talk to you later.' I hang up again.

'You're a terrible liar.' Sally swivels around on her seat. ' "It was just a groom. He was hungry, so we had a, um, working lunch," ' she mimics.

I laugh. 'Is that what I sounded like? I *am* a terrible liar.'

'I'll coach you some time.' Sally slaps her thigh loudly. 'Now, chop-chop,' she says. 'Finish up what you've got to do and I'll shout you a drink before you have to run off.'

'What are we celebrating?' I ask her.

She winks. 'Well, sweetie, fish like Drew don't come along every day. And to me he's certainly looking like a big marlin that you shouldn't waste any time reeling in.'

Funny, I think, as Sally grins at me. Advice on reeling in marlins from a toothy dating shark.

Y Y Y Y

I try to get the most out of the vodka, lime and soda that Sally buys me that afternoon, just in case.

Just in case the man that's sure to be sitting across from me at Rachel's dinner party is the kind of fish John West's sister would reject.

But this time Rachel happens to be telling the truth. There really is no extra guy. No ring-in. Just Rachel and Ryan and four other people (two couples) that I haven't met before. There's not even any mention of Valentine's Day—well, unless you count the heart-shaped crème brûlée that Rachel gives me with a big nudge. But heart-shaped crème brûlée I can deal with. Crème brûlée me up any day, whatever the shape, I say.

All in all, I have a really nice time.

I even manage to have a long chat with Ryan, which is nice. More like back to normal. Like the old days.

And as I back out of Rachel and Ryan's driveway for the second time in a week, I stop for a moment and wonder if things really are different this year…

I wonder if everybody really is going to leave me alone this Valentine's Day.

I wonder, just for a moment, what it would have been like for Drew and I to have been the fourth couple at that table.

And then I remember who I used to sit with at Rachel and Ryan's dining room table and I dismiss the idea just as quickly as it popped into my head.

Y Y Y Y

Back at the ranch, I take a quick shower and jump into bed, where I toss and turn for at least forty-five minutes before I give up and switch on my bedside light in order to read for a while. After my eyes have scanned the same page three times, I realise reading isn't going to help. I'm all worked up, and no amount of valerian, Tania's breathing and relaxation exercises or counting fluffy white sheep jumping over fences is going to see me nodding off.

I close my book and listen to Justine padding around her bedroom. When I finally hear her light switch off, I get up and tiptoe out to the lounge area. I get myself a glass of water and settle down on the couch to watch some mind-numbing TV. I only glance away from the screen for a second, to pick up my glass from the small side table, but when I look back…

I scream.

As hard and as loud and as ear-piercingly as I can. And when I run out of breath I do it again.

Louder.

This time the small, pink-suited man standing on my coffee table screams back.

I stop screaming and clap a hand over my mouth. The man laughs in a strange, effeminate manner and holds one hand out, offering me something—a rose. A red rose. 'For you, *mademoiselle*,' he says, with a bad French accent and a curt bow.

This makes me pause. I look from the rose to him, and back again. 'You're not French,' I say, the words popping out of my mouth, my brow furrowed.

He folds his arms, the rose suddenly gone. 'Damn. What gave me away?'

'Well, the bad French accent for a start.' My gaze moves down onto the floor and around the coffee table, searching for the rose.

'Right. Right.' He nods. 'Got to work on that one.'

Weird. I can't see the rose anywhere. Though not as weird, I have to admit, as the fact that a miniature man is standing on my coffee table.

OK. I turn and glance down the hallway. Where's Justine? Why hasn't she heard me scream and come running?

'Um, how much French do you actually know?' I say absent-mindedly, trying to keep the little guy talking until she gets out here. I've heard the police say that's what you're supposed to do in this kind of situation—(In this kind of situation? What am I talking about?)—make him remember you're a human being with feelings too.

He shrugs. 'The usual. The "How do you dos", the *"s'il vous plaîts"* and the "do you speak French" shit. The basics. Oh, and most importantly, *"tout le monde faire le danse du hamster"*.'

'What does that mean?' I say, turning back to stare at him. I don't remember the phrase from my high school French.

'Everyone do the hamster dance.' He grins a toothy grin.

Hmm. My gaze flicks sideways down the corridor, fast. Where *is* Justine?

'She's not coming.'

My eyes flick back rather smartly then, and my breathing starts to come a bit quicker. I remember Mrs Batty–Smith and gulp. 'Um, is this a dream?'

'Do you think it's a dream?'

I pause. 'I don't know. I guess so,' I say worriedly, concerned now that I didn't make time to go to the doctor yesterday or today. Maybe there's really something wrong with my health. Maybe I have epilepsy or sleep apnoea or something. Yes. Or something worse.

Even worse.

Like a brain tumour.

The little man rolls his eyes. 'Oh, come on. You don't have a *brain tumour…*'

Well, that's something. I glance back at the figure

on my coffee table for a second and try to assess the situation as level-headedly as someone can when they're facing a small man on their IKEA-ware who can read their thoughts.

I don't know what to think. I raise my arm to inspect the small pinching bruise. It's fading. Slowly. No, I don't know what to think—other than I must be completely and utterly stressed out to be having another one of these episodes. Anyway, none of that matters now. What matters now is, what to do? I've learnt enough from Mrs Batty-Smith to work out that where these apparitions are concerned I should roll with the punches and do whatever it is my brain's telling me to do. If I go against it, things tend to become nasty. I guess I'll just act as if my whole life is *Lucy in the Sky with Diamonds*-weird, see what happens and go to the doctor first thing tomorrow morning. If my brain hasn't haemorrhaged, that is.

'Fine with me!' the little man says cheerfully, and begins to inspect my apartment.

I'm starting to calm down until he turns around, and then I almost completely lose it. It's seeing his back that does it. The guy on my coffee table isn't just any dwarfish guy—it's Cupid. Cupid is standing on my coffee table.

It's the wings and the bow and arrow set that give it away.

I can't remember if I mentioned my hate of all

things Cupid before or not, but if I didn't I'm going to mention it again now.

I hate Cupids. And cherubs too, just to set the record straight. I hate their fat little protruding pot bellies. Their stuntedness. Their blindingly shiny goldness at weddings.

'Is that right, gorgeous?' he pipes up again, moving around to face me once more. This time he crosses his arms.

My mouth falls open and I move further back on the couch as he says this, wriggling away as far as I can from him. How does he do that? And, come to think of it, *what* is he wearing? I freeze, halfway through shuffling backwards, and stare. It can't be…but I think it is… Now I move forward again on the couch in order to touch it, not being able to help myself.

'Hey, hey, *hey*!' He takes a step back. 'Don't touch what you can't afford, darlin'.' He smooths his hands down his suit as he speaks.

'Is that really velvet?' I stare at him incredulously.

'Only the finest.'

'Pink velvet? The finest *pink velvet*?'

'Yes. The finest pink velvet. You got a problem with that?'

I pause. No, I think. No, I don't have a problem with that. It's my hallucination, after all. And, hey, at least I've had the good grace not to make *myself* the one who looks like a pimp. And really he *does* look like a pimp.

I mean, the guy—Cupid—is wearing a pink velvet suit complete with a pink-edged white carnation and a white ruffled shirt that's been dragged kicking and screaming into the new millennium from the seventies. It's a bit of a strange get-up, considering Cupid doesn't usually wear very much at all.

'An expert on it, are you? What would you do, honey? It's either nothing or a little strip of strategically placed red velvet. I decided it was better to subvert the patriarchy, if it's all the same to you.'

'And the comb-over?' I counter, staring at his balding head.

He shrugs. 'I think it gives me that little extra something. Takes ten years off me. Whaddya reckon?'

I don't know what to say to this—to someone who thinks a comb-over gives him a certain *je ne sais quois*, to quote some of that 'French shit', as he put it so elegantly before. I say nothing.

He says nothing back.

And it's in this brief silence that I finally have time to start paying more attention to the niggling thought that's been playing on my mind since I stopped screaming a few minutes ago. There's something about him. Something vaguely familiar. Something about that shade of pink…

'Oh!' I suddenly point at him, and wriggle so far back on the couch I actually end up sitting on the headrest. 'Oh!' I point harder—at his outfit. 'Oh!' It

takes me quite a while to form something like a co-
herent sentence. 'It—you—it…' I splutter, but then
take a deep breath and try again. 'It's you—*you* I've
been seeing. The pink flashes. I'd recognise that colour anywhere. I'm not going crazy…' I pause as I realise what I'm doing—talking to Cupid who's wearing
a pink velvet suit. 'I think.'

'Not quite yet, anyway. Guess I should introduce
myself, then, eh? Tony's the name. You'd know me as
Cupid normally, but tonight I'm filling in for the
Ghost of Valentine's Day Past.'

Valentine's Day Past? The words ring a bell in my
mind. Hang on, that was what Mrs Batty-Smith said
to me, wasn't it? That I'd be visited by three spirits? I'd
remembered them from my Dickens collection—the
ghosts of Christmas Past, Christmas Present and
Christmas Yet to Come. But *Valentine's Day* Past? Huh?
Oh, but wait. Justine was teasing me about my book
the other day, wasn't she? What did she say again?
Something about needing a forklift to get it into bed
with me? Ah, so that's it.

'This is ridiculous,' I say, swivelling around on the
couch so I can see down the hallway. 'OK, Justine. You
can come out now. And bring the TV cameras with you.'

Nothing.

I wait a long, long time before I turn back again. And
when I do I start laughing—crazy laughing. What else
can I do, after all? 'Hang on, did you say Tony?' I say.

'The one and only—in town for one show only.'
I laugh harder.

'What's wrong with Tony?' he says, arms crossed.

I remember I'm supposed to be keeping on his good side. 'Nothing. Sorry, I didn't mean to be rude. It's just that I didn't expect Cupid to, you know, have a name.' I pause and gather my wits. Roll with it, Liv. Roll with it. 'So, Tony, what are you doing here? On my coffee table, that is?'

'Like I said, filling in for the Ghost of Valentine's Day Past. He's busy. Hot date or something. I don't know. So I'm here to save you,' he says, nodding, as if I should know. As if I should have it down in my diary.

'And you would be saving me from…?'

'From yourself.'

Oh, but of course. I'd forgotten about the note I *had* made in my diary: Tuesday 9 February—remember to accidentally drop hairdryer in water while having relaxing midnight bath.

'Very funny,' Tony pipes up, having read my thoughts again. 'I'm here to help. You don't have to be so snarky about it.' He pushes one hand in his back pocket and pulls something out—a packet of cigarettes. 'You mind? Before we head out?'

'Um, well, kind of. You can on the balcony, if you want…' I only catch on to what he's saying halfway through my sentence. 'Wait. What did you just say? We're going out?' God, this really is the strangest dream.

'Going out? Surely are.' And with this he jumps neatly from the coffee table and starts off across the room. 'Come on.'

I sit and look at him.

He swivels on the spot when he gets halfway across the room. 'Come *on!* The sooner we go, the sooner we get back,' he says.

I chew on my lip for a second before I get up and take a cautious step or two across the room.

'Well?' Tony nods his head at the door beside him and I take a peek out on the balcony and consider his words about getting back. About getting it all over and done with. This at least makes sense—is something I can relate to. I tell myself this is all part of the dream, or the hallucination, or whatever it is I'm having here. And the sooner I go along with what has to be done, the sooner it really *will* all be over and I can get some sleep. And make that doctor's appointment.

I take another step forward, closer to the door. 'Well, OK.'

'That's the girl,' he says, reaching up for the lock. He's too short. He jumps, trying to flick it open a second time.

'Here,' I say, taking the final step forward to unlock it and slide it open. 'Let me do it.'

'Ta, love.' He steps out onto the balcony and immediately lights up. I watch as he takes his first big drag and then slowly exhales. 'Oh, I needed that, didn't I?'

I take one last look outside before I step onto the balcony, not wanting a repeat performance of what I'd seen in the powder room at the crematorium. There's nothing to worry about, however. It's quiet and still outside, nice and cool. There's the occasional noise from the apartment blocks around us—the odd person watching TV, talking to flatmates or friends—but that's it. I keep one eye on Tony at all times, having learnt my lesson with Mrs Batty-Smith. He puffs away joyously, and I realise, as I watch him out of the corner of my eye, that I should perhaps be more disturbed by all this than I am. Cupid is on my balcony. His name's Tony, he's wearing a pink velvet suit, a carnation and a ruffled shirt and he is making me wait for him while he finishes a fag.

He catches me staring at him and double takes.

'Right. Right. Sorry. We'll be off then.'

'Off?'

'Yeah, like I said. Give us your hand.' He offers me one of his.

I hesitate, not knowing where we're going or how we're going to get there.

'Oh, I forgot. You're one of those, aren't ya? One of the Cupid-haters.'

'It's nothing personal. I—'

'Not personal?' He snorts. 'Not personal? How can it not be personal, eh? Still, you're hardly the first. Seen hundreds. I've got something for the likes of you lot.' With this, he opens one hand, and in a flash something appears in it. It looks like a harness. The sort you put on children's backs at the shops so they don't go wandering.

'You've got to be joking.' I look at him. 'I'm not five. And it's a bit...'

'Kinky? Yeah, I know.' He looks downcast for a second, but then recovers and grins. 'I always try this one first. May as well have a go, yeah?'

There's another flash then. The harness disappears and something else appears in Tony's hand. Another type of kiddie harness, but this time it's the kind with the long curled plastic cord that Velcros onto the wrist.

'That's not much better,' I say, eyeing it, but I hold out my arm anyway.

'Right, then?'

'No.' And I'm not being snarky this time. I really *don't* think I'm ready for this—whatever it is.

He looks up and winks. 'Tough luck, kiddo.'

There's a pull on my wrist, upwards, and then everything turns black.

Y Y Y Y

It's still black when I work out my feet are standing on something other than the balcony tiles. Slowly it starts to get brighter, and I begin to recognise shapes around me. 'But…' I squint in the bright sunlight of day as I look at the chicken wire fence, the play equipment, the cream wooden building.

Tony takes my arm and rips the Velcro undone.

'This is my primary school. What are we doing here?'

He shrugs. 'Not up to me. You brought us here.'

'Me?' I look down at him, confused.

'That's what I said.'

I brought us here? So I *am* controlling what's going on.

'Primary school, you say, eh? Damn. Guess I can't take this in,' he says with a sigh, looking at his fag. He takes one last drag and then stubs the butt out with his foot. For the first time I notice he's wearing white suede shoes. My eyes widen. Whatever turns you on, I guess.

Without being told, I move forward and open up the latch on the gate that leads inside the school grounds. I let us both in and close the gate again behind Tony. Stepping off the concrete footpath onto the parched grass, I start to turn slowly, looking around myself, remembering.

'This is so strange,' I say quietly. 'It's like I'm really here. It's exactly the same.'

'It *is* the same. You *are* here.'

I glance down at Tony as the words leave his mouth, but I don't really take in what he's saying. In a daze, I walk over to the slippery slide and run my hand down the length of it, stopping when I get to the bottom, amazed at my ability to touch things. I've never had a dream like this before. I shake my head and keep looking around me.

'Leanne Johnson knocked two teeth out on that rock.' I point to the lump that's sticking out of the dirt at the end of the slide. 'She went down headfirst and couldn't stop in time.' As I finish saying this I spot the painted cement pipes a few metres away and run over to them, leaving the slide behind. I bend down and look inside, smiling as I remember. 'I kissed Ben Smart in there,' I say. 'My first kiss.' I stop then, thinking, and turn to look at the other pipe. 'Or was it that one?'

'This one,' Tony says, leaning on the pipe I'm still holding on to. 'I was there. Saw it all.'

'Is that right?' I say, giving him the eye as I stand up. I wonder just what else he's seen throughout the years.

'Wouldn't you like to know?'

'You...dirty little Cupid.' I try to sound cross, but can't help laughing a touch. Despite the trappings, there's something about Tony that you can't help but warm to. Pity Mrs Batty-Smith wasn't the same.

I catch sight of the school building that contains so many of my old classrooms.

'Want to go inside?' he says.

'Inside the building? Can I?'

Tony nods.

'OK.' I move quickly towards the steps I've run up and down a thousand times. Tony follows close behind me. We make our way across the bitumen, with its hopscotch stencils, and I run my hand up the worn-smooth railing as I climb the stairs. At the top, I open the silver-coloured handle on the door and let us both inside.

I know the smell as soon as it hits me. Vegemite and cheese sandwiches, spilled red and green cordial, disinfectant. Everything is as I remember it, down to the faded lino and the wooden bag racks along the wall. I stand still for a moment and breathe it all in before I cross over to the racks themselves.

'I used to put my bag right—' I stoop down and then stop cold. 'Wait.' Recognising it, I pull out the bag in front of me hurriedly and then sit down cross-legged on the floor, letting it thump into my lap. I unzip it and pull out the contents. I look up at Tony, who's standing by the door, entertaining himself by flipping the lid on and off his lighter. 'This is my lunchbox. This is my folder. This is my *bag*.' I hold the items up.

He nods, but says nothing. *Flip, flip, flip.*

I stare at the items in my lap one by one. How can this be? It's as if I'm really back at primary school again. As if…

I begin to hear voices as I think this. I start to crawl back up, using the bag rack to pull myself upright. When I'm standing again, I run the few steps down the corridor so I can see in the window of the classroom.

My eyes swing quickly to the right spot. And there I am—second row from the back, third seat on the right.

Me. With pigtails and a tiny uniform, and a pencil with one of those triangular rubber 'I'm learning how to hold a pencil correctly' things.

Me in Grade One.

I press my face up against the glass to get a better look at what's going on inside. I'm cutting something out, something red, my tongue peeking out slightly between my lips. Seeing this makes me smile, as it's something I still do today when I'm concentrating hard. My eyes move around the classroom, trying to work out what's going on. All the children are cutting, gluing and glittering away.

It doesn't take long for me to remember the day.

I'm still looking around, amazed at what I'm seeing, when the teacher says something at the front of the class, diverting my attention. Miss McClusky. I liked her. She was one of my favourite teachers. Dad's too. I smile again at this, realising that, now I'm seeing Miss McClusky from an adult's point of view, the reason he'd liked her so much might have been to do with the type of parent/teacher relations the school would have actively discouraged. She's very young and pretty and her skirt is—well, short. She glances over at the window while I'm thinking this and, worried, I take a step back, remembering what I'm wearing—my pyjamas. I hadn't even realised this until now.

'It's all right,' Tony says, beside me now. 'They can't see you.'

Oh. 'Can I go into the classroom, then?' I ask him.

'Knock yourself out.'

I walk down the corridor, past the windows and towards the classroom door. When I get there, I open it slowly, looking around carefully before I enter. A few steps inside I stop again and scan the faces around me just to make sure. They really can't see me, I think to myself.

'Nope—and can't hear you, neither,' Tony says, squeezing around behind me. He goes over to one of the children in the front row's desk. Julie Brodie, I think. 'What are you guys up to?' he says, moving his head up and down, above and below what she's cutting out.

'We're making Valentine's Day cards.' I start down the first row, heading for my desk. Everything seems so small. So tiny. The desks, the chairs, everything.

At the back of the classroom I stop in front of myself. In front of *myself*. I can't believe this.

I bend down so I'm kneeling, and rest my arms on the desk. My small self, myself twenty-two years ago, is still cutting out. Halfway through the outlined red heart, she looks up, glances around at the other children to see what they're doing, and then gets back down to business, her tongue peeking out again.

I smile and move my head around until I spot Tony...

He's standing very close to Miss McClusky, at the front of the class. Too close, I realise when I work out what he's doing—looking up her skirt.

'Get away from there,' I say, standing back up again. 'You *are* a dirty little—'

He jumps and steps away. 'Hey, I can't help it if I'm spatially challenged, can I? And her—' He jerks his thumb up at Miss McClusky, accidentally making her skirt lift higher. His eyes widen and he steps away. 'Oh, sorry, love,' he says, looking up at her before he turns his attention back to me. 'What I meant to say was that it's her fault too. Materially challenged.' He winks at me. 'If you know what I mean.' He tugs on her skirt with one hand and motions up and down his own legs with the other, suggesting that her skirt's not quite as long as it could be.

'Yes, yes, I get it.' I try to give him a disappointed look, but the truth is as he was giving his sad little explanation I was thinking that at least I could handle this guy. At least he didn't scare me, like Mrs Batty-Smith. Having brought it up, I then try to lose the image of Mrs Batty-Smith, of her poking her finger into me. Staring at me.

'Yeah. Not exactly a looker, is she, that Batty-Smith chick? But don't you worry about her,' Tony says. 'She's harmless enough.'

Harmless? I think. It wouldn't be the word I'd use to describe her. On my one-to-ten scale of pants-wetting scariness she rated a solid eight and a half.

Something catches my eye. 'Oh, look,' I say, stepping up to one desk in particular as I pass down the aisle. 'It's Louise.' I glance back at Tony, getting excited. 'I haven't seen her for years now.'

When I turn around again, the boy beside her is leaning over and whispering something in her ear. 'Snotty Scotty!'

'Snotty Scotty?'

'He used to wipe his nose on his sleeve all the time,' I explain, engrossed in the children's faces around me. They all look so familiar, but I can only remember a few of their names.

'Everybody?' Miss McClusky claps her hands together at the front of the classroom, startling me. I whip around on the spot. 'Everybody!' She claps again. 'That's all the time we have.' Her gaze moves around the room until it settles on a child in the second row. She moves forward, closer to the girl, and holds something out. 'Maria, could you take this plastic bag around the class, please, and collect the rubbish?' Maria stands up, takes the bag from Miss McClusky and starts off around the classroom obligingly.

I look back at my small self, who is feverishly gluing something onto the red heart she's cut out. She keeps gluing and gluing, stuffing her brush back into her gluepot every few seconds. Maria turns up for her scraps, but she doesn't look up. Maria waits and waits, until finally she reaches over and grabs the scraps herself. Still, there's more gluing to be done. Then, with one last stripe of glue, she sits up and the tongue goes back in.

Done.

I laugh at the importance she's given to the project. The importance of every last dab of glue, every tiny piece of paper. The all or nothingness of it.

'What?' Tony says, beside me now.

'Oh, I just miss that about being a kid,' I muse, still watching her. 'Knowing where you stand. Remember how you always knew your position on things? I *hate* this, you'd say. Or I *love* that. There was no in between. No shades of grey. I *hate* purple. I *love* licorice.' That's funny, I think as the words come out of my mouth. I'm still not that partial to purple, and there's no way I can resist a good bag of licorice.

'Couldn't say, myself. I'm just over two hundred years old.'

'Just over two hundred?' I know from my Valentine's Day research that Cupid is supposed to be slightly older than this.

'We stop counting after two hundred. It's like your twenty-one, you know?'

Ah, now I get it. I'm deciding whether or not to ask Tony his age directly when the bell rings and, startled, I pull my hand away and turn around to look at Miss McClusky.

'Home-time,' she says brightly, looking the most relieved out of anybody in the classroom. 'Don't forget your reading books. And I hope those tidy boxes are *tidy*.'

Suddenly there are kids everywhere. Pushing past me, running down the two aisles. And noise. Rattling tidy boxes. Chatter. I make my way up the aisle to the front of the classroom.

'No running in the corridor,' Miss McClusky calls out. 'That means you too, Stephen.' She grabs a child passing in front of her lightly by the shoulder.

I laugh as I watch him race out through the door and down the corridor to his bag. It's only when he's gone that I remember my small self up at the back of the classroom. I turn around to see what she's up to and why she hasn't left.

She's still sitting at her desk. This time with a smile slapped right across her face.

She has a Valentine's Day card.

'Look,' I say to Tony. 'I remember this.' I go over behind her chair and look at the card over her shoulder. 'There should be one from Louise and one from... Hang on.' I glance up again. 'I thought that—' As I say the words, I see him coming.

Stuart.

'Here he is. Oh, how cute,' I say as Stuart comes over and shyly gives my small self a card before turning and sprinting out of the classroom.

My small self giggles and looks at Louise, sitting a few desks away, who giggles back.

'Liv looooooves Stuart. Liv looooooves Stuart,' Snotty Scotty sings out beside her.

Louise whips around and gives him a good punch in the arm. 'She does not!'

'But I did,' I say to Tony. 'I had a bit of a crush on old Stuart.'

'Tell me something I don't know. Who do you think works these things out, eh?'

'Sorry,' I apologise. He seems quite offended.

'Well, I *am* offended. This is my job, you know.' He stalks off.

'Where are you going?'

'Outside.'

I'm about to argue and say I want to stay and watch my small self for a while longer, when she gets up and leaves the classroom, with Louise and Snotty Scotty following close behind. I follow the three of them out into the corridor, where Snotty Scotty leaves them. The two girls both grab their bags and run down the front steps.

'Now what?' I say to Tony, who's looking into the mirror above the handbasin near the door. He's fixing his comb-over.

'It's good, this kids' stuff,' he says, giving the porcelain bowl an appreciative slap. 'All the right size.'

'If you're six,' I point out, and this time it's me who's on the end of the withering look. 'Well? Now what?' I ask again, taking a step forward to the top of the steps so I can see outside into the playground. The sun hits my eyes and I close them for a second…

When I open them again, I'm at home.

'Hey!' I say, as my eyes adjust to the darker surroundings.

'Don't get your knickers in a twist. It's just a change of scenery.'

I consider telling him I don't wear knickers under my pyjamas, but then decide it would definitely be a bad idea. Knowing Tony, this is probably information he's already made sure he's acquainted himself with in my dossier. It doesn't need to be brought up.

My eyes having adjusted fully, I start to pick up on

things around me. A couch. A lounge chair. We're at my small self's home. The home I lived in when I was six. The house we lived in when my mother was…still around.

Tony and I are standing in the living room amongst the brown velvet lounge furniture. Even though I haven't seen it in years, I remember it now for its softness, for how I liked to lie my cheek against it and would fall asleep on its cushions within seconds. Looking at the shadows around me, I guess that it's late afternoon. It's still sunny outside, but cool, and there's a breeze moving through the French doors that lead onto the front balcony.

When I don't see Tony for a moment I swivel around, looking for him.

'I'm here,' he says, and I finally see him sitting in Dad's easy chair, his tiny frame engulfed by cushions.

'Liv?' I hear a voice and my breath catches in my throat. 'Olivia?'

'Here!' I hear my small self's voice call out. 'I'm in my room.'

'I've got something for you!' my mother says. There's movement in the beaded curtain that separates the living room from the kitchen, and then she's there.

My mother.

I haven't seen her for twenty years.

And though I always thought the first thing I'd do when I saw her was yell—yell and scream at her for the pain she put both me and Dad through when she disappeared without a trace, leaving nothing for us bar divorce papers at a lawyer's office—I can't yell at all. The only thing that comes out of my mouth now is a croak.

'Mum,' I say, my voice drying up.

'What is it? What is it?' My small self runs into the room like a whirlwind at the slightest hint of a present.

My mother bends down, with something behind her back, nose to nose with her daughter. With me. 'Pick a hand,' she says.

'Um, that one,' my smaller self says, pointing to my mother's right hand.

'Right the first time!' my mother says as my small self and I mouth the same words. That was our joke—mine and my mother's. We always both knew whatever it was would be in her right hand, because right was—well, right. Somehow that saying made a lot more sense at six than it does now.

My mother produces something and passes it over.

'What is it?' my small self asks, taking it from her.

'It's a gingerbread heart. For Valentine's Day. There were some ladies selling them at the shops. Aren't they pretty?'

My small self nods, inspecting the gift.

I go over and take a look for myself. I don't need to see the heart to remember it, however. I recall that gingerbread heart in perfect detail. Peering from above my small self, I study the piping, the soft pink iced roses. It's beautiful. Someone put some real love into that piece of baking. A lot of time and effort. And I remember now how, even though I didn't like gingerbread back then, it didn't matter. I was hardly going to eat the thing—I was entranced by it. It wasn't of this earth; it was obviously some kind of fairy gingerbread heart from the bottom of the garden because it was so beautiful. In the end I kept it till it went mouldy and my dad had to secrete it out of my bedroom with a pair of tongs and hand it personally to the garbage man on bin day.

'We have to go,' Tony says, breaking my attention span.

'But I haven't given her her card yet…' I look up at my mother's retreating back as everything around me fades to black again. 'And…'

As the light fills in around me once more I realise we're back in my primary school corridor. The same one as before.

'Different class this time.' Tony waves a hand and, rubbing my eyes, I follow him down to the next room.

I look inside. 'Ugh. Miss Hopkinson.' There's no forgetting a teacher like her.

'Yeah. I know. I haven't been able to help her out much. She's a bit…'

'Frigid?' I try, the word springing into my brain from nowhere.

'You could say that.'

I did—even back then, I think. Snotty Scotty came to school with the word and had started bandying it about in the playground one morning. Apparently his father had said that was what Miss Hopkinson was after one parent-teacher meeting that hadn't gone so well. I don't think any of us had a clue what the term meant, but we all thought it was the funniest thing we'd ever heard.

Looking inside the classroom, I'm surprised to find we're making Valentine's Day cards again, just like last year. I locate myself in the classroom and find that I don't look very happy.

'Remember, class,' Miss Hopkinson calls out from the front of the room in her clipped voice, 'we're only making one card—for our mothers. We're not going to spend all day cutting out red hearts, are we? We have some Social Studies to do, and heaven forbid we should actually *learn* something today...' She trails off, the last sentence muttered under her breath as she turns around to the blackboard.

I look back at my small self. She's not gluing with much enthusiasm. And then I work it out. Miss Hopkinson. Grade Two. February.

My mother left in early January.

I turn away from the window and look for Tony. He's standing in the corridor, and as I spot him the sun hits my eyes just like it did before. I squint and turn my head back to the classroom.

Except it's not the classroom.

Now we're in the living area of a flat. The tiny, miserable, one-bedroom flat I shared with Dad because our family home had sold so quickly. We rented the place while we shopped around, before we bought another house in a different suburb across town. A house and a suburb where his wife—my mother—hadn't left any kind of presence.

My dad, a younger version of the one I know today, is standing at the front door holding it open. 'Hello, pumpkin,' he says, scooping up my small self when she hurtles up the final few steps and hits the landing running.

'Hi, Daddy.'

He puts her down and peels her backpack off her back. They go into the living area and he sits down in the same easy chair Tony had been sitting in before, now squashed into this tiny room.

'What have you got for me today?' my father says, rummaging through my small self's backpack. He takes out her lunchbox and opens it up. 'So you don't like peanut butter sandwiches any more?' he says, looking at its leftover contents.

'I hate them,' she says, like he should know this.

'You loved them last week. They were your favourite. As long as they were crunchy.'

'I love Devon now. Louise always has Devon. And she has the kind with the smiley face on it.'

'Oh, well, then. We'll have to get some of that. If it's got a smiley face on it, it must taste better.' He looks at her, eye to eye now he's sitting down.

'It does.'

'I might have to prise you off the ceiling when the preservatives kick in, but it'll all be worth it for that tasty smiley face, don't you think?'

My small self nods, even though I'm sure she has no idea what a preservative is.

My dad puts the lunchbox on the floor and pulls out a book. 'Got some reading to do tonight, do we?'

'Social Studies too. And we'd better do it. Miss Hopkinson screams at you if you don't do your homework.'

'And what's this?' He pulls out something red and scrunched from the bottom of the bag.

She doesn't say anything now, and my face tightens, remembering. I watch as he unscrunches the ball, knowing what's coming.

'Oh,' he says when he reads the three large letters on the front 'Mum' and realises what it is. 'Oh.' He glances up at her.

My small self steps forward and quickly grabs the card from his hand, ripping it in the process. 'I hate Miss Hopkinson. I hate her and I'm never going back to that stupid school.'

She throws the two pieces of red paper on the floor and then makes a dash for it, but in the small flat there's nowhere to go. She runs into the bedroom, but as there's no door comes straight back out again.

'I hate this flat too. And I hate Valentine's Day. I *hate* it. I'm never making one of those stupid cards again. They always make us do those stupid cards. I'm never doing one again. Ever. I hate it. I hate it. *I hate it.*'

I watch as her face turns red. Really red. Frighteningly red.

My dad, standing up now, and looking far too big for the small living area, goes over and grabs her. He picks her up and hugs her as she fights away, pummelling his chest with her fists. Slowly, very slowly, as the minutes tick by, she starts to quieten down.

And standing there in the cramped living room, watching them both, my hand held up to my cheek in shock, I close my eyes and recall just how hard my dad had held on.

Y Y Y Y

'Tony?' I say into the blackness when I open my eyes once more. 'Tony!' He materialises beside me and I look down at him. 'I want to go home.'

He shrugs. 'No time, babes. Things to do, people to see. And the clock's ticking.'

Suddenly I don't know if I want to see anything else. I feel completely and utterly drained. Why am I seeing all this? Bringing up the past. As if seeing Mike today wasn't enough.

'Last stop,' he says.

After what feels like quite some time, things start to lighten up around me and I begin to recognise things. 'Wait a second, this is Saffron.' Saffron. Mike's and my favourite café.

I stop looking around me then, not wanting to go on. I close my eyes. But when I open them again I'm still in the same spot.

'We have to keep going.' Tony pulls on my pyjama pants.

'I don't think I want to.'

'You have to,' he says. But then he sees the expression on my face and hesitates. 'Just take it slowly. Think about how things really were back then.'

Hesitantly, my eyes scanning the garden for Mike, I turn, taking the place in, remembering.

It's beautiful.

I loved Saffron. Truly loved it. It was like a home away from home. An old wooden house that had been converted into a café. Its garden outside was bliss. Simply idyllic. All English country, with poppies and herbs and bees and quiet times with iced tea. If you tried hard enough, and there were only a few people there, you could imagine it was your own garden and the other people—well, maybe they were old friends you'd invited over for the afternoon.

After Mike and I split up I never went back there. But I've missed the place. A lot.

I stand in the middle of the garden now, with the sun resting on my shoulders. It's not hot, but nice and warm, with a gentle cool breeze. It's early in the day. Maybe around ten.

'There we are,' Tony says, distracting me. He's walking away across the garden. Towards the side of the house.

I take a deep breath and follow him, spotting myself at a weathered table slightly hidden by a wooden trellis that's practically creaking it's so loaded down with jasmine.

I'm with Mike. I look happy. We both look happy. And I know immediately what I'm seeing—it's our first year together. Our first Valentine's Day.

Tony and I stop a metre or two away from the table. I can't believe this. Again, it's all so…real. Like I'm actually reliving the moment in time.

Sitting at the table, Mike and myself of three years ago are laughing at some shared joke. When they stop, he pulls something out of his pants pocket and gives it to her. To me.

'What's this?' myself three years ago says, surprised. She looks up at <u>him</u> from the small package. 'I thought we said no presents!'

'I lied.'

'But…'

'It's tiny. It's nothing. Really.'

'But I didn't even get you a tiny nothing really.'

'Just open it!' Mike laughs at her.

Hurriedly, ripping off the paper, she opens it up.

I turn to Tony. 'It was a lipgloss. A pinky-coloured lipgloss I'd been looking at on a cosmetic counter a few days before but had told myself I couldn't afford that week.'

Tony nods. 'Good choice. Pink's the bomb.'

We both turn back and keep watching.

'Thanks,' she says to Mike. 'That's really sweet.'

'There's something else too,' he says.

'Something else?'

He reaches down and pulls something up off the floor. A huge basket wrapped in cellophane which he passes over to her.

'Mike!' She looks at the basket incredulously.

'Don't blame me. It's not my fault. It's those cosmetic counter women.'

Myself three years ago pauses, waiting for an explanation.

'It's just that when I picked out the lipgloss they ganged up on me. One of them started telling me how if I spent a little…well, no, a whole lot more, I could get all this for free.' He gestures to the basket. 'They worked in a pack. The first one kept showing me all the freebies, the second one started ringing their most expensive products up, and the third one did the basket and made the ribbon all curly.'

I laugh at this now, remembering his feigned innocence.

'So it's not my fault!' Mike says again.

Myself three years ago opens the basket up and starts sorting through the bits and pieces, making discovering noises as she goes. Finally she gets to what the cosmetic counter women have made him buy along with the lipgloss, in order to receive the free goods.

'Wrinkle defence?' She reaches over and gives him a playful slap on the arm, then pulls herself up and kisses him. 'Thank you. It's very sweet—even though you think I have wrinkles, which I do not.'

When Tony looks at me, I'm surprised to find myself smiling slightly. He jumps up on the seat beside Mike and inspects the lipgloss. 'Doesn't take much to make you happy. Lipgloss. Even if it is pink.'

I look at him. 'Don't say that. Mike was a good present-giver. He always knew what to get me. He paid attention, noticed things I liked. Made an effort. And look how happy I am.'

Tony shakes his head.

'What?'

'Girlfriend, you have really got to let go.'

'Let go of what?'

Tony looks at me as if I'm a freak. 'If you don't know by now, I can't tell you.'

Oh, he means the past. Fine. Whatever. I've only heard that about a million times from everyone in my life over the last couple of years. But it's an easy thing to say, isn't it? Not such an easy thing, however, to put into practice. I shrug and glance over at myself again. My deliriously happy self. And was I ever—deliriously happy, that is.

I can remember quite easily how happy I was back then. When Mike came along I fell fast and I fell hard. I couldn't help myself. Maybe because Mike was my salvation in some ways—the end of a long line of bad encounters with men. Mike was such a *relief*. And he was what I needed. Not in the way that I was looking for a man to complete me—I'd never wanted or needed that; I still don't. But somehow he made the whole bad journey along the pot-holed testosterone highway of dating hell seem suddenly worthwhile. Like a pilgrimage.

I've never told my dad, but I used to think a lot about something he pointed out to me once concerning one of his friend's sons. The guy—Callum, I think his name was—was about ten years older than me. He was tall and good-looking and had been engaged three times to three different women who'd all broken the engagement off. And he was a paediatrician. Dad used to shake his head with wonder every time he spoke to his friend about Callum and his adventures in coupledom. One day, after he put the phone down, I watched him as he sat there and I'd asked him what it was about Callum that he just didn't get.

I'll never forget what he said.

'There's got to be something wrong with him,' my dad had explained. 'Something really wrong. He's a good-looking bloke, and a paediatrician for God's sake. They're hot property, those paediatricians—it's not like he's a used car salesman or something. But he can't hold a relationship down, can he? And it's the girls who keep calling it off. It's got to be him. Yep, definitely something wrong there. Jimmy can't figure it out, though, and I have to say it's got me stumped.'

I'd never met Callum, so I couldn't speculate on whether it was a 'special' closet of women's underwear he kept in the spare bedroom, late nights with 'the boys' (all three of them in a king-sized bed), or a strange way he ran through vast quantities of gerbils from the local pet shop. Anyway, I didn't really feel like joking about it. Couldn't joke about it.

Because this was the answer to why I rarely got past a first date.

It was me. *Me*.

With nothing else to go on, I'd believed it for years.

And then Mike came along and changed everything. Or at least he did until he ended it all and left me for his wife.

Tony raises an eyebrow at me.

'What?'

He shakes his head sadly.

'What?' I say again.

'Darlin', the guy was another one of those potholes. There were just some bits of gravel covering up the gaps that hid the fact. And I'm sorry about that. But you should know not only did he leave you for his wife, he barely gave a second thought to your feelings after he did it—he thought it was right. He didn't sit by the phone. He didn't remember your birthday. He didn't think about you at Christmas. And you can bet your sweet arse he never even glanced at your horoscope in the paper.'

My eyes start to water with this last comment. I still have to force myself to stop reading his horoscope.

'You deserve better than him. And the others. Much better. I'm trying for you. I really am. But you have to try too. You have to let him go.'

'That's what everyone keeps telling me, but I can't!' I start to cry now. 'I want to, but I can't, all right! I don't know how.'

Tony reaches up and gives me his hand. 'That's what I'm here for, love. To show you how. To show you the way.'

I bite my lip and look back over for a second at the happy pair. Myself three years ago is standing beside Mike, pulling him up. 'Come on, wrinkle boy, I'll buy you some breakfast. Let's go check out the specials board.' They walk across the garden and up the stairs into the house.

Tony and I follow them inside.

But when we enter the house, inside isn't inside. Or it isn't the inside of Saffron. It's the inside of my old apartment, the one near the park. I'm in the kitchen. Me now and me…then. It's morning, maybe around the same time—ten-ish.

Mike is sitting at the kitchen table.

I know what this is instantly. It's the morning I'd received the phone call.

'Tony!' I yell.

'What? Down here,' he says, from where he's leaning against the fridge behind me.

'Please, no. Don't. Not this. I want to go home.'

'I can't make you go home.'

'Tony, I know what happens. I remember. I don't need to see it again. Please…'

'I can't. It's you. Your doing.'

'No.' I shake my head quickly. 'No. If it was up to me I'd be back at my real apartment. The one I live in now. In bed.'

'You have to see how it really was. For your own good.'

I keep my back turned on Mike and myself two years ago. 'But I know how it was.'

'Shh. Listen,' Tony says. He comes over and puts his hands on my legs, making me turn around.

Mike is talking. 'It's just that Amanda and I have discussed it over and over during the past few weeks and we really think it's best for Toby this way. We have to try and make it work between us. For him. For his sake. I can't be sure it's going to work. I just know that I have to try.'

Myself two years ago nods. 'I know it's for the best. For Toby,' she says, her arms crossed, not looking at Mike but fixing her eyes on the tabletop to will back the tears.

There's silence as he waits for her to say something else, but she doesn't. And from my point of view now, looking back on the past, I know that myself two years ago isn't going to say anything else. What she's just said is it. There's nothing to add, considering she doesn't believe the words that have come out of her mouth herself—that what's about to happen is for the best.

The truth is, in her heart she knows it isn't going to last between Mike and Amanda. She knows that it will all come apart again, like it did last time, and that Toby will suffer for it. She feels like she should hate Amanda. Hate her for what she's doing to her relationship with Mike. He's been increasingly distant over the past few weeks…calling less, avoiding her…and then the phone call that morning. The morning I'm seeing played out in front of me again now.

Yes. Myself two years ago is standing there feeling like she should hate Amanda for what she's doing— keeping Mike and Toby at her beck and call—but the truth is she doesn't care about Amanda at all. She just hopes that she'll go away again soon. Leave the country like last time, when she 'just couldn't cope with it all' and everything will be back to normal. Myself two years ago won't say anything else. There's no point in arguing about it. That would simply be futile, because Mike made his decision long before he entered the apartment this morning.

Maybe even weeks ago.

Mike and myself two years ago exchange a few more words before he gets up to leave. I try my best not to listen, but I can't help but turn and watch as he rounds the corner into the living room, goes out of sight and then, a few seconds later, closes the door behind him. I jump when I hear the noise, because I know now just how final that sound is.

That it really is over. That this time Amanda doesn't leave.

Myself two years ago stands in the same spot she's been standing in the whole time and cries soundlessly now that he's gone. Big fat tears roll down her face and drip onto her shirt, the table, the floor. After a while she reaches forward and takes something out of the basket on the table that's holding letters and bills and pens and other junk.

It's a card. A Valentine's Day card.

Leaving it unopened, she goes over and throws it in the bin. Then, standing upright again and looking out of the kitchen window, she watches as Mike's car drives off.

He hasn't even remembered what day it is.

I watch myself two years ago for a long time, my heart breaking all over again and my tears mirroring hers, falling sadly onto the floor. I don't know how long I stand like this, but it seems like hours before I feel that I'm done. Finally, I look down at Tony. 'Are you happy now? Satisfied?'

He doesn't say anything.

'Take me home.'

He comes over silently and straps the Velcro back on my wrist. I close my eyes, feel myself lift again, and then, with a thump, we're back on my balcony in exactly the same spot we started from.

'I hate you,' I say to Tony, pulling the Velcro off.

'You've always hated me—remember?' he replies, not meeting my eyes. 'But this is for your own good, Liv. Your own good. It wasn't always like the day in the café. You tend to forget that.' He looks up then, and even though I try not to look at him something makes my eyes turn to his.

'I thought you were going to help me? How is this helping? I just want to forget.'

'It's not that easy. You have to learn from what happened before you can forget.'

'Why can't everyone just leave me be?' I sob, my chest heaving as I struggle to breathe.

'Everyone will, if you're not careful,' he says. 'But I can't. And I don't fail. I never fail. Remember that.'

So very tired, I don't reply, but head inside. I slide and lock the balcony door behind me, leaving Tony out there, and go and curl up into a ball on the couch, where I keep right on crying, making up for all the times that I was strong and held the tears back instead.

Y Y Y Y

WEDNESDAY 10 February—
here it comes...

When I wake up to the beeping of my alarm at seven-thirty a.m. I wonder why it's so damn loud this morning. It doesn't take me long to work out it's not my alarm clock at all, but my head beating away in time with it that's the problem. I've got such a head-ache. And little wonder, I think, sitting up. What was going on in my head last night was more than strange.

I start to remember the events of a few hours ago and my heart beats a little faster. I bring my hands out in front of me. Like I'd thought—shaky. Last night was…awful is the only word for it. It was simply awful reliving those moments. Especially the last one at my old apartment. I look around me then, at my bedroom. I don't remember getting back into bed at all. Hmm. I guess I shouldn't have had any wine at all at Rachel's dinner party last night. And especially not red. I know it gives me migraines.

Maybe I really should go to the doctor's today? Or make an appointment with Tania. But what would I say? To either of them? All they'll tell me to do is try and relax, and there's no chance of that happening for quite a few days yet. And, really, do the dreams, or hallucinations, or whatever they are, honestly mean anything? I doubt it, I think, recalling another very vivid dream I had a few months ago, after a day spent shopping for a new fridge—in that dream a deep freeze had *eaten* me. Yes. The only reason I'd seen Mrs Batty-Smith the other day was because I was at her funeral and I was upset. And the dream last night—well, I'd seen Mike earlier that day, hadn't I? That had been reasonably upsetting too. Especially as I wasn't expecting it.

So, while I'd love to take the day off and relax, I can't. Exhausted as I am, I crawl out of bed immediately, knowing that if I don't I'll fall asleep again, get into work late, and Sally will have my guts for garters.

I stand under the shower for as long as possible, trying to wake myself up. I tell myself over and over and over again that it was all just a dream. Just a dream like all my other dreams. All the other dreams I've told Tania about. I say the phrase 'just a dream' so many times I realise I'm not even saying it in my head in more and I've started to whisper it out loud. *Just a dream, just a dream, just a dream.* However, standing so long in the shower means that I then have to rush as fast as my poor head can go through getting dressed, throwing on a bit of make-up, reminding myself to take my medication (and resisting the urge to double it), preparing a coffee to take with me on the road, and stuffing my handbag full of Snickers and muesli bars. Snickers bars…

Again.

I shudder as I remember not only last night's dream, but Mrs Batty-Smith.

Just a dream, just a dream, just a dream.

Next week I'll start looking after myself. Next week I'll see Tania. Next week I'll make that doctor's appointment.

But now—now I have to get through to the weekend. Now I have to try and forget…

Y Y Y Y

I'm working reasonably hard for twenty-six minutes past ten (well, OK, maybe seventy-five per cent), when my mobile beeps, distracting me. When I finally locate it in my bag (there's that lipstick and tampon again…) I have an SMS from Justine.

U GET MY NOTES OK? BE HOME 7.

I start to reply, then, a few letters in, I clear the screen and throw the mobile back in my bag. It's easier to e-mail. It'd be even easier to call, but I think if Justine received as many personal phone calls at work as she does e-mails, it would be a firing offence. I begin typing away.

From: "Liv Hetherington"
<liv@sallyblissphotography.com.au>
To: "Justine Holden" <j.holden@graydaytaxation.com.au>

All right already, I'm coming, I'm coming, believe me! I got all three notes. The one in the kitchen, the one on the TV *and* the one on my pillow. This night out is starting to take on the kind of organisation usually reserved for NASA shuttle launches...

L

I spend the rest of the day working feverishly, trying to keep my mind off everything. Sally's out of the studio, booked up to her perfectly plucked eyebrows with engagement portraits, so sadly there aren't any 'can I have a fag/I'll get the coffee and biscuits/let's do boozy drinks from three onward' distractions.

By five-thirty-two, I've managed to finish off putting together a wedding album that's due to be picked up next week; de-flabbed and de-cigarette-packeted a whole slew of photos from the lot I was working on but didn't finish last Friday (as it turned out, that mother-of-the-bride could have auditioned to be the Marlboro *woman*); and have had a quick look through Kirsty and Shaun's engagement portraits from yesterday (I was right about the hair against that grass...).

All in all, a good day's work.

At five-forty-one, I close the studio door behind me. On my way home, I stop off at a bottle shop to buy Drew a birthday present of a nice bottle of red, and at six on the dot I'm banging shut the garage door at home.

Justine opens the door to the apartment just as I'm about to stick my key in the lock. 'Thank God you're home,' she says, holding the door back.

'Why? What's going on?' I scan the inside of the apartment to see what's recently been on fire.

'You've got to get ready,' she says, grabbing one of my arms and dragging me inside.

I check my watch in case I've read the time incorrectly. 'But I've got almost an hour.'

'Well, that's just enough time, isn't it? Go on.' She takes my bag off my shoulder and gives me a little push on the small of my back towards my bedroom. 'Go and have a shower. And wash your hair.'

'What's wrong with my hair?'

'Just wash it, missy. And no talking back!'

I pause in the hallway and look at her. She's obviously already had a shower and is dressed for going out, though she hasn't put on any make-up yet or done her hair (however, with Justine's short red crop this only takes a five second blow with the hairdryer, a slap of wax and she's done). 'Um, aren't you just a little too excited about this?'

She puts her hands on her hips. 'Yes. Yes, I am. I'm very excited about this. I'm very excited *indeed.*'

'OK, OK.' I wave both my hands in front of me, surrendering, before I turn and keep going down the hall.

I do as I'm told and go straight to my en suite bedroom, undress and have a long shower. And as I wash my hair I have to admit to myself that, like Justine, I really am looking forward to tonight. I find myself humming as I towel off, don my dressing gown and start blowdrying my hair. Product applied and hair done, I slap a bit of moisturiser on and step into my walk-in wardrobe to choose what I'm going to wear. I decide on my favourite pair of camel-coloured Lisa Ho pants, the sequinned glittery sandals I bought specifically to go with them, and a silky dark blue, green and camel Charlie Brown striped shirt. I put everything on and take a look in the mirror. Not bad. Not bad at all for a crusty old overworked wedding photographer.

I run my hands down the sides of my pants. All right! They'd been getting a bit snug lately, but all the running around I've been doing in the last couple of weeks seems to have worked off that pesky half a kilo I gained over Christmas. Either that or I forgot to send the pants to the drycleaner after I wore them last. Come to think of it… Damn.

Oh, well, make-up time.

Back in front of my mirror, I pull out the first of my cabinet drawers and bring out the big guns. The good stuff. My everyday make-up sits on the top of the counter in a tiny, free-gift-with-purchase toiletry bag. It consists of concealer, mascara, cream blush and a lipgloss. But tonight I go all out. I start by tweezing my Neanderthal-like eyebrows, which I obviously haven't paid much attention to in the last few weeks.

Or maybe months. I repeat the 'no pain, no gain' mantra as I go—something I picked up from a particularly cruel PE teacher I had in high school. At least it comes in handy for real life (plucking, waxing, those last two minutes on the Stairmaster at the gym…). That done, I move on to painting myself—concealer, foundation, powder, blush, eyeshadow, eyeliner, mascara, brow pencil, highlighter, lip liner, lipstick—then squirt, squirt with my perfume of the moment and I'm done.

I take a final look in the mirror.

I'm a vision. If I do say so myself. A vision with perfect timing to boot, I think as Justine yells out, 'You almost ready?' from the lounge room.

'Coming.' I grab my handbag from where I've left it on the bed and stuff my lipstick and a few tissues in. I do one last fluff of my hair before I leave. Definitely a vision—though, I remind myself firmly, I am not looking this way for someone else. A someone called Drew. Sometimes it's nice just to look…well, nice.

OK, then.

I go over to open the bedroom door with a flourish, take a few hip-sashaying supermodelesque steps up the hall and into the lounge and twirl in front of Justine.

'I have arrived.'

And then I spot Drew, standing over near the table. Shit.

'Very nice.' He nods.

Justine just laughs.

'Why didn't you tell me he was here?' I give Justine a look. 'I could have been running around naked!'

'That's OK. Nudity's fine with me,' Drew says. 'In fact, I'm all for nudity.'

I give him a look too.

Drew laughs. 'Wait right there,' he says, and turns and steps into the kitchen for a moment. He comes out with two white tulips, each one wrapped in clear cellophane. 'Ladies…' He steps forward and presents me with one, and then goes over to give the other to Justine.

'Um, thanks,' is all I can say as I reach inside the wrapping, stunned, and touch the tulip. It's gorgeous. I love tulips. They're so gauzy—even the green stems always look like you're seeing them through a soft-focus filter (sorry—the photographer in me…). 'Tulips are my favourite.' I look up from the flower to Drew.

'It's beautiful,' Justine says.

I wake up to myself slightly then, my brain kicking in. Tu-lips? Hmm. Isn't that a bit NG? As Sally would say. I mean, on the NG scale surely this would have to rate at least an eleven out of ten? And in my mind, just like Santa Claus, the Easter Bunny and the good old Tooth Fairy, eleven-scoring NGs don't exist.

It's all a bit too good to be true.

I take a step back and Drew looks at me. 'Liv?'

I put my flower down on the dining room table that bit too quickly, as if it's burning my hand. 'Um, I was just thinking…what are you doing giving us flowers? It's *your* birthday.' I look around for a moment, and then go over to the dresser and pick up Drew's present from where Justine's left it beside my handbag. I take it over and hand it to him. 'Happy birthday.'

'Thanks. You didn't have to,' he says with a smile, pulling the bottle of red out of its glittery gold hologram bottle-bag packaging. As he takes a look at the wine, I can tell he's genuinely surprised I've taken the trouble to buy him a present. 'Wow.' He looks at the label. 'You really didn't have to.'

Just as I'm standing around, starting to get uncomfortable and knowing I'm about to say something stupid along the lines of 'what kind of a birthday cheapskate do you think I am?', Drew says, 'We'll definitely have to drink it together,' and takes a step forward towards me.

At the same time something blinds me. A flash. At first I think it's the lightbulb going, or Drew's watch catching the light, but then I realise it can't be either of those things as the flash is pink and like a streak. Tony again. I stop myself with this thought. OK. That's it. I've got to see some kind of a doctor before someone finds me dead on the floor somewhere. I'm really losing it. I'm starting to think this is all real…

Confused, I blink hard. When I open my eyes again Drew is closing in, and as he keeps coming I finally wake up to myself and what's going on. My brain still caught up on the tulip, along with everything else, clumsily I step forward as well, moving in to give him a kiss on the cheek. But when I take that step suddenly everything seems wrong. Really wrong. Halfway there I work out Drew's not going for a kiss on the cheek. He's moving in for a hug. I reposition myself, turning my head quickly, and instantly know everything really *is* wrong here. He hugs me and, with my head pushed back uncomfortably, I kiss him on the lips. Right on the lips.

There's no getting around it.

It's not a slightly off-centre cheek-kiss.

It's not a 'whoops, sorry, I brushed your lips' kiss.

It's a 'bang, right there, no disguising it, hello, there you go' kiss, and for a moment we're all wrongly placed arms and legs and still kissing and—ugh, how embarrassing. I detach and step back awkwardly, opening my mouth to say sorry, but nothing other than a small squeak comes out.

'Well, thanks again,' Drew says with a short laugh. 'For everything!'

As for me, I quit squeaking and look over at Justine, who's grabbed a tall glass vase from atop the entertainment unit and is heading for the kitchen. She's either not noticed what's just gone on or is pretending not to notice as she fills the vase with water, unwraps her tulip and places it inside. When she's done, she comes over and takes mine from the table, unwraps it and puts it in beside hers.

'Right, then.' I clap my hands together three times, like I'm a kindergarten teacher announcing it's nap time. 'Let's get going, shall we?'

Justine and Drew both look at me and I try to melt into the floor unsuccessfully. I turn and glance down the hallway for a second, as if I've just heard something, and cringe as the moment I've just had with Drew replays itself over and over again in my head. I take what I hope isn't too obvious a deep breath, and compose myself before I turn back again.

Drew is looking at his watch, checking the time. 'The cab should be here in five minutes. Should we wait for it outside?'

I nod.

'All set?' Drew turns to Justine, who's in the kitchen again, this time shoving the cellophane from the flowers into the bin.

She gives her hands a quick rinse under the tap and then dries them on a hand towel. 'I am now.'

The cab arrives right on time and we head into town, deciding on the way that we'll go to the Guava Bar for dinner. Both Justine and I have been there dozens of times before, but Drew never has, and he must, Justine says, be introduced to their cocktail list immediately.

Soon enough we're sitting at the long steel bar, with three of the barman's finest in front of us. I've ordered a musk stick cocktail, Drew's gone for a toffee apple (we wouldn't let him have the dirty martini that he chose first up, as it wasn't 'birthday' enough) and Justine's playing with the frozen guava in her Guava Bar special, and prattling on to Drew about her day at the office at usual Justine top speed. Meanwhile I'm pretending to listen, but am actually still having an inward cringe about the incident back in the apartment. And as many times as I tell myself to get over it and move on, I can't. I don't quite know why—after all, I've had far more embarrassing moments than this.

I don't have to search very hard to come up with one.

Like the time at a wedding last year, when I was standing on a high cement wall taking a group photo of approximately one hundred and fifty people, and my skirt blew up at least to my waist, exposing my favourite white strawberry motif undies.

Yes. That was fairly embarrassing.

I glance over at Drew for a second, but he's still listening to Justine and laughing every so often. I try desperately to concentrate now, to listen to what Justine's saying, but I can't.

Jesus, I've got to sort myself out.

I stand up and push my bar stool back in the process. 'Off to the ladies',' I say to Justine and Drew, and head off across the polished floorboards.

When I get there, I push the door open and step inside, letting it swing closed behind me. I don't open the second door that leads through to the toilets, but stand and look at myself in the mirror. I look fine. Great, even.

But my head…

Ugh.

Right, Liv. I take a good, long, hard look at myself in the mirror and prepare to tell myself a few things. Firstly, the kiss was nothing. Simply one tiny, slightly embarrassing moment. Not that it was even a proper kiss. At the risk of sounding indiscreet, there was no wetness involved. No tongues. If anything, it was a misplacement of lips. And though I try not to, and though I look down and stare at the bench in front of me very, very hard, the moment comes back to me in vivid detail once more. As I get to the brushing lips my breath catches.

I look back directly at myself in the mirror, realising for the first time what the problem really is here. Working it out.

My problem is that I *liked* it.

I stare at myself, my mouth hanging slightly open. I *really* liked it.

I think back. Back to lunch. Back to last night at Rachel's. And then I grab my bag and pull out my wallet. Slowly I extract Drew's card.

When he handed it to me I started to give him the 'I'm not ready' spiel before my eyes made me stop in case they spilled over. I was about to do the whole bit. I'm not ready to date again. I'm not ready for another relationship. I'm not ready for another man to…

I lower my eyes to my hand, where the card's resting, and start to turn the piece of paper over and over, feeling its edges dig into my fingers. I remember my dream from last night about my past. My past and Mike. Maybe Tania's right. Maybe it did mean something after all… I stare at the card so hard the words end up swimming before my eyes.

And then, after what feels like for ever, my eyes flick up to the mirror again.

I start to smile. And it's a small smile at first, but as I watch it gets larger and larger and larger. Well, maybe I was wrong about what I told Drew after lunch. Because I think I might be—ready, I mean. I glance over at the closed door then, thinking what's on the other side.

When I turn back I'm still smiling. Yes, I think I really might be ready.

Ready to put Mike behind me. Ready to move forward. Ready to… Oh, everything. I might just be there after all this time. I might just have found that pretty *darn* special one.

I look at myself steadily in the mirror and I simply can't stop smiling.

But I do stop. Just for long enough to reapply that lipstick that I never bother to reapply before I hurry back outside. Maybe eleven-scoring NGs do exist after all?

Here's hoping…

Y Y Y Y

The cocktails, two bottles of wine, bruschetta, crab pasta, citrus tart and a short black are all delicious, as per Guava Bar usual. By nine-thirty-five the three of us are walking arm-in-arm through the city, Drew in the middle to keep us steady, towards the club we were supposed to meet his friends at five minutes ago.

When we get there, his friends are waiting outside. Drew does the introductions—Paul from work and John from too far back to remember.

We head inside and I'm surprised to see how busy the club is for a Wednesday night. The place isn't nearly as packed as I've seen it on a weekend, but still, for a Wednesday night...I think I'd forgotten people went out on weeknights at all. As I look around, it shocks me just how young everyone looks. Truly...youthful. Unlined. They all look so youthful that I wonder whether they've all procured fake ID at some place around the corner; so unlined that I'm surprised the bouncer didn't make an announcement over the club's

PA system that somebody's mother was here to pick them up when he gave me the once-over and didn't ask for *my* ID (bastard), at the door.

Justine and I hoist ourselves up on some tall stools sitting around a spare table and get down to business. Scotch and dry kind of business for me, and another glass of white kind of business for Justine. John stays with us while Drew and Paul go for the drinks. I wait for them to come back with a jug of a garish-looking pink watermelon-flavoured concoction, saying the bartender didn't know how to make anything else, but they don't. They must get adults in here from time to time, I think to myself, as I take my Scotch and dry from Drew.

'Thanks.' I smile up at him.

He smiles back. 'So, do you think it'd be illegal for me to dance with any of the girls out there?' he asks, putting his elbows on the table. 'You know, me being over sixteen and all?'

I laugh. 'They make you feel old, don't they?'

He nods. 'It's an illusion. You've got to remember what it was really like for us back then. At least we can afford to buy more than one drink with three straws between us these days. And we don't have to leave at eleven-forty-five to catch the last bus home. We can afford a cab.'

'I never thought about it like that.'

I look over at Justine, who's deep in conversation

with John. She's been talking to him for ages now, and it's then that I remember John's the single one, and it's Paul whose girlfriend wasn't able to come tonight. Typical Justine. She's like a bloodhound. She can sniff out a single guy at fifty paces.

I look down at my drink. Hmm. Maybe I should slow down. And I should *definitely* not say that out loud.

Drew and I chat as we polish off our drinks, while Justine does a line on John and Paul talks to someone he knows nearby.

When he's finished his beer, John puts his bottle down on the table. 'Well?' he says to the three of us, and looks at the dance floor.

'You two go.' I turn and look at Justine, and then back at John. 'I've got to talk to Drew about something.'

As Justine gets up she bends over and whispers in my ear. 'Sure you're not interested?' she asks.

I shake my head. 'All yours, babe.'

She gives me a surreptitious wink before she stands upright and grabs John with one arm. 'Let's go.'

Drew manoeuvres himself around the table and into Justine's vacant seat. We watch as she moves John onto the dance floor.

I turn to Drew. 'The nightclub dance floor. The habitat of the native Justine.'

We both watch for a bit longer.

Finally Drew looks at me. 'What was it you wanted to talk to me about?'

'Talk to you about?' I have to think hard before I remember what I said just a few minutes ago. I take a look down at my drink again, wondering just how strong it is. Or maybe it was the three glasses of wine and the cocktail before that did it. Could have been. 'Oh, that,' I say, finally remembering. 'It was nothing. I just didn't want to cramp her style.'

Drew's eyes widen. 'You already worked it out between you? That she was going to have a crack at John? That was quick. I've been with you guys the whole time and I never heard you say anything about it.'

I laugh. 'We use a sophisticated form of eyebrow communication.'

Drew looks at me blankly.

'Oh, come on! I'm joking.'

'I'm surprised they hit it off, actually. Justine's not really his type.'

'And you'd know?' I say. 'She wasn't your type either, but you went out with her.'

'On one date! And I know what my type is, thanks very much.' Drew grins and leans in closer to me.

'And that would be…?'

He leans in closer still. 'Oh, smart, beautiful…'

Hello! my soused mind starts to think and I lean in closer as well. I'm just starting to wonder whether we're going to misplace lips again when John comes running back over to the table and pulls us both up off our chairs.

'I warned you,' he says and pulls us both up and out onto the dance floor.

We don't leave until well past one a.m.

I share a cab home with Drew.

In no time somehow we're kissing drunkenly on the back seat, his warm hands running up the inside of my shirt. And I'm about to ask him if he wants to come up for coffee, or sex, perchance, when something stops me and I pull back. Way, way back, to the other side of the cab. I sit there for a second or two, looking at him, at Drew, with my head telling me how it is—how I shouldn't be doing this. How NGs, whatever their rating, don't exist. How it's just the alcohol. How I'm going to get hurt again. How Drew's going to hurt me. And then, almost as suddenly again, I reach out and pull him over to me.

Because the fact is, right now, in this moment, I just don't care.

Y Y Y Y

THURSDAY 11 February —
it's right around the corner...

My alarm goes off at eight-thirty and I hit the snooze button twice, knowing that I don't have any appointments today at all. When I do drag myself out of bed I have a bit of a sleepy smile at myself in the mirror as I remember last night. The perfect night out. And not a bad dream in sight. Maybe, with meeting Drew, I really have put my past behind me.

There's that smile again. Amazing. I can't seem to stop smiling these days.

Things are looking up for Liv.

Just after nine-thirty, I walk through the studio's front door with a yawn and a wave.

'Hey, there.' Sally swivels on her chair to greet me. 'Sleep in?'

I nod, still yawning.

'Oh.' Sally picks up a piece of paper from her desk and holds it out to me. 'I've, um, got a message for you. Mike called. He said it was urgent.'

I've started across the room for the note, but now I stop halfway, suddenly wide awake. 'Mike?' This certainly knocks the smile off my face.

Sally nods.

I continue over and take the message from her. It's his work number. Beside me, Sally passes over the cordless phone, but her hand lingers on it as I take it from her. 'Liv,' she says, giving me a worried look, 'just…be careful.'

I nod, taking the phone from her. And I've just started dialling Mike's number when Sally's voice makes me pause.

'Oh. My. God.'

I stop dialling when I hear her tone. It's not good. It's not good at all. 'What…?' I begin, but trail off when I follow her eyes out through the plate glass front of the office.

It's Mike.

In the flesh.

My eyes swing back to Sally, who gives me a look I've never seen before. 'Do you want me to send him packing?' she asks quickly.

I can't answer and only manage a shrug and a slight shake of my head. I've got no idea what he wants. What he's doing here.

Sally takes a deep breath in. 'Like I said, Liv, be careful.'

I nod, still silent.

And then we both watch as the door opens before us and Mike enters the room.

The first thing that pops into my mind is that he looks—well, he looks…the same. Maybe his hair is a little different—the sideburns are longer, maybe he has a few more tiny wrinkles—but apart from that it's the same old Mike. The Mike I used to go to sleep with, the Mike I'd wake up with in the morning. Looking at him, though, all that feels like a million years ago. Almost as if he wasn't my boyfriend at all, but a figment of my imagination. Something I've dreamt, or a character from a movie.

'Liv. Hi.' He pauses in the doorway. 'Can I, um, come in?'

I wake up to myself with another shake of my head. 'Sure, of course. Sally said you called?'

'Yeah, right. I did.'

At least he has the good grace to look uncomfortable, I think, as I watch him move from foot to foot. 'Oh, these are for you.' He steps forward and gives me something.

A bunch of flowers. A bunch of lilies, actually. I take them from him. 'Um, thanks.' I'm not quite sure where to look. What is he giving me flowers for? And what is he *doing* here?

Mike must see what I'm thinking, because he starts a bit then.

'Oh, sorry. I've come about Toby.'

Now I'm really awake. I take a step forward, bringing me closer to Mike again. 'Toby? Is he OK? Is everything all right?'

Mike shakes his hands quickly. 'No, no, everything's fine. It's nothing like that. It's just that he keeps insisting he saw you up a tree in the park across the road from your old place the other day. He won't stop talking about it.'

'Oh. Ah. Right.' Damn. I could have sworn Toby hadn't seen me in the park. He'd was looking at exactly the right spot, but he made no indication that he recognised me.

'He's made me go over twice to look for you in case you're still there. He's convinced we're all involved in an elaborate game of hide and seek.'

'OK.'

'I asked him why he didn't tell me when he thought he saw you, but he says he thought it was a game, and then when he looked again you were gone, and—'

'Mike?' I interrupt him.

'Yes?'

'Tuesday morning. I was up a tree in the park. Toby's quite correct.'

There's a long pause. Sally coughs in the background and both Mike and I look over at her. 'Don't mind me,' she says, and we both turn back again.

'Can we, um…?' Mike motions over to the kitchen.

'Sure.' I follow him over into the next room. It's

kind of pointless—the office is so small you can hear everything that's said wherever anyone stands in it—but moving our conversation into the kitchen will give the illusion of privacy at least.

I exhale when I reach Mike again. 'Look. It's not what you're thinking. I was doing an engagement shoot. Trying to get a different angle. It wasn't a social stalking exercise or anything.' As soon as the words come out of my mouth I regret them and my eyes shoot down to the floor. Social stalking? Where did that come from?

There's another pause.

'Oh,' Mike finally says.

I continue inspecting the floor, my shoe, the bottom of the kitchen cabinet. 'So Toby's telling the truth. Tell him I'm sorry. I didn't know he'd seen me.'

'You saw us, then?'

Ugh. I realise I've just given that much away. 'I didn't want to disturb you.'

'Toby would have liked to see you,' Mike says. Then, 'And me,' he adds as an afterthought.

I can't help but ask. 'How is he? He looks so big.' I get the courage to glance up now. Now that we're on a safe subject.

'He's good. Really good.'

'Great. And, um, Amanda?' I try to be polite, but even I can hear that my voice sounds cold when I speak her name.

'Well, um, that's also kind of why I'm here, actually…'

I try to move my eyes away again, but they're fixed. My mouth opens, as if to say something, but nothing comes out. But there's plenty, plenty going on with the rest of my body. Something inside my head says: *This is it, this is it, this is it.* And my heart—well, my heart starts racing, making me feel slightly sick. I place Mike's flowers down and rest one hand on the kitchen bench for support, hoping that I look casual instead of freaked out.

'Amanda and I kind of finished for good. A while ago.'

'Oh?'

'Yes.'

'Oh.' Behind me I hear the front door to the office open and close. Thank God, I think. Sally's gone out.

'I've been meaning to call you. Or drop in. Or something. Anyway, when Toby said he'd seen you, I thought maybe it was a sign…'

'Right.' I'm sweating now. Actually sweating. I can feel the beads dripping down my back, sliding until they hit my waistband. 'A sign? Sure, Mike.'

'Yes. So, I was wondering if you'd like to go out for dinner tonight. You know, to talk about things?'

'Um, sure. Yes. Of course.' I say the words on autopilot.

'Great!' Mike looks relieved. 'Well, how about I pick you up at seven-thirty, then?'

I'm about to say sure, yes, of course, or something

like that again, when a little voice pipes up and tells me not to. 'Um, Mike, how about I meet you instead? Rosalie Street? Seven-thirty?'

Mike nods. 'Fantastic. I'll see you then.'

'OK.'

He grins. 'I'd best be off, then,' he says cheerily, moving past me on his way to the door.

I try to turn, to watch him go, but my feet seem to be stuck to the floor. I can't move. Can't think.

'You're a lucky man,' Mike says behind me. 'She's the best photographer in the business. Comes highly recommended.'

I finally manage to turn to see him slap the guy standing in the main office area on the arm.

'Yep, a lucky man.'

And with that he departs. But the guy, the guy he slapped on the arm, is still standing there.

And the guy is Drew.

'Drew!' I unfreeze, taking a few steps forward.

Behind him, Sally stands up from her chair. 'I'm sorry, Liv. I went to the bathroom and…'

'I, er, came to give you these.' He places a stunning bunch of irises down on the bench beside him. Irises. My second favourite flower—right after tulips. 'And to ask you out for dinner.' There's a quick, tight smile with this. 'But it seems you have other plans…'

My shoulders sag and I take another step forward. 'No, Drew, it's not like that…'

There's a pause. His eyebrows go up. 'What is it like, Liv?'

I stop in my tracks. 'I… He… It's…'

'That's what I thought. So I'll be off.'

'Drew…' I start again, but it's too late.

Drew has already gone.

Y Y Y Y

Once again, just like last night, I'm standing in front of my bathroom mirror getting ready to go out. But that's where the similarity ends, because tonight feels nothing like last night. Nothing like last night at all.

Ever since Drew left the office, my stomach has been churning, turning around and around and around, as I think about Mike, tonight and the bad timing that saw them both meet in the office.

'You're a lucky guy…' The words come back to me, making my stomach flip-flop once more. Ugh.

I go through the movements—the same movements as last night. Powder, blush, eyeshadow. But it's half-hearted this time. There's no…excitement like there was last night. No anticipation. And even though I want to look good, I know it's for a different reason. I want to show Mike I haven't suffered. That I've been OK without him. That there are a few less tiny wrinkles on my face than his.

At seven-thirty-five I park my car and start the short walk down Rosalie Street towards the restaurants, my step faltering for just a second when I spot him. And when I do, *bang*, there's that churning again. I feel awful. Sick.

'Liv!' Mike gives me a wave when he sees me and steps forward a few paces to give me a kiss on the cheek. I almost take a step back, wanting to tell him not to, but then realise I'd look ridiculous. Like I still care. And I don't want to look like that, remember? I want to look breezy. As if this evening is effortless. As if it's something I'll have forgotten five minutes after I'm home. Just like I forgot him after we broke up.

Yeah, right.

'Hi,' I say back, and return the kiss awkwardly.

'I made us a booking,' Mike says, stepping back again. 'Guess where?'

I look along the row of restaurants. I've been to a lot of them, but since the last time I was here several of them have changed hands. There's a Greek, an Italian, a Vietnamese… I shake my head.

'Isis, of course.' Mike smiles.

I don't smile back. Isis? Is he joking? Isis used to be one of our favourite haunts. Of all the places he could have booked…

'I haven't been there for ages,' he continues.

I look at him in wonderment. 'Me either.'

'Right. Let's go, then.'

And before I can protest, Mike takes my arm and starts to lead me down the street.

'So, what do you think?' Mike asks from across the table.

I take a sip of my water, trying to calm my stomach down, before I answer. 'About...?'

'The restaurant.' He looks around. 'It looks exactly the same, doesn't it?'

I've noticed. My stomach has noticed. 'Yes. Yes, it does.'

His head returns to his menu. 'They've even got my lambs brains on offer.'

'Great.' Shudder. I'd forgotten about his love of lambs brains. Now I really do think I'm going to be sick.

I don't know if it's Mike, the restaurant or the lambs brains, but over the next five minutes or so my stomach goes into overdrive. The cramps get stronger and stronger until I wonder if I'm going to be one of those freakish women who delivers a baby when they didn't even know they were pregnant (though considering my sex life lately I'm really doubting it). In fact, the cramps get so strong I start to sweat again, like I sweated in the kitchen at work today. Thank God I didn't wear a silk shirt like last night.

I sit across the table from Mike and watch his mouth moving as he talks. And as the minutes pass I realise I have no idea what he's saying. No idea what he said a few sentences ago. Every so often I take a sip of my water and pray that he won't ask me a question. Like this morning, I'm on autopilot. I think that it's just a bit much. Mike turning up. Mike asking me out for dinner. Being back at Isis. Being across the table from Mike. And what's even more strange is how he's acting like this is all so normal. But it's not normal. It's not normal at all. It's all…wrong. Like a bad dream. Like the bad dreams I've been having lately.

But this time it seems there's no waking up.

Drip. Another bead of sweat makes its way down from my neck, running between my shoulderblades.

Cramp. My stomach contracts once more.

'…don't you think?' Mike asks.

I put my water down. 'Sure. Yes. Of course.' I blurt out a bit too loudly.

Cramp.

I get up. 'I'm, um, just going to the bathroom.'

Mike looks up at me. 'I'll order for you,' he says.

This makes me pause for a second. Order for me? I'd forgotten he used to do that. I always hated it. I still hate it now. But I don't say anything. Just like I didn't say anything about dinner. Or going to Isis. Instead I cross the restaurant, hoping my stomach and I will both make it to the ladies'.

We do, but only just.

I am not well. I am not well at all.

Inside the ladies', I close the door behind me, take

a deep breath and make my way over to a chair they have beside the hand basins. As my stomach cramps fade a little, I take a look around me and slowly shake my head. I am spending way too much time in bathrooms these days.

I sit quietly, thinking my own thoughts, the minutes ticking by. As time passes the stomach cramps fade until they're almost gone, and I stop sweating. When I'm feeling almost normal again, I remember that I have to go back out there and it all starts up once more. What am I going to do? I look down at my hands, which are shaking slightly as they rest on top of my clutch purse. For something to do, I open it up to check if I've brought a tissue or two to fix myself up with. And then I spot it. My mobile.

Sally.

My hands still shaking, I grab my lifeline and dial away. 'Sal?'

'Liv. Hi. Where are you? The line sounds weird.'

'I'm in the bathroom. I'm out at dinner. With Mike.'

There's a pause. 'Oh, yeah?'

'The thing is, I…' I stop, not knowing what to say. Not really knowing why I've even called her.

'What's the matter?'

'I don't know. I just feel awful. My stomach's cramping and I can't stop sweating.'

'God, are you OK? Do you want me to come and get you?'

I shake my head. 'No, no. It's not that bad. I'm just…I'm just not sure what to do.'

'Do you want to leave?'

'Yes. No. I don't know. I don't know what I want to do. It's so weird. He's acting like everything's…normal.'

'Why doesn't that surprise me?'

Sally never really liked Mike. She told me after we split up that she'd always thought he was a bit arrogant. I don't say anything, and Sally continues after a second.

'Sorry, sorry. That isn't very helpful. So, do you want to leave? Because if you want to leave, just leave. You don't even have to say anything. You don't even have to see him. Just breakout through the kitchen if you have to. I've done that myself many a time.'

This makes me smile for the first time tonight. 'I'll bet.'

'So?'

I look around me, my eyes finally resting on the door. Outside, Mike is waiting. Probably wondering where I've got to. 'I'm…I'm not sure.'

'Look. Just take another minute. Try and tap into what you want to do. Listen to your gut. And if you want to walk out, just walk out. You don't owe him any explanations, Liv. You don't need to see him ever again if you don't want to.'

'OK.'

'And call me if you need anything. It's no trouble to come and get you. Really.'

I exhale. 'Thanks. Thanks, Sally.'

'No worries. Good luck, chickadee. I'll be thinking about you.'

I hang up the phone feeling a lot better, and then, like Sally suggested, I take that minute. I take that minute and I take ten deep breaths as well. And at the end of the minute my stomach feels close to normal again. I've stopped sweating completely. And I feel…good. Because Sally is right. I have to do what I have to do. And now I know exactly what that is.

'Sorry I took so long,' I say breezily as I sit back down at the table. And this time it's not fake. 'I was chatting with someone.'

'Oh?' Mike looks up. 'A friend?'

I smile. 'An old friend. A very wise old friend.'

He nods, but is barely even listening to what I'm saying, I realise, as he continues, 'I ordered us some champagne. And here it is, by the look of things…'

The waiter brings over an ice bucket. We watch as he pops the cork and fills our glasses.

When he leaves, Mike leans over the table, glass in hand. 'Well, Liv, I guess we should make a toast. To us…' He looks straight into my eyes as he says this.

I pause before I hold up my glass. I think back to 'us'. And with Mike sitting less than an arm's length away from me the past is amazingly uncloudy tonight. For the past couple of years 'us' has been something I think I've seen in a haze. What had Tony said in my dream? That I had to 'see how it really was'. Funnily enough, I think I do now. Because now, now my past with Mike is so clear I could almost reach out and touch it, like I could reach out and touch him. If I wanted to, that is.

'To, um, us.' I clink my glass against his, meeting his gaze.

Just as I put my glass back down on the table the waiter places our entrees in front of us. Mike starts in on his directly, but I don't even look at mine. My gaze remains unbroken and my hand remains on my glass.

Eventually Mike cottons on to the fact that something isn't quite right.

'Liv? Is everything OK?' His knife and fork pause in mid-air.

I look up at the ceiling for a second before I exhale and bring my eyes back down to meet his. 'Um, no. No, it isn't.'

'But you love scallops.' He looks at my plate. 'Aren't they any good? We can send them back if you want…'

'Oh, for fuck's sake, Mike, it isn't the *scallops*.' And I think we're both surprised at the words that have come out of my mouth. Mike's so surprised he drops his fork. It clatters against the side of his plate and falls to the floor beside the ice bucket containing the champagne.

Champagne. Honestly.

I lean forward, resting my folded arms on the table as if we're simply having an intimate conversation. 'What did you think, Mike? That you could just pick up where you left off? That the moment Amanda walked out again, like I told you she would, you'd just waltz back to me? That I'd be waiting in the wings?'

Mike's mouth opens and closes. 'Liv, I never thought that… It's not like that…'

Suddenly Drew's words from this morning pop into my head. 'No? What is it like, Mike?'

'I…'

I smile then. 'That's what I thought.' I stand up, coolly placing my napkin on the table. 'So I'll be off.' I go to turn, but then stop. I rest a hand on the back of my chair for a second. 'But before I go, do me a favour. Don't call me. And don't drop in. Ever again. Oh, and one last thing. Do your son a favour as well. Take a good hard look at yourself before he turns out anything like you.'

I sit in the darkness of my car and catch my breath. At first I'm worried that Mike will follow me, then I snort. Mike won't follow me. I know him enough to know that. Mike will finish his dinner and then Mike will go home. He'll probably watch some TV. And then he'll go to bed. Maybe over the next couple of days he'll ponder on a few of my comments. Especially the one about Toby. But in the end he won't worry too much about it all. He'll expect me to call and apologise.

But, I won't.

Looking out into the darkness, I shake my head. What a waste of time. I'm such…an idiot. There's no other word for it.

After a while I remember Sally and find my mobile again. I'm scrolling through the numbers in my address book when one flashes onto the screen that I don't expect. Drew. I'd forgotten I put that in there. I pause, looking at it, then think about my gut again. What did Sally say? That I should listen to my gut. So, before my head can argue with it, I press the little green phone button and bring the mobile to my ear.

Drew answers on the third ring. 'Hello?'

'Drew, um, hi. It's Liv.'

There's silence on the end of the line.

'I'm really sorry about today. I just… Anyway, it doesn't matter. I was wondering if you could come out for a drink? Or coffee?'

'I can't. Sorry. I'm a bit busy.' His voice sounds like it's a million miles away. In another country.

'I just met with Mike. Told him where he could go shove his flowers and—'

'Look, Liv, I'm sorry, but I've got to go.'

I pause. 'Right. I'll…um…I'll…'

'Yes. Thanks for calling.' Drew hangs up.

And then, with my mobile in my hand, I sit in the darkness for a long, long time.

Y Y Y Y

FriDAY ♥ 12 February

too close for comfort...

'Well?' Sally spins around in her chair as I enter the office.

I dump my bag on the floor and go and sit down in my own chair with a thump. 'Well, I blew it.'

Sally pushes herself across the floor rather ungracefully. 'What happened?' Her eyes are wide.

I sigh. 'I listened to my gut and I went out there…'

'And?'

I remember what I told Drew on the phone last night. 'I basically told Mike where he could shove his flowers. Now and for evermore.' I've never liked lilies anyway.

'Yes!' Sally punches the air. She pushes herself over further still. 'Good girl.' She pats me on the knee. 'I knew you'd do the right thing.'

I shrug. 'If I did the right thing, why do I feel like such an idiot? I feel like an *idiot*,' I repeat, more to the studio itself, to all of humanity, than to Sally in particular. And then I grin a fake grin in order to stop the tears from flowing. What *is* it with me this week? Normally I'm not a crier at all.

'Well, you shouldn't feel like an idiot.'

'But I do. I mean, what was I thinking? What have I been doing these past couple of years?' I shake my head. 'I *am* an idiot,' I groan. And I am. I really *am*. I thought about it at length last night. I thought about what Tony had shown me in my strange dream. And I realised he was right—these past two years my life has been on hold. Like a fool, I've spent my time crying, yearning, hoping, longing. Waiting for the phone to ring. For Mike to drop in. For Mike to care. While I might have tried to tell myself that it was over for good when Mike went back to Amanda, while I might have tried to tell myself that there would be no second time around, at the back of my mind there was always that niggling little 'what if?'. What if she doesn't stay? What if he realises he's done the wrong thing? What if, what if, what if. What if he wants me back?

Well, he does. Did.

But the funny thing is the thing I'd cried, yearned, hoped, longed and waited for…

I don't want it any more.

I snort at this. How about that?

'Hey, what did you mean?' Sally breaks my train of thought. 'That you'd blown it?'

'Drew.' I bite my lip as the tears start to surface.

'Oh.'

'Yes. Oh. I called him last night, to see if he could come out for a drink or something.'

'And?'

'And he said he was busy. Oh, God, I just want to die. I want to curl up in a ball, right here on the floor, and die.'

'Like a cockroach that's just been sprayed?' Sally asks.

I give her a look. 'Yes. But without the flailing around. And don't try to make me smile. Or laugh. I'm never smiling or laughing again.'

Now Sally shakes her head at me. 'Liv, don't be so damn hard on yourself.'

When she says this, the tears really start to well up. I try as hard as I can to push them back. I don't deserve to cry. It's my own stupid fault. I sigh and look at Sally. 'I just can't believe I've done this. The other night…I realised that I was ready. Ready to, you know, date again and everything. And I was so excited! I mean, I really wanted to. And now Mike comes along and I just throw everything away. For nothing! Nothing!'

Sally pats my knee again. 'Look. Don't worry about it. Drew will come around. You'll see.'

My shoulders slump. 'I don't think so.'

'Well, I do. I bet he calls. Today.'

I give Sally a small smile, trying to look hopeful. But something tells me Drew isn't going to call today. Or tomorrow. Or the day after.

The fact is, I had my chance. And Drew isn't going to call ever again.

I spend the next hour or so working diligently, trying to keep my mind on the job.

It isn't easy.

Every time the phone rings, both Sally and I jump. But none of the calls is from Drew.

When, just after ten o'clock, my mobile buzzes in my bag, Sally wheels herself over to me again. 'This is it!'

I stick my hand in my bag hurriedly and pull out my mobile. It's a text message. But it's not from Drew. It's from Justine…

YOU ARE SO AVOIDING ME

Ouch.

Obviously she's spoken to Drew. I think about calling her, but decide I can't face the music yet.

Another half an hour passes. Another fifteen minutes. Finally, I whip around and face Sally. 'I've got to do something.'

Sally swivels around. 'Like…?'

'That's the problem. I don't know. I can't call.'

Sally points a finger at me. 'Don't you dare e-mail. Or text. That's such a cop-out.'

'I know. I won't.'

'What about flowers? No, that's lame…' She vetoes the suggestion as fast as it's out of her mouth.

'That's what I thought.'

'Umm… how about a note?'

I pause for a second. 'But how would I get it over there? I can't mail it; it'd take too long. And I can hardly fax…'

Sally shrugs. 'Courier it over?'

Something comes to me then. 'I've got it!' I say, rocketing out of my chair. I grab my wallet out of my bag. 'Call the courier. I'll be back in a tick,' I say as I race out through the front door.

Twenty minutes later, the courier picks up the note and the tall latte in its takeaway cup and starts carefully back out to his van.

'I guess you think this is a bit strange,' I say to him as I hold the front door to the office open.

'Sweetheart, I've had plenty stranger than a cup of coffee,' he says, leaving Sally and I to wonder just what kinds of items he's transported across town.

'So, can I ask what the note said?' Sally corners me as soon as he's gone.

I make a face. 'You'll probably think it's cheesy.'

'Try me.'

'Well, the note said, "It would be great to start

over. Just you and me. No Mike. No Justine. Just us. And coffee…"' I wince. 'Cheese rating?' One of my eyes peeps open.

Sally pauses. 'Camembert. It's not blue. It's not *stinky* cheesy.'

Phew.

The phone rings twenty minutes later.

'I've already had my morning coffee,' Drew says.

'Oh,' I hear my voice reply quietly. 'OK…'

'But I'm free for lunch. How about I pick you up in half an hour?'

Y Y Y Y

When the dark blue Jeep pulls up outside the studio, I'm already waiting outside, despite the heat. From the inside, Drew opens the door for me and I jump in.

'Um, hi,' I say shyly.

'Hi.'

'I'm really sorry about yesterday—' I start, but Drew butts in.

'Don't mention it,' he says. 'We're starting afresh, remember? Anyway, we've all got baggage of some kind. Mike's yours.'

'Was mine,' I say with a smile. And using the past tense has never felt so fantastic.

Drew laughs then. 'I have to say I feel kind of like a naughty schoolboy. Ditching work and everything.' He slaps a hand on the steering wheel and I see in him the same kind of excitement that I felt the other night. The same kind of anticipation I'm feeling now. 'So, where should we go for this ditching of work?'

'Somewhere fun, I think. If we're both ditching, we'd better make it worthwhile.'

There's silence as we stare blankly at each other. But just as I'm about to give up and suggest the movies Drew's face suddenly lights up. 'I do know somewhere. It's a bit of a drive, though.'

I shrug. 'I'm up for it.'

'Great.' He pulls the car out into the traffic. 'The girls at work were talking about this place the other day. Apparently it's fantastic.'

'What…? No, don't tell me. Let's make it a surprise.'

'A surprise it is.' Drew glances over at me.

'So, um, I hope I'm not dragging you away from anything too important?'

Drew grimaces as he changes lanes. 'Not in my mind. I'm supposed to be in a meeting. Nothing they really need me for. Right now they think I'm at the dentist.'

'The dentist?'

'Your courier came at just the right time, actually. The secretary had just topped up the bowl on the front counter with some Minties when she called me out. Anyway, I took a couple of them, chewed away and made a big song and dance about one of my fillings falling out. I told my boss I had to go to the dentist right away—that it was a workplace health and safety issue.'

I laugh. 'You've probably shot yourself in the foot.

From now on you won't get anything nice in the bowl. It'll be jelly beans or nothing.'

'Well, we *had* better make this trip worthwhile, then. I won't be popular this week as it is. Everyone else is having to work tomorrow to get a job done and I'm bunking off to go to a wedding.'

I groan when I hear this. 'You and me both. Though I won't be so much bunking off work as working my butt off.'

Drew and I chat away as he keeps driving and a good twenty minutes pass before I start to notice the signs. My brain begins to tick over. And then we take the exit and I know for sure.

'I suppose that gives you a hint.' Drew glances at me. 'Hey, are you OK? You look a bit green.'

I shake my head. 'No, no, I'm fine. Just a bit, um, carsick. I'll wind down the window and I'll be right.' Carsick. As if. I've never been carsick in my life. Don't be stupid, Liv, I tell myself, getting to the heart of the problem. Thousands of people live here. I try and look cheery as Drew continues staring at me. 'I've heard the restaurants along here are great.' This is true, but naturally that snippet of information has always been overshadowed by the other thing I've heard—that this is where my mother has been living for the past five years or so.

We turn right and drive along the esplanade of a small up-and-coming seaside development, my mouth becoming strangely drier by the minute. About half-way down the strip, Drew glances out of my window. 'Hang on—there it is,' he says, and pulls over sharply into a nearby parking spot. I turn and look out through the back of the car. The restaurant is called Blast from the Past. I've heard of this place—a kind of retro diner with a fifties feel.

'Feeling better?' Drew touches my arm and I almost jump.

'Sure! Great!' But I can't stop my brow from frowning as I exit the car. Let it go, Liv, let it go…

There's no doubt about it. Blast from the Past is amazing. The place is decorated with anything and everything Fifties. The walls are lined with groovy stoves, fridges and knick-knacks, while even the lino on the floor, the tables, chairs and mismatched cutlery are remnants from another era. It's as if you should suddenly start seeing in black and white rather than in colour.

Our waitress, Judy, complete with dinky cap, attached hairnet and appliquéd name badge, seats us and hands over a couple of huge menus. Drew and I decide to go with the flow and get the malted megamilkshake, with two straws, and a couple of burgers and fries.

We have a simply brilliant time. I completely forget about my mother and yesterday's events with Mike.

I forget about Dad, Eileen, Tania, Justine, Rachel, and how much work I've got on over the weekend.

I forget about everything. For once, I live for the moment.

Drew and I talk, laugh, drink our shared milkshake and clap wildly at the daily fifties fashion parade. And I have to admit it feels pretty good to live for the moment. Not scary at all.

After our meal we share a brownie and then stagger out of the restaurant. 'Got time for a walk?' Drew asks.

I puff my cheeks out. 'I think we're going to have to. I don't know about you, but right now I'm guessing I won't fit in the car.'

Together we stroll down the long, winding path that runs beside the waterfront, dodging the pine cones that have fallen from the trees above us as we go. When we reach the end of the path, we turn and walk back, this time crossing the road so we can glance inside the shops. It's quite crowded for a Friday afternoon, and Drew and I joke that everyone's had the same idea as us and has bunked off work for the afternoon.

We're about halfway back to the car when I see it. Her.

My mother.

It is her. Clear as day. Looking just like I remember. She exits the bakery just ahead of us and hurries away down the footpath, looking into her calico bag as she goes, checking her purchases.

I don't even pause for a second to think. Instead I start running, pushing past the few people in front of me as I go, my handbag dropping to my elbow, the soft leather scraping on the concrete below. I run so fast my legs start to burn, my feet making loud slap, slap, slap noises beneath me. And when I get to her I reach out in front of me and lunge, grabbing her arm hard.

She turns quickly, to meet my gaze with a gasp.

Our eyes meet.

It's not her.

In that instant my brain tells me to let go, but I can't get the message to my hand. I continue holding on to her, our eyes still locked. The woman is looking at me, confused, trying to figure out who I am. And then, as another second passes, fear fills her gaze and she pulls her arm away smartly as she realises she doesn't know me at all. I must be some kind of freak. As for me, I try to speak, to tell her I'm not, but nothing comes out. All I can do is wave my free hand, finally prise my fingers from her skin and step back—first one pace, then another and another, until I stumble back and finally hit someone standing behind me.

Drew.

Up ahead, the woman is still looking at me.

'Sorry,' Drew calls out. 'I think she, er, thought you were someone else.' With this, the woman gives me a final worried look and keeps going. When she's on her way, Drew ushers me aside, out of the flow of jostling pedestrians. 'Are you OK? What was that about?'

But I still can't speak. My chest has gone all tight again. I can't breathe and there are too many people around me. Far too many people. I've got to get out of here. I make another gesture this time, back towards the park.

'You want to go sit down?' Drew asks, and I nod.

When we cross the road this time it's with Drew carrying my handbag and holding me firmly by the arm. 'Come and sit down over here.' He guides me over to a park bench. 'Do you want a drink of water or something?'

I shake my head numbly, trying to ignore the feeling that's rising from my stomach to my throat.

Too late.

I stand up and race over to the bin beside us and am sick. It really is a blast from the past, I think miserably, now regretting my overly large lunch. Drew hovers behind me and I try and wave him away. I hate people watching me be sick, touching my hair and fetching me glasses of water afterwards. It's always something I just want to curl up and do by myself, then roll into bed afterwards and hide under my doona. Not that I'm sick very often. Hardly ever, to tell the truth. But this week—there's just been something about it my stomach can't handle.

I keep waving Drew back. Eventually he gets my

drift and goes to sit back down on the bench while I clean myself up with a tissue. When I finally make it back there myself, I don't know where to look.

'Bulimia. It's a bitch, isn't it?' Drew tries to break the ice.

I try to smile, but nothing comes.

'Do you want to tell me what's going on?'

No, my brain answers immediately. But then Drew touches my arm again, making me look at him.

'Liv?' he says.

I shake my head and look away.

'Liv, you've got to start to learn to trust me. Or there's no point in me being here.'

I turn back then. Turn back and look him straight in the eye. And, as much as I don't want to, there's something in his gaze that makes it all come spilling out.

So I tell him how it is.

I tell him about how my mother left my father and I. About how I know she's been living in this area for some time but haven't been able to work up the guts to do anything about it, even though I rehearse around a million lines a day that I want to scream at her. About how she probably doesn't know or care that she's screwed with my father's and my heads so badly it looks like neither of us will ever have a decent relationship again.

And when I finish with this little gem, I don't stop. I keep going. Right on going. I tell Drew about Mike.

About how he left me as well. About how everyone leaves me. And I tell him about Tania. And about how I know I have to stop being this person who's defined by other people—my mother's daughter, Mike's ex—but I can't seem to. I can't seem to stop anything, and I tell him how most days my emotional life just seems like an awfully fast bullet train ride to nowhere I want to be.

I have no idea how long I go on for, but it feels like hours.

When I'm finally done, I look up from the ground, fully expecting Drew to have run off into the sunset.

But, surprisingly, he's still there. Right beside me. And I realise the whole time I've been regurgitating my life story he's listened, and he's said all the right things. All the things I needed to hear.

'Finally,' he says after a while.

I look at him in silence.

'I knew there was more to you. There had to be.'

I keep looking.

'When I first met you, you seemed like such a great person. So together. Like you had it all. But then… God, how can I explain it? It was weird. Every time I saw you, I kept expecting more. You know how the more you see someone the more you know about them? I kept waiting for this, but nothing came. All there was was this outer shell, this kind of…scaffolding.' Drew pauses. 'Am I sounding too much like a stupid architect? Am I even making any sense?'

Still silent, I nod.

Drew shrugs. And then he smiles. 'Well, I was right, wasn't I? There is more to you, Liv Hetherington. Plenty more.'

We sit for a while longer, not saying anything, until Drew helps me up and we walk back to the car, his arm wrapped around me, holding me close. And I let him. Because, well, it feels right…

As if, for the first time in years, I've reached the end of that train ride and I'm home.

Y Y Y Y

Saturday 13 February—
oh, god, it's tomorrow...

Another morning, another smile on my face.

But, as much as I want to think about Drew and yesterday, I can't. I've got work to do.

And heaps of it.

I creep around the apartment until I leave at six-fifteen, not wanting to wake Justine up as it's her non-running morning and she's sleeping in.

Like I want to be.

I get the car out of the garage as quietly as I can and head for my first stop—Molly's house. Our first wedding today is a ceremony in the garden of a restaurant at nine, followed by a champagne brunch at ten. This is more than two hours away, but my day starts even earlier than the brides I photograph, as I have to get up, get ready, pick up Molly, my assistant, and be at the bride's hotel to shoot her and her bridesmaids donning their finery starting at approximately seven a.m.

After the restaurant wedding, it's going to be go, go,

go to get to the next bride in the next hotel by ten-thirty, to photograph her getting ready for her wedding at one, and also to take a few shots of the groom's lot preparing themselves as well. This bride and groom are then off for a late lunch at three. Following this it's go, go, go again, to shoot the next bride getting ready at her mother's house at three-thirty, for her ceremony at five-thirty, with a shoot afterwards at the wharves at sunset and then dinner at seven-thirty.

While this may seem like a lot—and it is—after the bride, groom and guests hit the reception, I can basically take off. What many people don't know is that hardly anyone ever pays for a photographer to stay past the ceremony and subsequent group photographs. A few, like my third couple today, want an artsy shoot somewhere, and it's only because the first two couples don't that I'm able to fit in three weddings.

It's quiet on the roads, being early, and I mentally map out the route to Molly's as I drive, trying to remember exactly where her house is. I've only driven there a few times, as I usually pick her up from the studio, but today she's directly on the route to the hotel we're going to. Coincidentally, she lives only a few streets away from Drew.

Just as I'm parking in front of Molly's place, my mobile starts ringing. 'Hello?' I croak.

'What happened to you? You sound terrible.' It's Sally.

'It's just early,' I say.

'I hope you didn't have a big night out before the weekend to end all weekends?'

'No, boss. So, are you just checking up on me, or is something going on that I should know about? Tell me my first wedding's cancelled and I can go back to bed…'

'Sorry, no such good news. But as it happens I've got some other good news. I found a great studio for you.'

A studio? 'Really?' I sit up in my seat a bit.

'Yep. I went out to dinner with an old friend last night and he's got a commercial place he rents out. We swung by after dinner. It's a gorgeous little cottage. Yellow. Made for you.'

I open and close my mouth, not knowing what to say. 'But it's too early!'

'I know, but with a few sexual favours I could probably get him to hold it awhile. The other people aren't moving out for a few months yet. Graham said he'll show us around some time, OK?'

Silence.

'OK?' Sally tries again.

'Sorry—yes,' I say, still stunned. 'That sounds great. Really great. Thanks!'

'Good luck for that second wedding. It's Troy and Lindsay, isn't it? Got everything you need? Camera, cattle prod, neurosurgeon for a lobotomy?'

I laugh. 'A lobotomy sounds great right about now. Anyway, I'd better go. I'm at Molly's.'

'OK. I'll talk to you later. Bye.'

'Bye.' I end the call. And as I put my phone back in my handbag, I notice I have four messages. I'm about to listen when the slam of a door makes me look up from the phone. It's Molly. She comes running down the steps at the front of her unit block, simultaneously shoving a piece of toast in her mouth and pulling a cotton cardigan over her sleeveless light blue T-shirt. She opens the car door and jumps in with a grin.

'Sorry I'm late, Liv. Let's go.'

'No worries,' I say. 'Just one second.' I turn my mobile off and shove it back in my bag.

Y Y Y Y

'Liv! Liv!'

I'm cut off from speaking to Molly mid-sentence. The bride beckons.

'Yes, Lindsay?' I turn around to look at her. She calls me over to where she and her now-husband are standing beside their bridal garbage trucks.

Yes, that's right—bridal *garbage trucks*.

Old, cleaned up (thank God), white-painted, festooned with garlands of plastic roses bridal garbage trucks. And, oh, I don't like this pair. I don't like this pair at all. But Daddy owns all the garbage trucks in the city, and Daddy's paying, so…

'Troy's got a great idea!' she squeals when I reach them both.

I glance up at Troy, the proverbial brick shit-house, today looking ridiculously like the Milky Bar kid meets the Hulk in his white three-piece suit. I seriously doubt Troy's ever had a good idea in his life. He may not have even had a standard, run-of-the-mill idea.

'You ready for it?' Lindsay smiles a bridal bleached-white-toothed smile.

'As ready as I'll ever be!' I try to up my level of enthusiasm to match hers.

'OK. I need you to stand over there to get the right view.'

I go over to the spot she points out, on the other side of one of the garbage truck's bonnets.

And then I watch in horror as the bride positions the groom behind herself, lifts up her skirt, bends down to rest her hands on the front of the garbage truck and forms her mouth into a large 'O', acting for all the world as if her new husband is doing unmentionable things in unmentionable ways up her $18,000 snow-white (ha—as if!) dress.

My mouth hangs open for just a second. But then I snap it shut and regain my composure. 'How about that!' I try to sound impressed with Troy's creativity as I take a few half-hearted shots. 'Right. All done,' I say, about fifteen seconds later.

Lindsay stands up a touch. 'Oh. Can we have a few more, Liv? Troy really wants these ones in the album.'

Shudder.

But, 'Sure!' I say brightly, and Lindsay bends down to position herself once more.

I've only taken a few more shots when Molly creeps up behind me and gives my ankle a tap with one of her feet. 'We've got to move on, Liv,' she says quietly.

'And not just because I think watching this may make me go blind.'

'OK.' I stand upright, happy to do exactly what Molly says. 'Lindsay? Troy?' I say. 'We've got to move on. How about you in the truck, Lindsay? With Troy looking up at you?'

'Great!' Lindsay pushes herself up and opens the door to clamber into the garbage truck. As she goes, she catches a string of the plastic roses in her heel. 'Whoops!' She sticks her head above the door to look at me and laughs. 'And don't you take any up my skirt now! I've got to leave some surprises for Troy later.'

Gag.

'Ha-ha!' I reply, before I turn and grab Molly. 'Save me!' I whisper. I position one hand in the air, making shot-like gestures with my thumb and forefinger as I speak to her, as if I'm talking technical. 'Right. After this, we're going to go around the side of the restaurant and you're going to stab me to death with the tripod, putting me out of my misery. OK?'

Molly shakes her head, glancing down at the piece of paper in her hand. 'Sorry, it's not on the shot list. No can do.'

Damn. I knew I'd forgotten something. And Molly's tough. There's no way she'll humour me if it's not on the shot list. I'll just have to live to shoot another wedding.

'Good luck,' she says. 'You finish up here, then nip

inside to take a few shots of the table settings. I'll go round up the rest of the bridal party.' She pats my back and is gone.

I watch her go, thinking what a godsend she is. Sally picked Molly the same way she picked me—asked around the photography department at the local art college and trialled a few students here and there, getting them to assist her on smaller shoots where an assistant wasn't really necessary. Molly stood out from the crowd—just like Sally said I had, which is nice. But even I can see Molly is different from me. She was right from the start.

Because, like I said, Molly is tough.

Her specialty is getting people to do as they're told without having to resort to arm-clinching manoeuvres. The little Rottweiler, Sally and I like to call her. And it's a gift, what Molly is able to do with a group of people. It may not sound all that hard, but it's a reasonably demanding job to get a bridal party of ten to stand in some kind of formation when they've downed a bottle of champagne each. Molly's a trouper, and Sally and I both feel that, even though she's got a year of her three-year photography course to go, she's going to be a star. She's got what it takes—nerves of steel, a smile she can keep plastered on her face no matter what, and she isn't afraid of heights. (We do a lot of climbing in this job— trees, electricity boxes, brick walls, ladders, garbage trucks... You name it, we've climbed it to get the shot.)

I finish up the garbage truck bride and groom shots and head inside to take a few quick snaps of the equally disgusting table decorations (silver *and* gold? What is it with this pair?). I do the rounds of the numerous tables, my camera winding on and on and on as I go. Finally I get to the head table and spend some extra time there, making sure I capture everything. It's only when I turn to leave that I spot her.

Hannah the Horrible.

She's standing in the middle of the room and I wonder just how long she's been there—watching me. Hannah is this wedding's pushy bitch in residence, Lindsay's older sister and Matron of (Hellish) Honour.

I'd had my first run-in with her at Lindsay and Troy's initial meeting at the studio. Hannah came along as she'd been married the year before and was, thus, still the expert on all things wedding. I remember quite distinctly how much trouble she gave me over the quote. The first thing I did after making us all coffee was to explain to Lindsay and Troy the added cost of being married around Valentine's Day, as I always do with all the customers who are interested in this time of year. But it was Hannah who insisted that the Valentine's Day weekend was the weekend it had to be, so I brought out the packages they could choose from and explained the limited times I had left—one spot on the Saturday, as it turned out.

Hannah looked at me as if I was an idiot. 'This isn't

any good to us. We want Sunday. Valentine's Day. You know—the fourteenth?'

I explained through gritted teeth that I couldn't do the fourteenth as I'd been booked out for that day by other couples a good six months before they'd even enquired.

'We don't care,' she said. 'We want the fourteenth.' Then she picked up the price list and given it back to me smugly, without even looking at it. 'It doesn't matter about the money. That's not a problem. Our father—' she glanced at Lindsay then '—owns all the garbage trucks in the city.' She kept one eye on me as she said all of this.

I think I was supposed to be impressed.

I took much pleasure in telling her that it was Saturday morning or nothing.

She left in a huff, with Lindsay and Troy in tow. And then, a few days later, Lindsay and Troy came back. Alone.

Now, across the room, Hannah, obviously still pissed off at me, gives me the once-over.

'Hi, Hannah,' I say, trying to smile.

'This is for you,' she says, coming over to hand me a small silver box.

I'm slightly taken aback. A present? But as I put my camera down on one of the guest tables I realise the box is exactly the same as the one placed on each guest's plate. On opening, I'm met with a T-shirt with a picture of Lindsay and Troy on the front, their names and the date of their wedding spelled out in cursive script below. And not just any picture. My picture. The picture I took as their engagement portrait. The picture I hold the copyright to.

My eyebrows rise.

'Aren't they great?' She looks at me. 'I arranged them myself.'

'Mmm. Fantastic. Very…original.'

But nothing gets past Hannah, who gives me a look. 'Hey, you know what?' she says innocently. 'You should put it on.'

The woman has got to be joking.

'Go on,' she says, nodding. 'It'd really make Lindsay's day.'

Oh, great. Teeth gritted (as they always seem to be around Hannah), I reach down, pick up the T-shirt and pull it on over my head. Fantastic. But look on the bright side, Liv, I tell myself as Hannah heads for the door, at least you'll have some concrete evidence to take to court when you sue them for breach of copyright.

'Um…' Molly says, sticking her head around the door into the reception room. 'Oh, there you are, Hannah.' She spots the Matron of Honour. 'It's you I was looking for. We need you outside.' She glances back over at me. 'You almost done? Now I've got Hannah, we're ready to go.'

I nod and move towards the door.

'Hey.' Molly gives me the thumbs-up. 'Nice T-shirt!'

I don't grace this with a reply.

Outside, I spend the next half-hour taking the necessary bridal party shots in front of the garbage trucks. Finally Molly moves everyone over to the lawn that leads into the reception area, and I climb up onto one of the truck's bonnets to take a few shots of all the guests with the bridal party standing at the front.

It isn't until I take the last shot, and Molly lets the crowd disperse to descend on the hovering drinks and hors d'oeuvres waiters, that I see him.

Drew.

Right up at the back of the crowd. He waves and starts towards me. Surprised, I forget to wave back, simply stand and stare, still on the bonnet. As he makes his way through the crowd I become even more surprised. Because it's not just Drew that's coming over. Someone else is following him. Someone tall and blonde and willowy.

'Er, I think you can come down now.' Drew laughs when he reaches the truck. He offers me his hand and I take it silently, bending down to hop off. It isn't until I'm back on solid ground, have smoothed down my pants and got myself together a bit, that I remember my manners. 'Um, hi,' I say, looking up and feeling my cheeks get hot as I recall our outing yesterday.

But Drew doesn't seem fazed at all. 'Fancy seeing you here,' he jokes.

I smile and nod, then look over at the willowy blonde.

'Oh, sorry,' Drew starts. 'Liv, this is Tiffany—Tiffany, Liv. Tiff's Lindsay's cousin,' he adds.

Tiff?

'Pretty funny, hey?' Drew continues. 'I tried to call your mobile when I realised it was you who was going to be the photographer, but it must have been turned off already.'

I nod again and Drew keeps chatting about the wedding.

But me, I can't keep my eyes from flicking over to Tiffany every so often. What's Drew doing with her at Lindsay's wedding? He's acting as if she's just anyone. But who is she? Besides Lindsay's cousin, I mean.

Drew keeps right on chatting, and my eyes keep right on flicking from him to his partner. And as he talks I begin to think maybe Tiffany *is* just 'anyone'. Drew certainly doesn't look as if he's been caught out here.

'Liv?'

I look up. 'Sorry?'

'I asked if you wanted a drink,' Drew says.

'Oh, right. Um, a mineral water would be great, thanks.'

'Another champagne for me,' Tiffany adds.

'I'll be right back.' Drew heads for the nearest drinks waiter and Tiffany and I both watch him go.

'So, Tiffany…' I turn back to face her. 'Have you, um, known Drew for long?'

'Oh, a while, I guess! I'm his girlfriend.' She stops

for a second and titters. 'Well, OK, I admit it—ex-girl-friend. This is our last date, I guess. Ha-ha-ha. But really I shouldn't joke. It's a shame. He was a real gentleman, you know?' She keeps prattling on, with 'I've got a few champagnes under my belt already' girl-ish confidences, but by this stage I'm not listening.

Because my eyes have snapped over to watch Drew across the lawn, taking the drinks from the waiter.

His girlfriend? Ex-girlfriend? Last date?

Suddenly the excitement and happiness I've been feeling over the last few days drain slowly from my head, out of my feet, sink right down into the bitumen and are gone.

Tiffany follows my gaze over to him and smacks her lips. 'You know, I have to tell you—' she nudges her elbow against my ribs '—he comes highly recommended, if you're thinking about it yourself...'

I look back at her in horror, but she trails off as Drew reaches us and passes the drinks around.

'Are you all right?' he asks. 'You look like you've seen a ghost.'

My mind flicks back to Mrs Batty-Smith, and then to Tony.

'God, you're not all right, are you? Are you feeling sick again?' Drew continues, starting to look worried. He reaches out to touch my arm. Just like yesterday.

And with this one movement everything falls back into place for me. The world makes sense again. I look up to stare him straight in the eye. 'Everything's fine, thanks. I was just chatting to Tiffany. She was telling me you come highly recommended, as a matter of fact...'

Drew glances over at Tiffany, then at me, looking like he's the one who wants to be sick now. 'Er...ah...' Finally, he turns back to Tiffany. 'Tiffany, could you, er, excuse us for a moment?'

'Um, sure—sure.' Tiffany looks flustered. 'I think I'll go and congratulate Lindsay. I haven't had the chance to speak to her yet.'

'Good idea.' Drew doesn't take his eyes off me as she speaks.

I put my drink down on the ground and wait for her to leave.

Drew reaches up and runs a hand through his hair as he exhales. 'Shit. Sorry about that. I wanted to explain, but I couldn't really while Tiff was here. We broke up about three months ago—not that we even dated properly. Only a couple of times, in fact. But she rang this week crying because her date for the wedding had dropped out at the last moment and she needed a partner. I couldn't say no.' He pauses then, and runs his hand through his hair once more. 'Ha ha. You know me. The quintessential nice guy. It's always getting me into trouble.'

I watch him, silent. This is where I tell him it's nothing, my brain says to me. This is where you put it all down to Drew doing a favour for a friend. An ex-girlfriend, yes, but so what? This is where you both have a laugh about how much champagne Tiffany's had. How if she has just one more she'll be on the wrong side of tipsy. But I don't listen to my brain. Instead I remain as silent as Drew was on the phone the other night. After my meeting with Mike.

'I'm, er, sorry about whatever she said. Tiff's a bit…talkative—a bit, er, open…I guess you could say. And she's had more than a few drinks.'

Still I say nothing. And the truth is I don't want to. Because, like I said before, the world suddenly makes sense again. Suddenly it falls into a pattern. A pattern I know all too well. God, I can't believe I let myself say all that…all that drivel to Drew yesterday. That I let myself open up like I did to someone I hardly know. I shake my head, furious. Furious with Drew for letting me believe he was for real. But most of all furious with myself, for falling for it. For falling for it all over again.

One more time, Liv…you're an idiot.

I mean, how could I have been so stupid? What I'm hearing now—the situation I'm in—it's exactly why I made a conscious choice to stay single. To avoid this kind of shit in my life. I spot Lindsay then, entering the reception area, and even though my work at this wedding is practically done, I remember where I am and my role.

I hold up my hand and Drew's voice halts. 'You

know what?' I look up at him with a dismissive wave. 'I think I've heard enough.'

Drew looks surprised. 'Sorry?'

I shrug. 'So you're here with Tiffany, who thinks you're on some kind of a farewell date, some last hurrah, and goes around telling everyone that you're fantastic in bed. Frankly, you don't have to explain anything to me, and I don't want to hear it anyway. I'm—how did you phrase it the other night? Yes, that's it. I'm *busy*.' I turn then and start to walk off towards Molly, who's chatting to one of the bridesmaids as she packs away some of the camera equipment.

Drew grabs my arm, stops me and swivels me around. 'Liv, wait. You're blowing this all out of proportion.'

I pause for only a second. 'Sure, that's fine. Maybe I am.' I brush his arm off. 'But this is just the tip of the iceberg. You know, I was starting to think that maybe we… Oh, I don't know. Really I should just shut up. Cut my losses. I'll tell you something, though. What I *do* know is that I've had it with shitty men. I put myself on the line for you. I told you I wasn't sure if I was ready for a relationship again and you blew it. You blew it! You call this a fresh start? This doesn't look like a fresh start to me. You're dicking me around just like the rest of them, Drew. Except this time I'm going to be smarter. I'm stopping at the tip of the iceberg. I'm sick of all that he said/she said rubbish. As you can see—' I swipe my arm in a wide arc, indicating the two garbage trucks '—I've got enough of it in my life already, without the kind the male of the species can dole out.'

Drew looks at me for a moment in silence before he starts up again. 'I should have told you, I know. But this isn't anything. It's nothing. Tiff's just a friend. God, not even a friend…'

'Don't you get it?' I shake my head at him. 'You can stop with the excuses now. With your tulips and your irises and your lunches and your "should we share a cab home?" and "I'm the quintessential nice guy" lines.'

Drew continues to look at me, dumbfounded.

I check the time on my watch. 'Like I said, I'm busy. And now I'm also late. So if you could just let me get on with my job, that'd be fantastic.' I turn and start off again.

I only take a few steps before Drew laughs.

'So that's it, is it?'

I stop in my tracks, but don't turn back. 'Yes. That's it. Thanks. Goodbye.'

Behind me, there's a pause. When he speaks again, the tone of his voice changes completely. 'God, you really mean it, don't you?'

'Yes. I really mean it.'

'Wow. You can really fool yourself when you want to, can't you, Liv?'

Now I turn.

Drew is shaking his head. 'Listen to yourself. That is if you can hear me through that scaffolding we were talking about yesterday.'

Scaffolding? I roll my eyes.

Drew walks up to me. Right up. So close I can feel his breath on my face. 'It'd be really easy to believe I had a girlfriend, wouldn't it? Wouldn't that make things simple for you? So convenient. So…risk-free.'

I don't look at him.

'Yes. That would be perfect. Because then you could just discount me, couldn't you? You could just cross me out of your life like I never existed and get on with it. Live your life on the surface like you were before. Not feeling…well, not feeling very much at all…' He moves in even closer then, and is about to whisper something in my ear when there's a tap on my shoulder.

'Um, hello? What do you think you're doing?'

I jump.

Hannah.

'Liv?' she says, as I turn to face her. 'Didn't you forget something?'

I look at her blankly.

'Lindsay asked you to take some photos of Troy putting his jacket around her like she's cold. What are we paying you for?'

My teeth grind together again into something my dentist will later on probably label 'The Hannah'. 'I don't know what it is you're paying me for,' I hiss at her. 'My saintly nature, perhaps?' After my little talk with Drew, I just can't help myself.

Hannah gives me a look and taps one mint-green dress-matching shoe. 'Do I have to remind you who my father is?'

Behind me, Drew snorts, and I swivel around quickly to give him a look that says 'Keep out of this. This is my *job*.'

'I'll have you know he's a very powerful man. He could cause you a lot of trouble.'

'Oh, come on.' Drew laughs, coming up to stand beside me. Every single muscle in my body tenses. 'What are you saying?' That Liv will never have her garbage collected in this town again?'

Hannah pauses, unsure whether Drew is having her on or not. 'Maybe.' Her eyes flash as Lindsay approaches.

The four of us look at each other.

'Who are you?' Lindsay asks Drew, breaking the silence.

'Oh, haven't you met? This is cousin Tiffany's fuck-buddy,' I reply quickly, and instantly hate myself for it. Of all the things I could have said about Drew, this wasn't the phrase I meant to come out with.

And with this Drew gives me a long look. 'Give me a call when you get real, Liv.' Then he turns on his heel and leaves.

The three of us watch him until he rounds the corner and is out of sight.

All too soon I spot the look on Hannah's face. Time for damage control. I forget about Drew and put on my you-poor-hassled-bride voice. 'It's OK,' I soothe. 'I'm sorry about that. I think he's had too much to drink. Oh, look at you, Lindsay!'

I try to divert some attention away from myself.

It works. Hannah looks over at her sister.

'Me?' Lindsay says.

I nod. 'Your face is all flushed. It looks great. Very virginal bride!' I hold up my camera. 'How about we take a few shots and then grab Troy and his jacket?'

But Lindsay's excited now. 'Troy! Troy!' she calls out to her husband, who's standing maybe fifteen or so metres away, talking to a group of guests. 'Come and look. The photographer says I look like a virginal bride!'

Every single guest on the lawn turns to look at Lindsay.

And there is dead silence. Except for one small snigger in the background.

'Well, I do!' she says, putting her hands on her hips.

I wheel her around and start snapping off shots until she's happy. When I've wasted enough film to pacify her, I grab Troy and his stupid jacket and take pose after pose until it's time for them to move inside for the entrée.

With everyone seated inside, I really am finished for the day.

I make my way across the lawn and lower myself slowly onto the pavement beside the second bridal garbage truck. Molly comes over to crouch down beside me. 'Some wedding, huh?' she says. 'Ready for the next one?'

I put my head in my hands.

'Um, Liv? What was all that about before? I was coming to get you, but I saw you arguing with that guy. Do you know him from somewhere?

I exhale slowly. 'He's someone I was… I mean, I…' I give up trying to explain myself. 'He's just someone I knew once.'

Molly must hear the tone of finality in my voice, because she doesn't say anything, just gets up and collects our gear, bringing my handbag over to me.

'Thanks,' I say. I open it up, looking for a piece of gum, or a mint—anything, really, to take away the foul taste that's in my mouth. But there's nothing. I start to close the bag again, but then spot my wallet and remember something. I pull it out and extract Drew's card from the pocket at the back.

And as Molly and I leave the car park I throw the small piece of buff-coloured cardboard behind my shoulder and into the back of the garbage truck.

As far as I'm concerned, I just *got* real.

Y Y Y Y

Molly and I are sitting eating lunch in a park when she just walks right on over.

'Justine?' I almost choke on my sandwich. 'What—? How—?'

'Sally told me where you'd be.'

Molly looks from one of us to the other and back again.

'Hey, Molly,' Justine says then.

'Um, hi. Did you want me to…?' Molly motions.

I shake my head. But Justine shakes her head too. Then she grabs my arm. 'I wouldn't want to disturb your lunch,' she says to Molly. 'No. *You* are coming with *me.*'

And with that I'm dragged up from the table and across the grass. 'Are you all right?' I say, when Justine finally stops.

'Oh, I'm fine. It's you I'm worried about. Well, you and Drew.'

I look over at the swings on the other side of the

park. Nice to know he got his side of the story in as fast as possible. 'Is that right?'

'Yes, that's right. I can't believe how rude you were to him! And, no. Don't think he rang up tattling, because he didn't. I called him.'

I don't say anything, but I can feel my body start to tense from the soles of my feet up.

'Well?' Justine finally asks.

I shrug. 'Well, what? What am I supposed to say? For God's sake, Justine, he was there with his ex-girlfriend—a bimbo of the first order, I might add—who thought they were on some kind of strange final date. She waxed lyrical on how great the guy was in bed. I didn't like it, and I'm not going to hang around to listen to that kind of shit.'

Justine points a finger. 'But you're not hearing "that kind of shit" from Drew, are you? You're hearing it from some bimbo.'

'What difference does it make? From Drew, about Drew—I don't care.'

'And you don't care that he feels terrible about what happened today?'

I look away again. 'He'll get over it.'

'Oh, that's nice. It's nice to know you care about him.'

'I did. For a while. But it's not about him any more. It's about me. I'm just not interested. He had his chance and he blew it.'

'What? He blew his chance by being a nice guy?

Drew doesn't even *like* Tiffany. He hasn't spoken to her for months. They went out a couple of times because his dad and her mum set it up. Then she called up crying because her date for the wedding backed out on her, and he felt bad, so he did her a favour and went along.'

I remember tall, blonde Tiffany. 'Mmm. She's a real charity chase, that Tiffany. What are you going to tell me next? That Drew was just trying to boost her self-esteem by sleeping with her?'

This catches Justine out. 'I don't know anything about that. All I'm saying is they're not seeing each other any more. That this was just a one-off thing.'

I sigh and look at the patchy grass beneath my feet. 'Fine. I'm not saying that's not true. But it's not about that. Like I said, I'm just not interested in playing those kind of games any more. When I saw them together today, I realised I'm not ready to go through all that again. I'm only trying to protect myself here.'

Justine laughs out loud at this. An 'I can't believe what I'm hearing' laugh.

'Yes?' I cross my arms.

'Too right you're trying to protect yourself.'

'And what's that supposed to mean?' It's getting hot out here in the sun. Hot and tedious.

'Just yesterday you were begging Drew to give you a second chance. *Begging*. And now that *he* needs one, what do you do? Run at the first sign of trouble, that's what. The truth is you're not protecting yourself. You're just plain scared. You're too scared to give him *his* chance like he gave you yours.'

I shrug.

'Oh, please.' Justine shakes her head now, a bemused look crossing her face.

'What?'

'How are you ever going to find him, Liv?'

'What? Who?'

'This perfect, perfect guy who never takes a step out of line. This white knight in shining armour.'

I raise my eyebrows. 'He should be pretty easy to spot in a crowd. On his horse and all.'

Justine throws me a dirty look.

'Fine,' I say then, wanting to get this over and done with. 'Obviously you've got a point to make. Would you like to make it? I'm getting burned. And I've got a wedding to get to...'

Justine pauses for a second, and I can tell she's wondering just how candid she should be. 'Sure. I'll make my point. Relationships are messy, Liv. That's all there is to it. They're never perfect. There are always things to discuss and work out. You *know* that.'

Did I ever. 'So I'm supposed to settle for second best right from the get-go. Is that what you're saying?'

'No, but you can't fly off the handle when everything doesn't go your way either. Drew had a good explanation for what happened today and you just dismissed it.'

'Well, that's my prerogative, isn't it? When I saw him with Tiffany, it just all came back to me—what happened with Mike. I promised myself that this time around I'd be more cautious. That I'd wait until—'

'But that's just it!' Justine butts in, voice raised, carrying across the park. 'All you ever end up doing is waiting! It's like you gave up men for Lent one year and forgot to start back up again.'

I throw up one hand, thinking I really, really don't need this right now. My head's pounding, I'm tired. I just want to shoot what I have to shoot and go home.

Justine and I eye each other off.

'What?' Justine says eventually. 'Go on—say it.'

Oh, hell—why not? May as well get this over and done with. 'I just didn't expect to get the "it's terrible to be single so you'd better grab the guy that's in front of you and hang on tight" argument from you, that's all.'

'What are you talking about? I never said there was anything wrong with being single! You're deliberately avoiding my point.'

'The one about Lent?'

Justine's jaw tightens. 'Forget what I said about Lent…' She pauses. 'What we're talking about here is Drew. Drew *is* the guy. The one you've been waiting for. He's perfect. But you're throwing him away because of one little thing.' She holds her right index finger up.

'No.' I shake my head. 'No, that's not true. It's like

I told him today—this is just the tip of the iceberg. If it wasn't this it would have been something else. Something else further down the track, when I was more…involved.'

'Yeah, that's right. Some other *excuse*. Some other excuse you could have used to ditch him before it got too serious, just like you did with the very few guys you've dated since you broke up with Mike. God, Liv, I have to give it to you. You're good at it—protecting yourself. You've been practising for years. You're getting so good at it I'm surprised you haven't branched out on the evolutionary scale, joined the insect world, and started having sex with all the guys you meet so you can have the satisfaction of eating them after you mate.'

My brain stops dead when I hear this. Eating them after I mate? This is ridiculous. I've had enough now. My mouth opens and closes a few times.

But it's Justine who speaks first. She sighs. 'Liv, I know you're scared of being hurt again, but Drew's not like that. He's really worried that he's upset you. Why don't you call him? Or try and get away early tonight and come to the ball with us and…'

Ugh. That's it. I am so, so sick of everyone being the resident expert on what's going on in my head. I hear enough about it all from Tania as it is. 'That frigging ball,' I mutter, staring at the grass.

'Sorry?'

I'm about to blow the whole thing off, but then

look up to clock the expression on Justine's face—all innocence and 'I just want what's best for you, Liv'—and I decide to tell her how I feel once and for all. To have my say.

'It means I thought I was finally home free. I thought that Dad was going to leave me alone, Rachel wasn't going to set me up and you weren't going to make me go to your stupid singles events any more. I'm sick of everyone pushing me and pushing me and pushing me. I thought that I'd got lucky, that you'd all made some kind of pact to give me a break from being set up this Valentine's Day. Or hopefully for the whole year. For ever, even! I thought you might all let me forget. Finally. But, no, I should call Drew, date Drew, go to the ball with Drew. Why can't everyone just leave me be?' As the words exit my mouth I remember what Tony said in reply to this question in my dream other night: *I can't. And I don't fail. I never fail. Remember that.*

Stop thinking about it, Liv. Stop it! It was a dream. Just a dream.

Justine's voice raises again. 'You have no idea, do you? Why do you think everyone keeps at you about the guy thing—tries to get you to date, tries to set you up?'

'Gee, I don't know.' I make a mock-dumb face. 'To make my life a misery?' Ugh. Why do these things keep coming out of my mouth?

Justine looks away, disgusted.

'Right, then,' I say. 'Why don't you tell me your great motive, if it's so wonderful? I'd love to hear it. Can't wait. I bet it's almost as good a fairytale as whatever you told Drew about Mike. Because I'm sure you did. Not that you ever *met* him, that is.'

'I didn't need to, did I? I've been living with him for the past two years through you! And, fine, you want to hear it like it is? I'll tell you. OK. So Mike and you decide to split. You pine—and I mean really *pine*, as in you don't go out of the house except to go to work for ages—then you rebound and date like a thing possessed for six months, you wear yourself out, then go into dating hibernation for well over a year. You think that's normal? It's not. It's a bit... I don't know, *extreme*. Your dad, Rachel, me—we're all just trying to help you get back into the swing of things. To get you to see that not all relationships have to be like yours and Mike's was. Valentine's Day coming around each year just reminds us what you're missing out on.'

'Oh, yes—the dating slump. Don't think I haven't heard it all before. But as far as I'm concerned I'm not missing out on anything, so you can stop. You can all stop. I'm not going to date Drew. I'm not going to call Drew. I'm not going to the bloody ball. I'm going to go to my final booking of the day, then to bed, and tomorrow I'm going to get up and go to work...'

'Ugh.' Justine lets out a frustrated noise from her throat. There's a pause as, once again, our eyes do battle. 'I can't believe you!' There's another pause before she points a finger at me again, angrier now than I've ever seen her. 'Right, Liv. Fine. You do that,' she says. 'You keep busy. Really busy. You fill your days up with work and Spanish and the gym, and whatever else you can find. And then it'll all be OK, won't it? Because that way you won't have time to stop and think about what you threw away so readily today. About the chance you couldn't give to someone who could so readily offer the same thing to you.'

I feel terrible almost immediately.

And every fifteen minutes or so that afternoon I check my mobile for messages.

Nothing.

Or close to nothing—there's one that happily informs me that, come Monday evening, I'm going to be the proud parent of two ancient cats named Betsy and Shu-shu.

Great. I can't help but grimace as I think of the cats' owner. And the grimace quickly turns into a frown as I start to worry—all the things I've been dreaming this week are starting to seem scarily like premonitions of some kind. Premonitions that are getting harder and harder to discount.

Eventually I stop checking my mobile. Because I realise I'm not getting a second second chance. Not from Drew. And not from Justine.

I drop Molly off at home at the end of the day, and when she closes the door to her house behind her I bend forward, resting my head on the steering wheel.

All this fighting has drained me. Especially fighting with Justine. I never, ever argue with Justine. She's such an easygoing, hard-to-get-a-rise-out-of person.

The awful thing is, some of the things she came out with this afternoon—she was right. Some of the things I said to Drew today were just plain wrong. But I was angry and, like I told Justine, I was—*am*—trying to protect myself. I can't deal with relationships like she and Sally are able to. I just can't. This week—it's just been a bit too much for me. A bit of a rollercoaster ride. I need some time to decompress. I need some…

Panadol. I think, as my head throbs.

I push myself up off the steering wheel then. OK. That's enough. I'm only making my headache worse by sitting here and going over everything. I turn the ignition back on and pull out.

Y Y Y Y

Almost fourteen hours after I last closed it, I'm standing outside my front door again, fumbling around in my pants pocket for my keys. Finally, I locate them, and stick my house key in the door. It's as I go to turn it that, in one swift movement, the bag on my right shoulder falls onto my arm.

'Ow!' I yell, then, 'Bloody, damn it…' I mumble more quietly, rearranging my bag and reaching out for the door again. Just as my fingers touch the lock, the door magically opens in front of me. I look up. It's Drew. Drew in a tuxedo.

He looks—well, I hate to admit it…fantastic.

'Er, hi,' he says.

'Hi,' I say back, pulling my key out of the door awkwardly. Shit, oh, shit, oh, shit. My heart *thumpa-thumps* as I recall our fight and all the things I said. I didn't think he and Justine would still be here.

'Here—let me take a few of those bags.' He reaches

over and starts to unload me. First my left arm, then my right.

'Um, thanks.' I push the door open a bit wider with my foot. When he's taken a few more bags I follow him inside. With the lighter load, for the first time in hours my shoulders feel like they're more than a few inches off the ground.

'I didn't think you'd be back this early,' Drew says, stacking the bags on the floor near the dining table, not looking at me.

I check the time. Seven-forty-eight. And even though I can't see the expression on Drew's face, I get the impression from the tone in his voice that he thinks I've lied to both him and Justine about what time I'd be home, telling them it wouldn't be until late so I can get out of going to the ball.

'Well, usually I head back to the studio to sort a few things out, but I've got a headache I just can't shake. I think I need some extra sleep. And I *definitely* need to sit down.'

Drew looks at me now, concerned. 'You're probably dehydrated. It was pretty hot out there today. Er—here you go.' He pulls out a chair at the dining table for me.

Hot out there? Tell me about it. I've downed six bottles of water and only peed twice. I decide, however, that this is information no one else really needs to know. Especially not Drew.

'I've had a headache for days. This week—it's been a bit much.' And then I wince and look away, knowing Drew's probably thinking about this morning almost as much as I am. I try not to squirm in my seat. I change the topic. 'Aren't you going to be late for the ball?'

'Er…it doesn't start till eight. Justine and I thought it'd be better to go from here, being closer and all.'

I nod and watch as Drew pulls out one of the chairs from the opposite side of the dining table. He undoes his jacket with one hand in an undeniably sexy move before he takes a seat. It's quite a while before he looks at me. 'Liv, I'm, er, sorry about this morning. But it's true. Tiff… It was all a favour, nothing more.'

'You don't have to—'

'I want to,' Drew cuts in. 'I've got a few things to say. Firstly, I don't want you to believe there's something's going on that isn't.'

'I—'

'And I wanted to tell you that I'm not trying anything on here. I'm not hiding things from you, or pretending. What you see is what you get. I know it's bad timing, and you've…had a lot to deal with this week, not to mention a lot of work on, but that's just the way it's worked out. I've, er, had a really good time getting to know you better, and I think it'd be a shame for us to stop seeing each other now.'

'I—'

Drew smooths the tablecloth out with one hand. 'So what do you think about all of that?'

'Um…' In the nick of time Justine comes into the room, attaching an earring.

'Hey,' she says, giving me a quick wave.

'Hey,' I say, turning around in my seat to face her. 'You look great.'

'Thanks.' She keeps her eyes on the floor, concentrating as she fixes her earring. Obviously she's still angry at me. 'We'd better get going. Don't want to keep our dates waiting.'

Drew pushes himself up from the table. 'Definitely not. If I keep mine waiting she might set the poodles on me. And if we fall out, you know what that means.' He looks at Justine, raising his eyebrows.

'What?'

'No romantic walks along the beach in the moon—light for me!'

'And what a shame that would be,' Justine says, with a laugh. 'Imagine all the fun you'd miss out on, scooping up poodle poop off the sand.'

The pair say their goodbyes and continue chatting as they make their way out through the door. Drew gives me a final look before he closes it behind them. As it clicks shut I suddenly wish we'd had a few more minutes together.

A few more minutes to sort things out.

Alone now, I get up with a sigh and head for my

bedroom, ripping off my shirt as I go. I can't wait to get my nastiest of nasty bras off. I knew it was a mistake wearing the one with the underwire that cuts into my chest on a day like today, but at five-thirty this morning, when I couldn't find the one I really wanted, I thought I'd just deal with it.

Wrong.

I strip off, have a quick shower, then put on my most comfortable pyjamas to console myself. And I have to admit that life looks just that little bit better now I'm out of the pinching nasty bra and into comfort wear that I can breathe in. I pause and look at myself in the mirror as I comb my wet hair.

If only the rest of my life was so easy to fix.

Well, maybe it is. Maybe it isn't as bad as I think, as Tania would say. I know what else she'd say, too. She'd tell me that the situation I've got myself into could be easily fixed if I just wanted to fix it. And I guess she might even be right. I mean, all I've really got to do is sit down with everyone involved and talk things over. OK, so maybe I'll take Justine out for dinner or something on Monday, to make things up to her. And Drew—I'll call him tomorrow.

I start combing again.

Yes, I'll call him. But what will I say?

Well, for a start I'll definitely apologise for the awful comments that came whizzing out of my mouth this morning without the stamped approval of my brain.

I can't believe some of the things I said. I wince as I remember a choice couple of lines, including the lovely 'Tiffany's fuck-buddy'. Ouch. But what about Drew's words before—about us continuing to see each other? I'm not so sure about that. I'm not so sure it's going to happen.

I know Justine is right, and Drew deserves exactly the same kind of chance he gave me. Tiffany's his baggage, just like Mike is mine. But Drew and I…we're different people. He hasn't had the same experiences I've had. Where Tiffany and Mike are concerned Drew's baggage is carry-on while mine's in the hold with 'oversize' and 'heavy' stickers plastered all over it. Like I told Justine, I need to protect myself from having my world shredded into little pieces again. Seeing Mike again this week, having him finally make that visit that I'd been subconsciously waiting for for so long, it's brought it all back again—what happened between us. What happened to me. And even though I'm finally—once and for all—over him, that doesn't mean I want to live it all over again.

So, while I feel bad that Drew was telling the truth about his innocent date with Tiffany, and I understand that I shouldn't have changed my opinion about him, the fact is I have. Well, maybe not about him as a person—he's a nice guy—but I think I *have* changed my opinion about where he fits into my life. Where we stand. And in my eyes, at the moment, we should be standing an arm's length apart.

Plus, I remind myself of Sally's phone call this morning. By the sound of things I'm going to be too busy for a relationship anyway. I can't let anything distract me from setting up my own studio. The statistic of fifty per cent of small businesses failing within the first year is too scary to even contemplate.

So maybe that's it.

Just friends.

I cringe when this thought passes through my head, because I've always hated that term 'just friends'. It's such a meaning-loaded term. How can it not be? The whole point of its existence is that both the parties involved in being 'just friends' want different things— one wants more than friendship and the other doesn't. This being the case, how can a real, true friendship ever happen at all? Personally, I don't think it can—that difference in feeling will always be there, playing piggy in the middle. Still, that's the way I want it to be. Just friends.

I finish combing my hair and make my way to the kitchen, grab a Lean Cuisine out of the freezer, stab it a touch too gleefully in the appropriate places and chuck it in the microwave. While I'm waiting for it to heat I drink a large glass of water and then refill it again, thinking about Drew's comment on dehydration.

When the microwave beeps, I forget about my headache and concentrate on my stomach. I empty my salmon and cheese sauce sachet onto my pasta sachet better than a celebrity chef ever could (there's a certain trick, a flick of the wrist, that I use to get all of the sauce out). Then I take my bowl and fork out to the living room and turn the TV on. I channel-surf until I find something my brain can cope with tonight, settling on *When Family Pets Turn Bad*. Yep, I think, I should be able to cope with that.

I watch as dogs, parrots, rats and ferrets have a go at their owners, their owner's friends, neighbours, children and other pets in ways I've never thought about before. A story about a cat attacking both its owners in their sleep worries me—should I have asked about the soon-to-be-arriving Betsy and Shu-shu's criminal record?—but I don't fret for long. Veronica said Betsy and Shu-shu were twelve, didn't she? If she's right, their furtive pouncing and eye-gouging days are probably long gone. I placate myself with the thought that as long as I feed them they probably won't resort to chewing off any of my appendages for sustenance during the night.

The show finishes and the news headlines come on between programmes. I'm reaching forward for my glass of water again as I hear it. Something about Valentine's Day. I choke on the pasta in my mouth and have to take a big gulp of water to unstick it. I can't believe this has surprised me, caught me unawares. Valentine's Day is tomorrow and is, essentially, what this weekend is all about for me—what I've been photographing all day today and will be photographing all day tomorrow. But on a personal level I haven't made the connection until now.

Valentine's Day.

I'm going to get through it unscathed. No set-ups, no dinners, no dates with my dad's friends' kids. And I'm floored. Because, for me, this feels like an absolute first.

I sit, stunned, staring at the TV presenter, who's gabbing on about some couple who are going to get married as they abseil down a cliff somewhere tomorrow, but I don't really take in what he's saying. Slowly I work back through the years. Last year, the year before, the year before that… My God, I think, as I scroll through time, it *is* an absolute first. The absolute first and only time in my grown-up, single-girl life that my family and friends haven't arranged something hideous on Valentine's Day.

I don't know whether to laugh or cry. Laugh, I guess—this should be a cause for celebration, a breaking out the Bolly moment.

But it's not.

I can't laugh, because for some reason Justine's words from this afternoon keep ringing through my aching head: *You getting what you want—it's not a good thing…* Over and over again.

I lean forward, grab the remote and switch the TV off.

Uneasily, quickly, I shovel down the rest of my

pasta. When I'm done, I get up and put my dish in the sink to soak, then grab my Dickens collection off the dining room table in the hope of occupying myself. I'm almost finished, I realize, when I look at the page I've marked with a folded corner. I've only got another fifty or so pages to go. I take the book and myself back over to the sofa and read almost four pages before I let my eyes rest closed, just for a moment…

Y Y Y Y

My eyes flick open the moment I hear the noise. I look around the room nervously.

Everything seems fine.

Breathing a sigh of relief, I get up off the couch. I really should go to bed and get some proper rest.

It's only when I take my first step down the hallway that I see the light. Not in a 'I'm having an epiphany' kind of way, but a real light. The study light. Seeping out from under the partially closed door. I stop mid-step, place my foot back on the floor and listen. Someone's typing.

Hearing this, I start to think that everything isn't fine, like I'd thought only seconds before on the couch. I reach out and put one hand against the wall to steady myself. The other hand I cover my mouth with. My breathing suddenly sounds extraordinarily loud. Someone's typing. Someone's typing in my flat. And it isn't me and it isn't Justine. I keep listening. Every so often the typing stops, and sometimes there will be quite a long pause before it starts up again. Slowly I start to creep down the hall, one step at a time, keeping my hand against the wall.

Slowly, slowly. The typing pauses and so do I.

Clickety-clack. It starts up again and I move down the hall once more. Who's in there? It *can't* be Justine or Drew. I'd have heard them when they came back in.

Oh.

I get a sick feeling in my stomach as I remember back through my week. All the way back to Mrs Batty-Smith's funeral and the bathroom—three spirits.

Slowly, slowly, I creep towards the door. When I finally get there I extend my hand and carefully push the door open just the tiniest crack, so I can see in the room. Then I inch forward and peek through the gap.

There's a man in there. A man sitting with his back to me and typing away on my computer.

At least I think it's my computer. Because my study…it's changed. Very changed. The last time I left it it was serviceable. A desk with my computer, a swivel chair, some bookcases, a filing cabinet. Now all those things are still there, but in different places in the room—which seems to have morphed from its standard rectangle to something like an oval. It's changed colour too—the new colour is… Let's just say it's kind of different. It used to be a not very interesting cream. Now it's a vibrant blood-red and has been stenciled with gold hearts. There's a heart-shaped gold clock where the normal clock used to be, red curtains where the white ones were, and the carpet—that's changed as well.

Red, of course.

I *must* be dreaming.

Because this—this is exactly like a room you'd see in your dreams and still recognise. It's happened to everyone, I'm sure—you're dreaming and recognise you're somewhere in particular, your kitchen, or your bathroom, or in my case your study—but the surroundings aren't like anything you've ever seen before. It's that kind of feeling. This isn't my study, but it is. I know it is. I keep looking around the room in wonder. Even the computer has some kind of a wacky heart-shaped border attached to it. It's as if they gave the contestants on *Changing Rooms* an extra forty-eight hours and an unlimited supply of LSD.

And this is the end of the line. I'm handing myself over to Tania come Monday morning. I may not have a brain tumour (if Tony's to be believed...), but there is definitely something wrong with me. This just isn't normal.

The typing starts up again then, and I move my attention back to the guy whose fingers are clacking away on the keyboard. As I watch, he moves his right arm away from the keyboard for a moment to use the mouse and...

Hang on a second.

He's looking at porn!

I forget about everything then, and step forward into the room, pushing the door wide open as I go.

'Hey, I hope you haven't downloaded any of that!' I say, remembering the charming computer STD Justine's little brother left us with last time he visited.

He turns on the swivel chair and looks at me.

Oh…um, wow.

As soon as I see him my eyes probably widen to something that looks pretty much like pre-roadkill staring into oncoming headlights. Because the guy sitting in my swivel chair is categorically, undeniably, squiffingly, lickably, the most handsome man I've ever seen.

'I'm so sorry,' he says, standing up and turning the computer off. 'I was…' he coughs discreetly. 'Passing the time. Tony has been teaching me about the Internet.'

'Tony,' I sigh. I should have known. 'Look, it's all right,' I say quickly, any viruses forgotten as I stare at his gorgeousness. 'Don't worry about it.' I take a big whiff. What is that? He even smells delicious. He stands in the middle of the room, adjusting his cuffs, and I, quite willingly, keep staring at him.

Divine.

And I don't mean in the Hugh Grant kind of way.

I could like this dream. I could like this dream a *lot*.

This guy looks great, smells great, is over four feet tall, has a perfectly fitted tux and, to top it all off, a gardenia in his buttonhole. Not a red rose, a gardenia. Very classy. You've got to love a man who knows his flowers.

The guy buttons his jacket up. 'If you'll allow me to introduce myself, I am the—'

'Ghost of Valentine's Day Present?' I butt in.

He nods.

'Right,' I say, and keep on taking him in (there's probably dribble running down my chin by now). After a while I notice something strange as he looks back at me. Every few seconds his face looks different. And I don't mean his expression, I mean his face. His actual face. As if he has several different faces that keep changing from one to the next. When I walked into the room he looked rather like Keanu Reeves. But now he's more Ben Affleck-ish. And, wait, that looks like a bit of Brad Pitt there. And is that Jude Law? I try to catch the change time and time again, but it's seamless.

Hopefully he'll rotate back to Keanu Reeves sooner or later.

'Shall we?' He steps forward, one arm bent for me to take.

I remember then that I'm in pyjamas, just like I was with Tony. They don't really go well with his crisp tux.

'Um—' I start, but when I look down I don't have pyjamas on any more. I'm now in a glamorous light cream beaded evening dress that matches his gardenia perfectly. 'Um, er, OK,' I stutter, and take his arm. He escorts me down the hall, out into the living room and opens the front door for me.

Hey, no Velcro bungee-jumping off the balcony this time. This guy knows how to treat a lady.

As he closes the front door behind us I become curious. 'So, do you have a name? Or is it just the rather formal Ghost of Valentine's Day Present? Sounds a little ominous, don't you think?'

'You can call me James,' he says as he leads me down the stairs.

'James,' I say. 'James is great. It's a nice name, James.' Don't babble, Liv, I tell myself. Act as if men with movie-star looks miraculously appear in your study every day.

I wish.

Outside, we keep walking down the path towards the road. Where a limo is waiting. James opens the door for me and I slide in across the tan leather seat. Inside, there's a glass of champagne waiting for me in the drink-holder resting within the armrest.

Even better. No leaping from the balcony, a free outfit, and champagne to boot. This kind of ghost I could get used to.

As James lets himself in on the other side of the limo I notice there's only one glass of champagne. 'Oh, sorry…' I begin to say, because I've already picked it up, but James waves my words away.

'I won't be partaking this evening,' he says.

Partaking? OK. I look down at the glass and consider whether or not I should drink it, with my headache. But then I realise my headache's gone. Finally. I lift up my left hand. No shaking. I feel…OK. Good, even. As if all my troubles have suddenly lifted. I frown, thinking of my emotions and how they've been up and down like a rollercoaster this week, then take a sip from my glass, nodding when I'm done.

'It's good,' I say to James. He doesn't look over. I take another sip. 'I can't even taste the Rohypnol,' I add. He nods back, ignoring the Rohypnol comment, and I watch as he adjusts his cuffs again, noticing that the silver cufflinks are shaped like small love hearts.

The limo moves away from the kerb. 'So, where are we going?' I ask.

'You must decide,' he says.

Hmm. Just like Tony said. I pause, glass in hand, thinking of the other night's stumble down a muddy memory lane, and wonder how I can make tonight a little more pleasant.

But wait a second.

This is the Ghost of Valentine's Day *Present* who's sitting beside me. Valentine's Day *Present* I don't have as many issues with. Well, good. And with this thought I snuggle back into my seat. Maybe tonight I really will be able to go with the flow. Anyway, for the moment I'm warm and comfortable, I'm holding a glass of champagne, and I'm ensconced in a great-looking dress. I take another sip from my glass, letting the champagne warm me even further, and gaze out of the window as the world passes by.

If I'm supposed to decide where we're going, I'm not doing a very good job of it. I have no idea where we're off to. My stomach rumbles and I think about food for a moment. It's been a while since that Lean Cuisine. If we have to go somewhere, dessert wouldn't be a bad idea. Something tells me, however, that keeping my stomach happy isn't going to be James's main objective in life.

I turn away from the window and look at him—the Ghost of Valentine's Day Present. I think back to Tony again. Maybe I *have* been wrong discounting these dreams. Especially since they keep right on coming. Maybe repressing them is making everything worse? I snort now, with this thought. Ugh. Listen to me. Pre-Tania, I would never have used a word like 'repressing'. Still, maybe I can get something out of all of this? Maybe I can pump James for some information?

'Um, am I supposed to be learning something here?' I ask James slowly, already guessing the answer.

He nods.

'About…?' I pause. 'About Valentine's Day?'

'You are, as they say, half right.'

'So there's something else as well?' I sit forward a little, almost spilling my champagne.

He nods again.

I think about this for a moment or two. Something else. I glance over at James in the hope that he'll fill me in and see instantly that he's not going to. He is, after all, a man of very few words—as I'm quickly discovering. He might look a treat, but he's hardly one of the great conversationalists of our time. I start to wonder if it's true, what they say about beautiful people—that they're not all that bright or interesting. That they just look good. Rather like ornaments—pretty, but useless. I never really believed that before, but now I'm not so sure. After all, he's been a lot of different beautiful people in a matter of minutes, and none of them have exactly been chatty.

'I don't know what the other thing is,' I say eventually.

James doesn't reply, but I let it go as he's looking like Keanu again (the buff version, not the in-between-movies guy). Fine, be like that. I shrug and, after a while, sit back again to concentrate on polishing off my champagne.

We keep driving. And driving. And driving.

But my champagne keeps filling itself up, so I don't really mind.

After what seems like an eternity, we pull up. Outside Rachel and Ryan's townhouse.

'But their house is only five minutes away from mine,' I say, as I realise where we are, not understanding what's taken us so long. But when I look over at

James somehow I know what his answer's going to be. 'I know, I know. It's all up to me. I brought us here.'

He inclines his head in his usual regal-looking nod. Yes.

I reach for the door handle, but just as I touch it it opens from the outside. James is standing there, holding the door open. I look back to where he was sitting just seconds ago. There is no way he had time to get out and around to my side of the car. Damn ghosts. But I try to do the regal incline of the head thing back as I princess-exit the car in my fancy dress…

And hit my head on the car roof.

That's it, I think, trying to look like it doesn't hurt. I'm booking myself into charm school as well as the loony bin.

'I guess we're going inside.' I start up the path towards the front door, wanting to rub my head but being too stubborn to actually do it. Halfway up the path, as Rachel pops into my thoughts, I stop. James bumps into me.

'Excuse me,' he says.

'No, excuse *me*,' I say absentmindedly as I hunt around in my mind for the details I'm looking for. This is the present, right? And Rachel told me she was going to be away on some conference for the Valentine's Day weekend. She told me that she was going to be away on the Saturday night but would be back Sunday morning. I look up at the house, knowing she's not there, and start to wonder if I'm going to like what I see inside. Ryan had better not have another woman in there, I think to myself, before I start up the path again.

The screen and front doors are both unlocked, and in a reversal of roles I open them and let James in before myself. I wonder for a second if he'll die from the shock, but he seems to take it OK, and doesn't even feel the need to adjust his cuffs again.

Inside the entry, I stop and listen. I hear voices almost immediately. A man's and a woman's voice that definitely isn't Rachel's. They're arguing. And there's some kind of other noise as well. A kind of... whirring.

I try and catch what the voices are saying, but I can't quite make the conversation out. They're downstairs, though. I narrow my eyes and start the investigation. On my right, the lounge is empty, but as I head through the dining room towards the kitchen the arguing and the whirring get louder. And then I see why.

Ryan is in the kitchen, hand mixer in hand, mixing something in a large bowl. He has something propped up in front of him—a recipe book—and is leaning forward and squinting as he reads it, because he doesn't have his glasses on. As I watch he leans forward even further, then glances sideways for a moment at the TV, where the arguing is coming from, and reaches over and turns the sound down.

'OK,' he says, squinting at the recipe book again.

'That's done, that's done and that's done. So it's dunking time.' He stands back then, obviously pleased with himself, and wipes his hands on his jeans.

I look on, amazed, as he starts to pick up meticulously cut-out pieces of heart-shaped bread, dunks them into the mixture in the bowl and then carefully lays them out on a baking-paper-lined tray. When he's done, he washes his hands, wipes them on his jeans again, covers the tray in cling-wrap and puts it in the fridge. After this, he starts the washing up.

'Is this really Ryan?' I say to James.

He regals again.

I move forward so I can see the recipe book. French toast. *Low-fat* French toast. Requiring numerous extra steps to get it that way, like buying and defrosting large quantities of frozen egg whites.

'That's Rachel's favourite,' I say, recognising the recipe book. We've made it before.

'Heart-shaped, also, may I add,' James adds.

'You may.'

'Thank you.'

'You're welcome,' I say, trying to add a tone of finality to my voice. If I don't, this could go on for ever.

I take a step back and lean on the bench, watching Ryan go about his washing up. And I have to say I really am amazed. Surprised. Aghast. This isn't like Ryan at all. He's always been the kind of guy who thinks the more expensive the gift, the better someone will like it—that presents aren't worth giving if you're not going to impress someone. At the start of his relationship with Rachel he showered her with the best champagne, the most 'in' restaurants, and weekends away at exclusive resorts. Of course she enjoyed it—who wouldn't? But I know the truth about Rachel—the most exciting present she's ever received was from an old boyfriend who went to quite a bit of trouble tracking down a boxed set of Chevy Chase movies that she'd always coveted. Diamonds really were never going to be Rachel's best friend. So this—the French toast—for Ryan is so…ordinary. And an *effort*. That's the big thing here. It's an effort. An effort for him to find the recipe, buy the ingredients and cut out the heart-shaped bread. It's the effort that surprises me the most.

I shake my head slowly, still not believing what I'm seeing. There's only one thing to think, however. If all this is real—maybe Ryan *has* changed. Maybe he really did mean everything he said to me about his and Rachel's relationship being so important to him.

I glance over at James, who's been sitting on one of the dining table chairs for the past five minutes while I've been inspecting Ryan.

Oh. Colin Firth. Nice touch.

'Shall we?' I say, offering him *my* arm this time.

He nods, stands up, and rebuttons his jacket again, leaving me to wonder how often he wears out his suits. It's open, closed, open, closed with the buttons, and pull, pull, pull on the cuffs. Dizzying stuff.

I take one last look at Ryan over my shoulder as we retreat. He's humming as he finishes tidying the kitchen. I shake my head one more time and keep going. Well, good for him, I think, stepping out of the townhouse and onto the front path. Good for him.

Soon enough, we're back in the limo and the streets are whizzing past my window once more. As we go I think of Ryan and what he's doing, and start to imagine what everyone else is up to tonight. If Ryan's making low-fat heart-shaped French toast, all kinds of strange things could be going on.

It doesn't take long before we pull up again.

'Hey, this is Dad and Eileen's house,' I say, as the limo stops. I don't waste any time getting out of the car, but nimble-toed James still manages to get around to the other side and open the door just as I touch the handle. 'You're a tricky one, aren't you?' I say to him as I step out, watching my head this time, and he suddenly seems a bit startled, as if he doesn't know how to answer my question. I give him a hint. 'Just nod.'

He nods.

I head for the house, and the closer I get towards it, the lighter it gets outside. By the time I reach the front door, night has turned into day—or, more specifically, afternoon. People appear around the houses in the cul-de-sac, mowing their lawns, talking over the fence, washing their cars.

I start to feel a touch overdressed in my cream beaded fashion story.

At the front door, like before, the closed screen and front doors open for me with the slightest touch. Even though I know Dad and Eileen always keep both the security door and the front door locked since they had someone steal Eileen's purse when they were out at the back gardening.

Inside, I go from room to room, James following close behind. Finally I see Eileen in the main bedroom. She's sitting on the bed wrapping a present—a pair of glow-in-the-dark 'Yes/No' boxer shorts, I see as I get closer.

Oh.

Considering these are a present for my dad, I revert to childhood and try to convince myself that the message suggests something different. Like Yes/No to watching the late night movie with a bowl of popcorn. Or Yes/No to pancakes in the morning.

I take a seat beside Eileen on the bed while James stands beside me.

'Can I come in yet?' my dad calls out loudly from the kitchen, making me jump. I hadn't seen him in there.

'Not yet,' Eileen yells back. 'I'll tell you when, don't you worry.' She smiles as she turns back to her wrapping. 'Never could stand a surprise,' she whispers to herself. She pulls two last pieces of sticky tape off the roll and fastens each end of the present. Then she gets up and puts it in the third drawer of her dresser, with her winter clothes, right at the back. 'You won't find it there Neville Hetherington.' She laughs softly to herself. 'You'll just have to wait till the morning.' When she's finished, she opens the bedroom door and sticks her head out. 'All clear!'

Dad comes in then, licking an envelope closed. A red envelope.

'Oh, is that Liv's card?' Eileen asks.

My dad nods and puts it on top of the dresser with something else. A chocolate heart, I see, and smile. Dad always gives me a chocolate heart. When he's finished, he turns and pauses.

'What's the matter?' Eileen says, looking up at him. It would have been my next question too, if I was able to ask it. Even I've noticed that my dad has been un-usually quiet in the thirty seconds he's been in the room. Licking an envelope closed you could still count on my dad to be jabbering on about something at a hundred miles an hour.

'It's just this ball thing and Liv,' he sighs. 'I wish she'd decided to go. She's been missing out on too much lately, what with how she carries on about work and fills her time up with everything else. It's not healthy.'

'What do you think she should be doing? Besides the ball?' Eileen asks.

'Well, it'd be nice if she went out more with her friends. Like Justine—she's a laugh, isn't she? She's good for Liv. And if she managed to introduce her to some nice men it wouldn't hurt either. But all she seems to talk about these days is work.'

Eileen waves a hand. 'It's nothing. With all her saving and having to buy equipment for her own studio, she probably doesn't have a lot of money to throw around.'

'That's what she keeps telling me, but she doesn't have to go anywhere expensive. It's just an excuse.'

'Maybe she's going through a stage.' Eileen looks doubtful.

My dad huffs at this. 'If she is it's one that's lasted over a year now. That's a long stage.'

Eileen doesn't say anything, but pats him on the shoulder.

'I just wish she'd lighten up a bit. Get out more. That's all.'

'It'll be OK. She'll pull out of it, you'll see.' She pauses, waiting to see if he's going to say anything else. 'I don't know about you, but I'm filthy after that gardening. I'm having a shower before we go out.'

Dad nods.

'Sure you don't want one?'

'Not yet. Maybe in a while.'

'OK,' she says, as she grabs her bathrobe and moves towards the door. She pauses when she gets there. 'I'm off, then.'

'Right, love.' He sits down on the bed.

'Oh, come on,' she says, going over to him and bending down so they're eye to eye. 'Cheer up. Liv doesn't have a terminal disease. She just needs to get out more. It'll be all right—really.'

'Yeah, I know.'

'Good. Now, no present-hunting while I'm gone!' She gives him a slap on the knee as she leaves the room.

Dad laughs.

With Eileen gone, I stand and watch my father, arms crossed. I can't believe what he's just told her. That he's worried about me working so hard. That I'm not going out enough. After all, he was the one who instilled the work ethic in me in the first place—*and* he was always telling me about the long hours I'd be putting in when I set up my own business!

'Can you believe him?' I say to James.

James stays silent and good-looking.

I turn back when there's movement from Dad. He gets up off the bed and goes over to the bedroom door, where he pokes his head out just like Eileen did before. When he sees she's not there, and he can hear the shower running, he goes over to the dresser and opens the first drawer. The top left-hand one.

'Hey! The lady said no peeking!' I defend Eileen in her absence, thinking he's present-hunting like she said he would.

But he's not. Because he finds what he's looking for

without much effort. He takes it and goes back to his place on the bed. And then he opens his hand.

It's a small box. A small black velvet box. I move over quickly as he opens it up and looks inside.

It's a ring. A beautiful ruby ring with two small diamonds on either side. Rubies are Eileen's favourite.

'Oh, my God, you're going to propose?' I say to my dad, before I realise he can't hear me. I turn to James instead. 'He's going to propose! My dad's going to propose to Eileen! After all this time he's actually going to do it! I never thought he'd…' James is just looking at me as I babble. 'It's just that he said he'd never get married again when he signed the divorce papers, and… Oh, you wouldn't understand.' I wave a hand.

'But of course I understand,' he says. 'I helped to arrange it.'

'What?' I turn and look at him. 'Really? Getting him to propose, you mean?'

He nods.

'Well…' I don't know what to say, but step forward, my hand outstretched. 'Let me shake your hand, because you succeeded where I failed. For ten years!'

James shakes my hand.

'Gosh.' I stand around for a bit, stunned, as James keeps eyeing the door. I think he wants to go. 'Shall we go?' I ask him, when I can form the words.

'If that is your wish,' he says.

'It is,' I say seriously, suddenly feeling full of energy.

After what I've seen so far tonight, I wouldn't mind seeing a bit more. I take one last look at the ring before we leave the room. 'Good luck, Dad!' I call out as we go. 'Not that you'll need it. I think Eileen knows the answer. She's been practising her answer every birthday, anniversary and Christmas for ten years.' I stop halfway across the lounge room when something makes me turn and run back. Dad's putting the box back in his dresser drawer when I enter the room again. 'And don't worry about Eileen. She won't...you know, leave. I know she won't.'

And when I say this my dad looks straight at me, just as if he's heard me for real.

As I walk back out to the limo everything turns dark again, just as it turned light before. The neighbours disappear one by one and the streetlights flick on. It reminds me of one of those time-delayed pieces of video footage where you can watch a city go from dawn to dusk in thirty seconds or so. I look up ahead at James, remember Tony, and then wonder about the next ghost. About what it will show me.

It's as if time means nothing any more. As if it's a pack of cards you can flip through and pull one out at random—some scene from your life, past, present or, of course, future, which I have to admit I'm more than slightly curious about. Who knows what that dream will be like?

Sitting back in tan leather heaven, I wonder where

we're going to go next. I know better than to ask James, of course. He'll only tell me it's up to me, like before, so I sit back and think of nothing. After all, it's not like I'm actually deciding anything here. Even though James, like Tony, has told me I'm making the decisions, we seem to be turning up to places without me having to consciously think about where we're going, so there's no point trying to work it out beforehand, is there?

I turn and look at James as the limo pulls out of Dad and Eileen's driveway and something occurs to me. 'Who's driving this thing, anyway?' I ask him, nodding my head in the direction of the dividing screen that's separated us and the driver the whole trip.

'You are,' he says.

'No, I don't mean who's deciding where we go. I mean who's physically driving. As in, who's up front?'

James presses a button and the dividing screen whirrs down.

There is no one there.

I stare at the blank space for what's probably a very long time before I can speak. 'Let's put the screen back up, shall we?' From now on I'm just not going to ask the obvious questions. And I'd better think of somewhere to go—quick.

I don't come up with many ideas. I wouldn't mind seeing how Justine and Drew are going at the ball, or… The car changes lanes and I remember the driver up front. Or lack of driver. I stop thinking about where we're going then and watch the road, trying to visualise how I'd be seeing it if I was driving.

'This is a really bad intersection,' I say to James, as we pass by a place I know. 'Watch out for the zebra crossing,' I add, as we approach one I know many pedestrians have been hit on.

'You don't have to worry.' James turns to me.

'I'm thinking it's a bit late for that,' I reply, my mind's eye picturing the vacuum at the front of the car.

A few minutes later we pull up. Thank God.

I open the window a little, hear the noise, read the signs and work out where we are—the Cupid's Choice Ball. I start to push open the limo door, but James beats me to it once again. As I get out, I notice I've already managed to dirty my beautiful cream dress on something.

'Oh, no,' I say, picking up the skirt and inspecting it.

James bends down to touch the spot, and as I watch the mark miraculously starts to disappear.

'Hey,' I say, watching it inch away. When it's all gone, I let the dress fall back down. 'You could save me a lot on dry-cleaning.'

James smiles and nods.

I doubt if he knows what dry-cleaning is, I think, looking at his squeaky-cleanness. There's not a spot on his tux, a hair out of place or a blemish on his now John Cusack-looking face.

Ah, lovely.

James starts off across the road quite quickly and I realise he's forgotten to take my arm—in fact, he seems eager to get inside the function. Far more eager than he was to see Ryan or Dad and Eileen.

The ball's being held in one of the large brick exhibition buildings attached to the city's show grounds, and from the noise emanating from inside it sounds like there's a good few thousand people in there at least. We round the corner and come to the entry, which is decorated with silver and gold hearts. An oversized plastic Cupid, taking aim with his bow and arrow, hangs above the two bouncers' heads. I notice the neatly placed piece of velvet Cupid is wearing and think of Tony. Hmm. Maybe he *was* right about going for the pink ensemble.

I follow James inside, almost losing him in the sudden burst of noise and flashing lights. When my eyes adjust, and I catch sight of him again, I notice that he's lost any semblance of his suave act—he's excited to be in here. He seems brighter now, more alert, and has a strange Mona-Lisa-type smile stuck to his face that isn't giving anything away. I start to wonder what he's up to, but then, as I take a quick look around, it becomes obvious what he likes about this place.

He's in his element.

I mean, the guy's the Ghost of Valentine's Day Present, isn't he? Of course he's going to like this place.

It's full of people celebrating Valentine's Day and trying to get together. What more could he ask for?

Well, maybe for computer matching to actually *work*, but still, at least they're making an effort...

After James sees that I've caught up, he moves off, the crowd parting for him and closing behind him as he goes. I step up closer to him when I find they're not going to do the same for me.

It's such a pain being mortal.

I shuffle close behind James and am trying to spot Drew and Justine when something flies into my eye.

'Ow!' I say, cupping my hand over it. 'What was that?'

But in front of me James is busy, and it doesn't look like he's heard. The thing that landed in my eye, whatever it is, is on my cheek now. I can feel it. I pull it off and have a look. It's a tiny pink metallic heart. As I'm looking down at it, another few land on my hand. I drop them all and look up to see where they're coming from.

James.

James is digging into his pants pockets with both hands, pulling out handfuls of these things and throwing them into the air. He notices me looking at him. He turns around. 'Is something the matter?'

'You kind of got me in the eye.'

'I am sorry,' he says, dropping the rest of his hearts and truly looking, well...sorry, I guess. 'Forgive me.'

'Um, sure. Of course,' I say. How could any girl *not*

forgive Ethan Hawke's baby face and big brown eyes? 'What are you doing?' I add. Scattering pink metallic hearts in the wind doesn't seem a very James thing to do.

He pauses. 'Er, to help, er…'

It's the first time I've seen him at a loss for words. He looks caught out, as if I shouldn't know he's doing this. Or maybe he *shouldn't* be doing this? 'Ah.' I give him a nudge with one elbow. 'A bit of an aphrodisiac, hey?'

James looks shocked at my suggestion.

'Oh, come on.' I wave my hand and start to think I might be a little bit tipsy. 'It's not cheating. You're just helping move things along a little. Like you told me you helped Dad and Eileen. You know—kind of spreading the spirit.'

'Yes, that's it.' He nods. 'Spreading the spirit.'

'Well, that's what we'll call it.' I reach up and swivel him around by the shoulders. 'Off you go, then. Do your job, like a good ghost. I hope you've got plenty of those hearts.'

As we continue through the crowd I start pointing out potential couples to James. 'Don't miss those ones,' I say as we pass by a man and a woman, both blondes, who look perfect together. 'They could even share their hair dye later on in life.'

James sprinkles a little extra on them.

'And those two.' I point out a girl about my age who's comparing her computer match print-out with her date.

James sprinkles even harder.

I turn to my left, in the hope of finding another couple worth sprinkling, and come face to face with Drew, who's carrying four drinks. 'Stop.' I tap James on the back again. 'It's Drew. And Justine,' I say, spotting her as Drew finds their group and passes around the glasses. I walk over quickly, curious to get a closer look at their dates.

It's Michelle, Drew's date, the poodle enthusiast, that I walk up to first. She has long curly blonde hair that I'm guessing is permed, and is wearing a lavender-coloured shapeless old-lady dress with some beading around the hem and neckline. I stand between her and Drew (there's more than enough space) and eavesdrop. Or maybe it isn't eavesdropping if the love gods have decreed I'm supposed to be here. I don't know. Either way, I'm not going to miss my Invisible Man chance to listen in.

Michelle is talking to Drew about her website. About how many hits it gets and the photo competition she's just started, where people can send in pictures of their poodles dressed up as famous people and win a prize. She adds that next year she's thinking of running a dog and owner lookalike competition. Beside her, Drew smiles and nods and asks questions politely, though I don't think he's really that interested. It's the glazed look in his eyes that gives him away.

After a while, Michelle still talking a mile a minute about her website. I walk back over to where James is waiting. 'So, are you going to sprinkle them?' I watch him carefully as I ask my question.

He looks cagey, as if he doesn't want to answer.

I ask again. 'Drew and Michelle, I mean.'

'No.' He shakes his head slowly and I feel relieved when he says this for some reason, even though I've decided 'just friends' is it where Drew and I are concerned.

There's a pause and James glances away for a second at a couple behind him. When he looks back, I see...

Robert Downey Jnr.

'That's it! You've finally got it! Now, stay *right* there,' I say smartly. 'Just like that. And no taking illegal substances when I'm not looking. They'll wreck your complexion.'

His face reads confusion.

'Oh, don't worry about it.' I sigh, and check back on the group. 'Well, if you're not going to sprinkle Drew and Michelle, how about these two?' I ask him, as I go over to Justine and her date.

'Justine and Gary—yes.' James follows me and gives them a good heart-sprinkling before he steps back again, leaving me some room to step in and listen.

They're sharing bad date stories. Justine is telling Gary about the guy she was set up with who stood her up three times, each time coming up with a plausible story, and how they never even got to meet before he broke the relationship off. Gary is telling Justine about a girl he took out to dinner whose right breast kept trying to sneak out of her dress. He didn't know whether it was a 'your skirt's tucked into your pantyhose' kind of situation, where you tell the person, or not. In the end he told her about it, to be polite and she just looked down and tucked herself back in. Five minutes later, there it was again. The second time he didn't say anything and let the breast do what it wanted.

Halfway through the story, Drew and Michelle start listening in.

'Was there nipple?' Drew says, laughing.

'No.' He shakes his head. 'I was getting scared there would be, though.'

'And she didn't care she was hanging out there?' Drew asks—a little bit *too* interested in all of this, I note.

'She didn't seem to,' Gary says. 'I think it was a free-range breast.'

Everyone laughs except for Michelle, who looks shocked. 'That's disgusting.'

'It didn't put me off my dinner,' Gary adds, and everyone laughs again. Everyone except Michelle, that is.

I move back over beside James. 'That girl needs another drink. A double. And fast,' I say.

James doesn't say anything, however, and we continue watching the group. As they laugh and chat together, I start to feel a bit sad. As if I *am* missing out, like Dad said before.

I turn away from the group and look at James. 'Can we go now? Can I go home?'

He nods and we start to make our way out to the entrance again, James sprinkling as we go.

I'm still feeling a little sad as the limo pulls out for the last time. 'They looked as if they were having an enjoyable evening,' James says, staring out of his window, away from me.

This time it's my turn to nod. 'I know.' And as we drive off I think about Ryan, Dad and Eileen, Drew and Justine, and I realise at last what James has been trying to show me about Valentine's Day—that it *doesn't* have to be expensive or over the top. Everyone I've seen tonight has been having a good time, making some small gesture towards the day for the fun of it, to show other people they're important. For them it's just a silly day that comes around once a year that they make a little bit of an effort for. Unlike me. But I guess that's the thing about my job—it brings out the worst of Valentine's Day. The overcharging, the over-sentimentality, the spectacularly large gold Cupids. And, thus, it brings out the worst in me as well.

I guess James has served his purpose. I've taught myself a lesson here—I've seen tonight that Valentine's Day isn't so bad if you do it for the right reasons with the right person. Looking out of my own window, I remember Ryan and his French toast again. The ingredients probably cost less than ten dollars, but it's the effort that Rachel will remember. The trouble he went to. The thought he put in and the fact that he realised it would mean more to her than an expensive dinner out that he could just whack on his credit card.

'Yes,' James says, making me look over.

I lose my train of thought when I catch sight of his face. He's gone all Sean Connery on me. A young Sean Connery, but still...

'You're getting grey hair,' I say, sliding over the seat closer to him. 'And wrinkles! What's happening to you?'

'I must leave,' he says. 'Valentine's Day is passing.'

I shake my head, confused. Valentine's Day is passing? It can't be Valentine's Day yet. When I nodded off on the couch it could only have been nine-thirty at the latest.

The limo pulls over and I look out to see my apartment building, even though we hadn't been close to my suburb at all seconds before.

I wait for James to open the door, which he does with one hand, buttoning his jacket with the other as I get out. He closes the door behind me and then moves over and gives me a perfunctory kiss on the cheek. He has a few more grey hairs, I notice.

Damn. I should have pushed my point about the Robert Downey Jnr thing.

'Well, thank you for a nice evening,' I say, remembering my manners.

'It was lovely to meet you,' James says in parting. I

watch as he makes his way back over to the limo and unbuttons his jacket before he gets in again.

I shake my head.

And people think *I* need to lighten up.

Y Y Y Y

I hang around in the driveway and watch as the limo indicates and pulls away from the kerb. Well, that wasn't too bad a dream, I think. At least James was a well-mannered, well-dressed ghost. A well-mannered, well-dressed ghost who'd soon be needing a nose and ear hair clipper set, the way he was ageing. But a well-mannered, well-dressed ghost just the same.

As the car turns right at the end of the road, I know I should go upstairs and try to get some proper rest. But with James gone and only my thoughts left to talk to suddenly everything doesn't seem quite so cheery and 'let's get on with it, then' easy.

I go over and sit down carefully on the apartment block's low brick letterbox, minding the beads on my dress. I don't want to go upstairs yet. My headache hasn't returned, but somehow I don't feel right. I need some time to think.

I look back down the street to where James's limo has just disappeared and think about the ball once more. About Drew, really. Well, Drew and Justine. I wonder if they're both still in the same spot, talking to Michelle and Gary, or if they're talking to other people. I wonder if they're even still there, or have left and gone on elsewhere. It doesn't take much brain-power on my part to work out what doesn't feel right. I still feel like I'm missing out, and I really *do* wish that I'd gone out tonight like my dad thought I should.

If, after yesterday's debacle, I'd still been invited.

Oh well. I take one last look down the road before I push myself up and make my way upstairs. I can't stay out here all night, dreaming or not.

Inside the main door, everything is quiet apart from my stomp, stomp, stomp up the steps to my apartment. I open the door and expend the least amount of en-ergy possible as I take the three steps over that I need to fall onto the couch, feeling as if I now know what Superman was talking about when he whinged about Kryptonite. The couch is as far as I'm going. I just don't think I can make it to my bedroom, let alone save the world using my superhuman strength.

I do manage, however, to turn my head and check out the time on the VCR—12:23. James was right—it *is* Valentine's Day.

I snuggle back, rest my hands on my lap and close my eyes. But, again, just as my eyes shut, there's a noise outside the door. I sit up and look at the VCR clock, startled.

12:24. I thought so. I didn't think I'd actually gone to sleep. I mean, you hear about people closing their eyes and waking up eight hours later, thinking they've only just gone to sleep, but that would have been ridiculous.

There's another noise. A different noise. The door handle rattles.

Three spirits. I remember Mrs Batty-Smith's words.

I get up warily and go over, not knowing what's on the other side. And when the door handle rattles one final time I wrench it open.

'Agh!' Justine and I both yell at each other. Then, 'Shit—sorry,' we say together.

'I didn't expect you to be up,' she says, looking me over.

'I didn't expect you to be home so early,' I reply.

Justine checks her watch. 'It's not that early.'

I move aside to let her in. As I shut the door I look down and realise that my beautiful dress has disappeared and that I'm back in my pyjamas.

Damn. I really liked that dress.

Justine leans against the wall and puts one hand on her chest. 'My heart's going a million miles an hour. You scared the life out of me,' she says. 'I thought you would have been asleep hours ago.' She takes her shoes off, then pushes herself off the wall.

I snort at this. 'Yeah. Me too. I just, um, can't sleep.'

'Phew.' She lets out one last final breath and flops down on the couch. 'I've had it.'

There's an awkward silence.

'So, um, how was the ball?' I ask, and sit down on the opposite couch, the one I was trying to nap on only minutes before. I'm curious in all kinds of ways. Firstly, I want to find out if what I saw was real, and if it was I also want to know what happened after I left.

'Good. Fine. Fun, I guess.'

'You guess?'

'No, it *was* fun. My date was really nice.'

'Gary?'

Justine gives me a look. 'How did you know his name? I don't remember telling you.'

Oh, bugger. She didn't, either. I wing it. 'I, um, saw your computer matching sheet on the side table.'

Justine nods. 'He was nice. A builder.'

'And how about Drew's? The poodle-lover?'

Justine laughs. 'She was OK. I've had enough poodles for one night, though. I've had enough poodles *for ever*.'

'What did she wear?' I just need one more test to make sure.

Justine gives me a look, knowing I wouldn't usually care what anyone wore. 'You want to know what she wore?'

I nod.

She shrugs. 'I don't know. Some purple thing?'

'With beading?'

Justine pauses. 'Yeah, I suppose so. Why did you think that?'

Second wing of the night. 'Oh, I just knew another poodle-lover once. She always wore, um, purple beaded things.'

Another look. 'Right.' But then Justine becomes engrossed in staring down her top. 'I knew something was in there!' She pulls something out from around her cleavage. 'God, it's been scratching me all bloody night.'

'Cheap tissues?' I say.

'Very funny. No, somebody was going around throwing these in the air.' She holds out her index finger.

There's a small pink metallic heart on the end.

This freaks me out a bit. I don't think I need any more tests.

'So, um, Gary? Are you going to see him again?' I ask.

Justine nods enthusiastically and then stops, her gaze sliding sideways to meet mine. 'If that's all right with you,' she says, and I know she's making an abstract reference to our little 'discussion' this afternoon.

I cringe.

'Oh, I'm only joking,' she says, waving one hand. 'I've been wanting to talk to you about that.'

'I've been wanting to talk to you about it too.'

'I'm sorry. I didn't mean to come on so strong. Whatever's going on between you and Drew is none of my business.'

'That's OK. I'm sorry too.'

'So—friends?'

'Friends,' I say with a nod. There's a pause before I have to ask, 'Do you think Drew will see Michelle again?'

Justine groans and rests her head back on the couch. 'I doubt it. I felt so sorry for that poor girl.'

For *her?* All I saw when I was there with James was Drew being ear-bashed about the pleasures of poodles. 'Why?'

She turns her head and eyeballs me. 'You should have heard him. It was all Liv this and Liv that.'

'Me?' I say, a touch too squeakily for my liking.

Justine sits up. 'Yes, you. "You should see Liv's photos—she's such a good photographer—Liv, Liv, Liv,"' she mimics. 'Liv's *very* in this season.'

'Um…' I don't know what to say.

Silence.

Finally, Justine sighs. 'Liv, I'm not trying to butt in, really I'm not, but what *is* going on? Between you and Drew, I mean?'

I shrug. 'I had a really good time when we went out for lunch. Twice. And at dinner for his birthday. But seeing him with Tiffany—it just brought the whole Mike and Amanda thing flooding back. And I've had enough of that for a while…'

Justine pushes herself up a bit. 'Look, Liv, if I tell you something, will you listen to me? As in really listen to what I'm saying and consider it?'

Umm.

'I'm not going to attack you, like this afternoon, and I don't want to nag. So this is why I'm only going to say this once—because I really think you need to hear it. Will you listen?'

She's going a bit over the top here, even for Justine, I think. But she looks so earnest I decide to give her a chance. 'All right. If it means so much to you, I'll listen.'

'It does. It really does.'

There's a pause.

'Well? Are you going to tell me or not?'

Justine gives me a look.

'Sorry,' I say.

She takes a deep breath before she begins. 'OK. Here goes nothing. I think you have to quit with this overly careful business. This trying to prevent anything awful from happening in your life.'

I go to open my mouth and Justine holds up a finger.

'You promised.'

I didn't, actually—promise, that is. But I close my mouth again anyway.

'OK. That didn't make sense, so I'm going to go from the start. With the dating. Drew told me you'd been trotting out this "guys don't like me" stuff again. He was asking me what you meant, and because I had to explain it to him it gave me a sort of fresh look at the whole situation. It made me see that the reason you keep getting rejected when you date is because you pre-empt the break-up *every single time.* You think each and every guy is going to reject you way before it could even happen—even before the first date—so you find any kind of excuse you can to break it off. And then, when it happens—the break-up—you think your theory's been proven. The thing is, though, it's not true. It's just inevitable. You're not open to anything happening and that's why it doesn't.'

I raise an eyebrow, but don't say anything.

'Right. OK. So you do this over and over again. What do you call it? Crazy-dating—that's it. You notch the failed dates up on your bedpost, and when it gets to be too much you stop dating to try and protect yourself. You say that you'll date if something better comes along. More than a year passes and there are a couple half-decent ones that come along, but you let them go because it's easier to date the ones you aren't really interested in. Remember that photographer? He seemed lovely, but you had a dozen reasons for never asking him out. Anyway, more than a year goes by, and something really, truly better does come along—Drew. And you go out a few times, and you really enjoy each other's company. And then, just when it gets to the critical stage, you use some bullshit piece of nothing incident as an excuse to go back to good old safe singledom again.'

I raise the other eyebrow, but still say nothing.

'I think the only reason he's got as far into your life

as he has is because you were open to getting to know him because he's my friend. If he'd just been some guy who asked you out, he'd be long gone by now. But he's lovely, Liv. A really nice guy. He'd never intentionally hurt you, and you two would be great together. It wouldn't kill you to date him a few more times, would it? Just to test the water...'

This time, I open my mouth.

Justine raises the same finger again. 'That was a rhetorical question.'

I close my mouth once more.

'Anyway. The whole point of this is it's not about you dating Drew or not. It's about me being worried about how you're living your life. And I know that it's really none of my business, but I *am* worried, and as your friend I can't just keep out of it. God, Liv, sometimes you have to take chances, you know? Give people a chance. Maybe even a second chance. I understand that you don't want to get hurt again, and I can't promise that things will work out with Drew if you date him, or with anything in your life, but you have to stop being so scared. You have to jump into the deep end once in a while. It's scary, but it can be fun too.'

I'm starting to get increasingly angry—right up until this last bit. The bit about taking chances. About giving people chances. Second chances. It's this that hits home. I knew she was more than right when she said that this afternoon—that I needed to give Drew the second chance he'd given me.

And as she keeps talking I can't stop thinking about what I've seen tonight. About Dad and Eileen. About how he's going to propose. And how, even though he's scared that things will repeat on him, and that if he marries Eileen she'll leave him like my mother did, he's going to ask her to marry him. He's jumping in the deep end.

I think about Rachel and Ryan too. About how Rachel took a chance on Ryan and believed him when he said he wouldn't cheat again. She listened to what he had to say and trusted him despite everything. I didn't believe him, but Rachel did. And from what I've seen tonight it looks like he meant what he said. That he cares, that he is putting in an effort, that he does love Rachel as much as she deserves. Imagine if Rachel hadn't taken that chance on him—she'd never have what she has now. A husband, happiness, *and* heart-shaped low-fat French toast. Just about everything she's ever wanted in life.

Then there's Justine and Sally. I was thinking about them only the other day as Sally and I drove to the crematorium, wasn't I? About how they live their lives, taking chances that I never would. And, yes, like Justine said, sometimes they get hurt. But they also get over it, whatever the hurt is, and keep going. So maybe it wouldn't be so bad for me to date again. To date…

Someone like Drew.

I tune back in to Justine then, who's still talking. 'You know dating, Liv, it's like a sushi train. You can't just watch all the nice things pass you buy. When you see one you like, you have to reach out and pull it off the conveyer belt, not just admire it as it goes past.'

When she says this, an image of me standing outside the studio as Drew left the other day, card in one hand and cheesecake box in the other, comes to mind.

'You've got to be ruthless,' Justine continues. 'You've got to get in there and grab away before someone else takes it.' She looks at my blank expression with a sigh. 'You don't get it, do you? The point here is Drew *is* the good one. He's the guy you're supposed to get back on track for. He's perfect for you. Perfect! But you're so used to shrugging them all off, you can't see it.'

I look back at her. I try to say something, but every time I open my mouth to let a word or two out nothing comes.

Justine stands up. 'Anyway, that's all. I'm just worried about you.' She pauses and snaps her fingers together. 'Oh, and one more thing. You hating Valentine's Day—that's the biggest load of rubbish. You don't have a reason to hate it any more. Not now you've given Mike the flick once and for all. Sally told me. So, yes—I know you.' She leans forward and looks at me, eye to eye. 'And you wish you'd come with us tonight, don't you?'

I still can't get anything out of my mouth, but I point a finger and waggle it. I'm sure she knows what I mean.

She reaches over and pats the top of my head. 'How about you sleep on it and yell at me in the morning? I need a shower.'

At least this time I manage to nod.

It's only when Justine's walked out of the room and down the hall that I manage to speak. 'Hey, I've had some pretty crappy Valentine's Days, you know!' I call out.

'You're female. We all have,' she sings back, and then laughs.

There's not much I can say to that, so I resume my resting position on the couch and try to keep up with my thoughts. As I settle back in I can't help thinking that maybe what Justine says is right. About the deep end and taking chances.

But then there's me and Drew.

I know several things where we're concerned. I know that we have a great time together. I know that he wants to see me again. I think I'd like to keep seeing him. But the thing I don't know is the most important thing of all…

I don't know if taking that leap into the deep end is truly right for me.

For *us*.

Y Y Y Y

Tired, and trying to figure it all out, I accidentally let my eyelids droop.

Just as my eyelashes hit my cheeks, there's a rustle from the other couch that makes me think Justine has come back from her shower. That was quick, I think. Maybe she decided not to have one after all. I open my eyes up and glance over.

Right. That's it. I am never closing my eyes again.

Because it's not Justine. It's a woman. A woman I've never seen before, who is lounging on my couch like my living room is her second home.

She doesn't look at me, but I look at her all right. Stare, more like it. And there's plenty to stare at. I give her the sideways once-over (well, she's lying down), from her head to her feet and then back again. The best way to describe her look would be Barbara Cartland wannabe. It's all there. From the diamonds dripping around her neck, offsetting her pouffy white hair, the glittery too-tight silver dress pulling at the bust, the overloaded blue eyeshadow, seventies-streaky blush and trowelled-on mascara to the martini resting on the coffee table and the box of expensive handmade chocolates she has sitting on her lap and has half finished.

Yes. It's all there. On *my* couch.

Including a very pink romance novel, complete with Fabio cover, which she's holding in the hand that isn't busy transferring chocolates to her glossy pink-lipsticked pouty mouth.

'Um, hello?' I say.

Nothing.

'Over here?' I wave.

Still nothing.

I give up and talk to myself instead. 'You know,' I say, thinking of Tony on my coffee table and James surfing for porn, 'you guys have really got to stop doing this. Why don't you just knock on the door like normal people?'

Now she looks up. But only for a second, before she goes back to her novel and her chocolates.

'I take it you're the Ghost of Valentine's Day Yet to Come?' I try then.

She nods, but doesn't look at me. Instead, she pops a rectangular chocolate in her mouth. A hard centre? Peanut brittle, maybe? There's a loud crunch.

Hey, peanut brittle's my favourite.

Crunch, crunch, crunch.

'I suppose you're going to show me my future?'

Maybe if I get her to acknowledge my presence she'll offer me one. But, no, she simply nods again and pops in chocolate number... I don't know, she's had too many for me to keep count.

Another crunch.

I decide to call her Barbara.

I watch as she reaches into the box again. There are three chocolates left now.

Crunch.

Crunch.

Crunch.

All hard centres.

Bitch.

The chocolates finished, she places the box on the coffee table and stands up. My eyes follow her as she walks over to the balcony and opens the sliding glass door. It's only when she's out there and glancing back at me that I realise I'm supposed to be using my initiative, and that when she hauled her large silver behind off the couch I was supposed to follow her outside.

I guess she's not the talkative kind of ghost, like Tony, or the arm-taking kind like James.

OK. I can deal with that.

I get up and go out onto the balcony, stopping a metre or two away from Her Glitteriness. When I halt, she glances at me—a loaded glance that tells me I am, basically, nothing. A small turd to be stepped over on the footpath that is her life.

Fine. I'm *definitely* calling her Barbara now.

Barbara motions to the back of her silver dress, indicating the train-like appendage that's hanging off it.

'Mmm, it's lovely,' I lie.

I get another small turd look for this. She motions again, and this time I realise she wants me to pick it up.

'You've got to be joking,' I scoff. 'I'm finished with bridesmaiding.' What she doesn't know is that by not offering me a chocolate, giving her lip has become compulsory.

She looks away. And for the next five minutes or so we stand on the balcony not looking at each other. Stubborn vs Stubborn. There may even be some foot-tapping involved. From both parties.

It's about halfway through minute number six when I remember Tony's Velcro gadget and James's limo and put two and two together. Picking up the train is going to enable me to go into the future with Barbara. Not picking up the train is going to mean I spend a lot of time standing around on the balcony.

I pick up the train.

Whammo.

There's a flash of light and in an instant we're transported to a coffee shop.

I don't even bat an eyelid. In fact, I act quite blasé about it all—I'm practically an old hand at this now.

A jaded time-traveller.

Barbara obviously is too, because the first thing she does now we're at the coffee shop is not to explore, but to go over and help herself to a macadamia and white chocolate chunk cookie from one of the glass jars on the front counter. Then she takes a seat at the closest table.

I want to go over, sit down and start grilling her on the future. On what I was thinking about on the couch before I was so rudely interrupted. Where does Drew fit into my future? But Barbara doesn't look like she'd be too happy if I disturbed her cookie frenzy, so I let it go for the moment and turn in a full circle to inspect the coffee shop.

I don't think I've been here before. No, I definitely haven't.

Ah, hang on. Of course I haven't. It's the future, isn't it?

There are only two people in the coffee shop—a young couple flipping through some brochures, sitting by the window. It's bright outside the café, and as I go over to them I check the time on the clock on the wall—ten-fifteen.

When I reach them, I stand over the table and take a look at what they're flipping through. Wedding photography brochures. Wedding photography brochures from the future—this should be interesting. I lean over and look more closely.

'What did you think of this one?' The girl holds up

one of the brochures. Her fiancé takes it from her and opens it up.

Geoff's, I note. I know him. He's good, but over-priced.

'Oh, him. He was OK. A bit pricey, though, don't you think? Compared to the others?'

She nods. 'Mmm. I guess.' She puts the brochure back on the pile and holds up another one. 'I liked her. She was really nice. And her sample albums were great.'

I crane my neck to take a look at whose brochure this one is. It's Sally's.

The guy takes it from her. 'She was the one with the car?' He glances up. The girl nods and he laughs. 'She was fun. I wouldn't mind having her. At least she wasn't as serious as some of the others. They're only photos.'

'Only photos we're paying thousands of dollars for...'

He nods. 'Well, yeah. But some of those photographers—it was like they were doing us a favour even seeing us. She was friendly, her samples were good, and her prices were comparable with everyone else's. Way less expensive than that Geoff guy's, anyway. Why don't we go with her?'

'Are you basing this decision on her work, her car, or her skirt?'

I laugh at this. Sally's skirts must get even shorter and more daring in the future.

'Her work, of course,' he tells his fiancée, with a smirk.

She laughs as well. 'Well, if you're sure… OK. I'm happy with that.'

'Yeah, I thought she was good. Her other photographer seemed nice too.'

His fiancée nods. 'I'll give her a call later.'

'Great.'

I smile when I hear this, thinking it's nice that they liked both Sally and myself. But then I pause. Again, this is the future. Maybe the other photographer isn't me? I crane my neck, trying to catch a glimpse of Sally's brochure. But, their decision made, the girl is now tucking all the glossy paperwork away in her handbag.

One brochure falls to the floor and she opens it as she picks it up. When she sees what it is, she snorts. 'Well, we can get rid of this one.' She shows her fiancé the brochure before I can see whose it is.

He takes a look. 'Oh—her. Wasn't she a freak? I couldn't wait to get out of there.'

'Me either.' She takes the brochure from him and stuffs it in her bag with the rest of them. 'The way she looked at us as we walked in—it gave me the jitters.'

Jesus, that's a bit harsh, I think, my eyes widening. I wonder for a second if it's Trudy's brochure. I mean, she's not exactly much to look at, with that ever-developing mono-brow, and I heard she threw a photographic tanty at someone's wedding not long ago, when the grooms-men got too drunk to stand in any sort of a line…

The couple start talking about their vows then, and I take a few steps back, figuring this was all I'm supposed to see and hear.

I go back over to Barbara, who now has the jar of macadamia and white chocolate chunk cookies sitting on her table and is taking out the last one.

She stands up when I reach her, and I realise soon enough that she's not going to explain anything. We're simply going to move on to the next moment in time.

I pick up her train.

I'm right. There's another flash. As the brightness dies down I see that it's still daytime and we're now standing on a busy road in front of what can only be a pawnbroker's shop. It has bars on its shopfront windows behind which all kinds of goods—fishing gear, jewellery, computers, etc.—are displayed. The name of the place kind of gives it away. 'Cash, Cash, Cash' the sign above the door reads.

Barbara moves forward and up the few steps, pushing open the front door and jangling the bell. I drop her train as she pulls away from me and follow her inside.

There's not much going on. Apart from some serious dust collecting.

It's a shop that doesn't look like it's been cleaned in a while—there's dust forming on all the surfaces, and there are plenty of surfaces. TVs, guitar cases, stereos, fans—you name it, it's there with dust on it. Besides Barbara and myself there's one sufficiently dodgy-looking customer, who exits right after we enter, leaving only the also dodgy-looking man behind the desk, who's writing prices on small tags and attaching them to the items he has placed in front of him, which I see are mostly cameras and lenses.

Hey, good cameras—really good cameras. And good lenses—really good lenses.

Interested, I go over and take a look at how much he's charging for them. The answer is: not enough.

I turn each tag over after he attaches it and become more and more shocked as I work my way down the line.

I should come to these places more often. I pause. More often? I don't know if I've ever even been in a pawnbroker's shop before, so I can't go more often, but I'm definitely starting now. It's bargain city in here. For example, the two Nikon camera bodies he's just tagged are a steal. You'd pay at least three or four hundred dollars more for those from a proper second-hand camera dealer. And one of the lenses is so cheap I wonder if he thinks it's actually a View-Master.

I look around for Barbara. 'I guess I can't buy anything while I'm here?'

Turd look number three.

Well, it was worth a shot, wasn't it? Imagine the interest-free credit I'd get, purchasing in the future. Now that's my kind of shopping—whack it on the credit card and get five to ten years interest free.

I turn back as he marks up the medium format camera. The one I was really coveting. When I see the price I almost faint. 'Hey!' I say, the tag in my hand. 'What are you doing? This camera's worth a bloody fortune!'

Of course he doesn't look at me. Instead, he starts transporting the pieces of equipment to a space he's made for them in the window. I watch as he carries them inexpertly and almost want to cry. I would love to have that equipment. Whoever's let it go for this price is crazy.

When every last piece of equipment is in the window, and the guy's placed signs there as well, indicating the 'too low to be believed' prices, I finally turn and look at Barbara. 'Can we go now?'

I get turd look number four before she flounces out of the shop as fast as a very large, chocolate-coated-arteried, diamond-encrusted old lady can flounce.

Outside, I pick up her train again. 'Let's motor,' I say sourly.

Bang. Barbara doesn't waste any time, and we turn up in front of another shop. This time it's on a road that isn't busy at all, and the shop itself is very different from 'Cash, Cash, Cash'—it's a gorgeous little old-style yellow-painted shop with a tin roof and a creeper crawling up its left-hand side. It's lovely. Warm and welcoming in the lazy afternoon sun.

'Davo!' I hear a voice above me and raise my eyes, wondering where it's coming from. The roof, I guess.

'Yeah?' another voice calls out.

'Want to start on the other end?'

I walk out from under the covered front of the shop onto the road and look up. Barbara doesn't follow. I guess she knows what's up there and, as it isn't food based, she's not budging.

There are two guys up there in white overalls. Tradesmen.

'The other end? Yeah, no worries,' Davo says.

'Probably only take two coats. Should be able to start on the new sign as well. It's hot enough. Paint'll dry in no time.'

Davo agrees, takes a roller, and starts painting down at the other end.

What they're doing is painting over the shop's sign. The first man has already painted over the business name at least once, and is halfway through painting it again. I can only make out the last word—'Photography'…

Something 'Photography.'

Something Photography… I mouth the words. And then I freeze.

The brochure. The pawnbroker. The yellow shop. Something Photography.

I want to sink down slowly, my knees suddenly unable to carry my weight, but I can't move. Something, or someone, is keeping me stuck to the spot, my eyes glued on the sign above my head. Something Photography. The words flip over and over in my mind. Something Photography. Something Photography. Taunting me. Torturing me.

And I don't know what that first word is, but I can guess.

I flick my eyes over at Barbara now, who's looking at me with pure and utter loathing. Then suddenly I'm unstuck again. I make my way over unsteadily and pick up her train.

But after the flash we don't land somewhere in the future. Instead I'm back on my apartment balcony again. Home. I drop Barbara's train, confused. I don't understand. That's it? All I get to see of the future? What about my family and my friends? And Drew? I look over at Barbara, but she's already making her way up to the other end of the balcony. She isn't interested in me, and it doesn't look like I'll be able to get any answers from her.

I take a deep breath, trying to quell the nasty, nauseating feeling I still have in my stomach. I start to look around me. And as I look I realise that something's wrong here. It's dark, night, but even though there's only a little light to go by one of the first things I notice is that the balcony's looking a bit tatty. There are a few tiles that have come unstuck here and there—which is funny, because I hadn't noticed them before now, and I spend a lot of time on the balcony. I look down as something makes a noise under my feet. Wow, I really need to sweep, I think, when I work out I'm standing on quite a large pile of leaves. Hosing it down wouldn't be a bad idea, either, because I keep getting a whiff of some foul smell. Like cat pee or something. Ugh.

There's a noise from up above then, from the balcony of the floor upstairs, and I glance up. It sounds as if they're having a party. A good party. And that's kind of strange as well, because the apartment upstairs has been for sale for ages and I didn't think anyone had bought it yet. While I'm thinking this, something falls from upstairs, and because my balcony is longer and wider than the ones on the upper floors the something hits the tiles almost in front of me. It's a packet of cigarettes.

'Oh, shit,' a voice says, and when I look up I can just see some long hair dangling over the railings.

'What is it?' another voice says.

'I dropped my fags on the balcony down below. Almost a full packet.'

'Downstairs? You've lost them for good, then. That's Auntie Social's place. Catwoman. Cut your losses and buy a new packet. She'll never give them back to you.'

'What?' I turn and look at Barbara, who's moved back towards me now something's going on. 'Why wouldn't I give them back? People are always dropping things over onto my balcony. Towels, stubbie holders, pegs. I always give their things back. Or at least I put them at the bottom of the stairs, so they can grab whatever it is as they go past.'

Barbara just looks at me. I shrug and glance back upstairs, but they've stopped talking now. I shake my head. Barbara moves away once more, her dress trailing behind her. I follow her and try to pick up the train again, but she swishes it away just as my fingers are about to touch the fabric and turns her head to glare at me.

'What?' I shrug. 'You mean this is really it? We're not going to see anything else? This is the end of the line?'

I'm expecting turd look number five when, instead, Barbara points inside. As if I'm supposed to go inside the apartment. I'm about to protest when suddenly I get it. All too well.

The bile rises again.

I glance over at the door that leads inside my apartment and the hairs on the back of my neck stand on end. I feel the leaves scrunch under my feet. I hear the people upstairs...

And realise I'm still in the future.

I'd assumed once we landed on my balcony again that I was home free. Safe. That I'd reached the end of the ghost train and could go to bed and hide under my doona.

But I can't. I might be back at my apartment, but it's not my apartment as it was when I left it. This is my future apartment. The apartment I live in years from now.

The leaves scrunch again, and I look down to see just how dirty the balcony is. Instantly I know I really don't want to go inside.

But I have to, because right before my eyes the screen and the sliding glass doors open and a gust of wind pushes me forward.

It's dark in the apartment. Very dark. At least on the balcony there was the moon and some light from the balcony upstairs to see by. But in here the only light is emanating from two candles—one on the dining room table and one in the kitchen. I reach over and flick on the kitchen light, but it doesn't work. I try the balcony light instead. It doesn't work either. Something brushes past my leg and I yelp. It's a cat. Two—no, three—no, four cats.

Ugh.

I turn and look at Barbara, who's sitting down at the dining room table. She points again. This time to one of the couches a few metres away in the living room.

When I look over, my eyes finally adjusting, I see that there's a woman in here. A woman sitting with her back to me on the couch. In the darkness, I didn't notice her before, but now I know she's there I can hear something—a low noise—as if she's muttering to herself. Either that or she's talking to someone softly. Maybe the cats, because there doesn't seem to be anyone else in the room. I notice then that there are another two cats standing on one of the sofa arms. That makes six cats that I've counted all up.

Six cats? That can't be City Council legal.

I stand and watch her as she keeps muttering. 'Catwoman,' I remember the girls upstairs said. I pause and shake my head. No...

It can't be. This isn't right.

And it's strange, but from where I'm placed, near the dining table, I could swear that it's Mrs Batty-Smith sitting on that couch. Not the ghost-like dusty one, though, from the crematorium bathroom. I mean the real one.

The dead one.

Quickly I reach out, grab the candle off the dining room table and take a few hesitant steps over towards the couch. My heart starts pounding, as I'm remembering Mrs Batty-Smith's bony finger pushing into my chest. A few steps closer and I'm able to see her more clearly.

Jesus, it does look like Mrs Batty-Smith. Hair in a loose bun. Dark-coloured clothing—not grey, but dark enough nonetheless. I take one last step forward, holding out the candle out so I can see better.

Oh, my God. The place is a pigsty.

There are newspapers all over the floor in the living area. And when I say newspapers I don't mean 'Hey, let's give the place a lick of paint' properly laid down newspapers. I mean dirty, old, half-shredded newspapers.

And the cats. The cats! There has to be at least eight writhing around in here. Not six, like I'd thought before.

A clattering noise from the kitchen makes me turn around. I pause, then decide to investigate further and take the few steps over I need to see. I hold up the candle.

Another cat. Or one of the ones who brushed past me before? Who knows? Not that that's the most important thing here, because what the animal is actually doing is standing on the kitchen bench top and eating something off one of the plates that are stacked high in the sink, cockroaches crawling over them.

Disgusting.

'Cuddles, Snookums, Cutie, Whiskers…' The woman in the lounge calls out in a husky voice.

The cat on the kitchen benchtop looks up at her voice, then jumps off and pads out of the kitchen.

I follow it back into the lounge room to see what the woman is up to. I go as close as I need to with the candle, to see, but not one step more.

She has something in her hand. A packet of something. I move just a fraction closer. Cat treats, it looks like. I move back again and hold the candle close to me.

'Come, my darlings,' she croons, and I almost gag as the cats start to gather. She shakes the treats into her hand and then holds them out. The cats move in for the kill, pushing and squabbling and shoving to get to the food.

My eyes bulge as I take in the scene. It doesn't look like she feeds those cats at all. They're all kind of scrawny and unkempt-looking, with dull coats and sticky-out ribs. Also, by the way they're diving into those cat treats, I'm guessing they're not receiving their daily bowl of vitamin-enriched Happy Cat, fresh water or regular cat flu boosters.

I keep watching until the cat frenzy stops and the treats have obviously all been eaten.

The woman pats a cat here and there. 'That's it. No more,' she says, and after a while the cats begin to move away from her, realising this themselves. 'Time for bed.' She pushes herself up off the couch with an old-person noise. I take a few steps back again, towards the dining room table this time, so I won't be in her path as she heads down the hallway.

She stands for a moment, brushing off her skirt and running a hand over her hair.

And I'm waiting, waiting for her to turn around, frozen, stuck, glued in place again just like before. She brushes off her skirt again. Pats a cat.

Barbara comes over and hovers beside me just as the woman starts to shuffle towards me from the living room.

I hold my breath and lift my candle up higher to get a better look. Just as I'm about to see the woman's face for the first time, Barbara pushes me from behind. I stumble forward a few steps, looking at my feet. Finally I stop. And then I look up.

The woman is right in front of me. Inches away

from my face. I yelp in surprise, even though something inside me knew what I was going to be confronted with all along. Still I can't believe it. Can't believe what's right before my eyes.

It's me.

Me.

As she passes by I stumble again, backwards this time, away—away from her, away from Barbara—feeling my way to the wall. Vomit rises in my throat and I put my hand over my mouth, willing myself not to be sick. Once a week is definitely enough. I keep backing away, and when I hit the two walls that form the corner of the room, I stop. There's nowhere else to go.

Barbara follows me closely.

Me.

No. I shake my head. No. It can't be. How can that be me?

'How can that be me?' I look at Barbara.

She stares back at me, unblinking.

'It's not me. I'm not like that. It can't be me. I won't believe it. I won't!' I stammer and stutter my way through my words.

Barbara thrusts something at me. It's a book. Her book. The pink romance Fabio-covered one from before.

'What? I...'

I start to turn the book over to the front, but before I can she takes it from me, turns it over to the back again and thrusts once more. I look at it dumbly. She thrusts the book at me a third time and then points. The blurb, I realise. She wants me to read the blurb. Barbara makes a motion with one hand to her mouth. She wants me to read it out aloud.

I put my candle down on the floor, my hand shaking, and bring the book up closer to my face. I begin reading. "'When Liv and her partner, Mike, break up, and he returns to his ex-wife and child, Liv is distraught. Eventually she decides to date again, but quickly makes up her mind that men simply are not for her. She believes she is wasting her time dating man after man, and decides that she will stay single and wait until a decent male crosses her path. She tells herself that she will concentrate on developing her own interests and her potential business. However, instead of letting this new situation enrich her life, she starts to protect her independence too fiercely, and becomes blinded to the happiness new relationships and love could give her if she would only let people into her world. Can she overcome her fears and open her arms and heart to what life has to offer her? Only time will tell…'"

When I'm done, I slowly turn the book over so I can see the cover.

Fabio is gone.

Now, instead of being pink, the cover is grey and muted. There is a picture of a woman—the woman

I've just come face to face with—in a darkened lounge room. Surrounded by cats. One last time I turn the book over. I stare at the blurb.

This is me? What my life's become? I can't believe it. I can't.

I look up at Barbara again as the blurb, the cover, start to sink in for real. 'This is me? It can't… I can't…' I babble at her quietly. I point to the book and then down the hallway, where the woman has disappeared. 'Me? My life? My work?'

Barbara nods.

'No.' I look back down at the blurb, the words hitting home. 'It's not right. I can't believe it. I won't believe it. How can that be me?'

There's a long, long pause as I stare at the book. I think about the couple in the café, with what must have been my studio brochure. I was the weird photographer. The freak. I think about the pawnshop and all the beautiful equipment. The beautiful equipment I obviously pawned. I think about the gorgeous little yellow studio. My studio. The one that Sally was talking about. I'd taken it. It was my studio. The studio I'd lost.

Me.

'No…' I start again, looking up at Barbara. I was going to say I couldn't believe it for about the millionth time—but how can I *not* believe everything I've seen? And that connection. That connection I'd always felt with Mrs Batty-Smith. Tell me this isn't it. What

I'd felt all along. And now the ghost, Barbara, is show-ing me the future. This is the other part of the lesson James wanted me to learn. That the spirits all want me to learn. This is me. *My* future and…

Wait. *Wait.* I stop with this thought. Hang on a minute. Maybe I'm not just babbling here. Maybe I'm right. Maybe this doesn't have to be my future. Maybe it doesn't have to be like this. After all, if this really is my future, it can only be this way—I can only end up this way—if I take certain actions. Do certain things.

Right?

I move forward and grab Barbara by the arm. 'This future? Is it changeable? Do my actions from now—in my real life, I mean—can I change this? All of this?'

Barbara doesn't say anything, but she looks away shiftily.

'I need to know!' I plead, practically begging now. I'd get down on my knees if I thought it would work. 'Tell me!' I bite my lip as I wait for an answer.

But she's silent.

I let go of her arm and try to make some sense out of my thoughts, grabbing at ideas, my thoughts whirl-ing. The future. My future. If it really is my future I *must* be able to change it. If I refuse to become like her, that creature, then I can't become her, can I? If I move away from, instead of towards her life, then I can't have her life. Like the newspaper, I think, step-ping on a piece on the floor. If I never lay down a sheet of newspaper on my carpet there will never be any there. Or the dishes in the sink. If I do the dishes every day they can never pile up like that. Or the cats. If I never buy a cat…

Damn, I remember Betsy and Shu-shu.

But they don't matter. I can cope with two cats. Two cats is normal. Normal people have two cats. Two I can deal with.

I *must* be right. I don't care if this is a dream, or what it is. If I make a promise to myself now that I won't take any of these steps, if I refuse to, then I won't be like that. Like her. I'll change. I will.

I won't have her life.

I'll change everything. I won't be that woman the couple was talking about in the coffee shop. I won't be the woman who pawned her equipment. I won't be the woman who lost her beautiful studio. I won't become bitter and twisted.

I won't.

I look up at Barbara again. 'I will change. I promise. From now. Right now. I understand what you're trying to tell me. You and James and Tony and Mrs Batty-Smith. I'll change. I'll be…open to opportunities and new people and love and relationships and happiness. And everything. I'll take chances. I'll…'

Y Y Y Y

'I'll…jump in the deep end.' I finish my sentence, as the loud *beep, beep, beep* of the clock radio on my bedside table wakes me up.

'I'll take chances. I'll jump in the deep end,' I repeat drowsily, not really knowing what I'm saying as I roll over and look at the time.

6:42.

Shit. *Shit!* 6:42? I sit straight up. I have to pick up Molly at seven, and it takes at least ten minutes to get there. The alarm must have been going for ages.

I swing my legs out of bed and start to get up, but something pushes me back. I frown as a voice comes into my head. For a moment, I struggle to hear it. Change. Something about change…

And then everything comes rushing back.

Mrs Batty-Smith.

Tony.

James.

Barbara.

My future self.

And finally my own words—*I will change. I promise. I'll take chances. I'll jump in the deep end.*

Now I really do stand up. 'I have to change,' I say out loud, to no one. I spot myself side-on in the mirror and turn around fully. 'I have to change,' I say. 'This is my last chance to change. My last chance to save myself.' I take a step forward. And with that one step, that one look, I put it all together. 'This is my last chance with Drew,' I whisper, standing there staring at my lopsided pyjamas and troll-like hair.

My last chance with Drew.

This scares me so much I get goosebumps.

Because now I know what all the fuss I've been making about Valentine's Day over the years has really been about. I know what the ghosts have been trying to make me see. What Justine has been trying to make me see. What Sally has been ever-so-quietly trying to point out. What Tania's been pounding into my brain on a weekly basis.

I want the kind of relationship I had with Mike. But I've been protecting myself from the pain of a relationship ending by stopping it from getting anywhere in the first place. By thinking that it's never going to happen again. By making myself believe that love and relationships will always be for other people. I've been stopping it from happening all by myself. No partner required.

And now I don't want to stop it from happening with Drew. What I mean is, I want it to happen.

Quite a lot.

Finally I understand what everyone's been going on about. What Dad's been trying to say. And Rachel. Everyone, in fact. Everyone close to me. Everyone involved in my life.

Especially Tony. I realise now that this is all Tony's doing, really—whizzing in and out of my life, in and out of my dreams, with his pink flashes. Without him I wouldn't be standing here, thinking what I'm thinking right now. Without him, I might have just let Drew pass me by. He's really gone all out for me. Cupid. Cupid has made a special case out of *me*. And if Cupid's pulled out all the stops, showing me my past and my future, it must be right.

Wait... Hang on...

Maybe.

I pause as the finer details of last night's escapade start to sift through my mind. I catch another glimpse of myself in the mirror. My eyes have turned into suspicious little slits.

Tony.

I remember the last ghost very clearly now. Barbara. The one who showed me myself. In my living room. With my cats. My future-to-be. I remember the story I've just finished reading—Dickens's *A Christmas Carol*. I remember Scrooge and how, by the end of the story, he comes to love Christmas. Hmm. I think I may have been the victim of Cupid scare tactics.

Scaremongering for singletons. That's what it is.

After all, do I really believe that if I don't date Drew I'm going to turn into that thing…that walking cat treat I saw last night? That I'm going to lose my business and that gorgeous little studio and that brilliant camera equipment and have people talk about me in cafés like I'm a loon?

No.

No, I do not.

I shake my head.

'Tony!' I say out loud. 'Wait till I get my hands…'

And then I see my expression in the mirror and start laughing. OK, so I might not believe all that Tony cooked up for my future last night, but you have to give it to the little man—he's good. He knows how to hit where it hurts, and whatever methods he's had to use to get me here, to this morning, to not hating Valentine's Day any more and opening myself up to something happening with Drew, he used them for the right reasons and they worked.

Because as I stare into the mirror now I know beyond any doubt that, dodgy old cat lady or no dodgy old cat lady, this really *is* a chance I have to take. In fact, I'm so sure of what I have to do there's no choice to make. I can't let Drew pass me by. I can't and I won't. This time I'm going to follow through. I'm going to grab onto my chance and hold on tight. Like the choice my dad's made by deciding to propose to Eileen. Like the choice that Rachel made in trusting Ryan. Like the chance Drew gave me with our fresh start…

Yes. This is it. I'm going to jump in the deep end— head-first and risking spinal injuries if I have to.

And I don't know if I'll be able to swim like a champion once I make the jump, but I *do* know that this is something I have to do.

OK. I'll just stop here. I look back at myself slowly in the mirror, my forehead now well-lined. Have I gone completely nuts? What am I talking about? Do I really think this is for real? That Cupid exists? That he's been hanging around giving my love life a helping hand?

How am I going to explain this one to Tania?

Time. 6:47 the clock reads. Holy crap! I *really* have to change now—my clothes, I mean.

I whip into action, wrenching open my wardrobe door and picking out the first likely items of clothing I find that are clean and ironed—a black cotton skirt and a short-sleeved red linen shirt. Then I race over to my dresser. I find a bra and start searching for my black undies.

I can't find them. I glance over at the clock again. 6:49. I hunt faster. Harder. No undies. So I stop.

Fuck the undies. They don't matter.

I have more important things to do this morning. And if I know guys like I think I know guys, my chances will probably be better without the undies anyway. Come to think of it, not being able to find my undies is probably Tony's doing as well.

Stop it, Liv!

6:50!

No time for undies—well, OK, I lie. I settle for some pink ones—it's a reasonably short skirt, after all!—and no time for a shower either. Instead, I grab my washcloth from its hook in my bathroom and birdbath over the sink. I scrub my face and my armpits, then run some water through my hair, brush it and pull it back into a ponytail. I slap on some tinted moisturiser, lipgloss and mascara, and hope that I look like I've made some kind of effort.

I race back into my room and pull my clothes on. 6:54.

Got to go. Got to go. If I don't go now, I won't have time.

Shoes. Shoes!

I find the pair I want at the bottom of my wardrobe and stumble out through my bedroom door as I try to put them on and walk at the same time.

Out in my clean, cat-free, newspaperless living room, I grab my handbag, keys, numerous camera bags (this morning I don't even notice their weight on my shoulders), locate my sunnies and run, run, *run* out through the front door and down to the car. I put my gear into the boot and jump in.

The car starts first time.

'I love you,' I tell it as I back out of the garage. The fact that it's never failed me before doesn't cross my mind. I knew that if it was ever not going to start it would be now, but it hasn't. It's started. I love it. Today I love everything. I screech out of the driveway and speed off in the direction of Molly's house.

6:56.

Every set of lights turns red as I approach, but I don't care. I can't stop smiling. My smile is back and this time I know it's here to stay. At one set of red lights the guy next to me stares when he sees my expression. I wave and toot the horn at him when I drive off. Not a loud, obnoxious toot, but a happy, 'see you around' toot.

I'm three quarters of the way there when I see the first one.

I pull over with another screech, grab my wallet from my bag and jump out of the car. Maybe this Valentine's Day it's OK to spend a bit of money, considering all the other times I've bypassed the day. Anyway, what's money for if you can't spend it on the people you care about?

'Um, three dozen, thanks,' I tell the woman.

'Sure, love. Do you want them all together?'

I nod. 'That would be great.'

She moves over to her small portable table and starts wrapping.

I dance from one foot to the other on the spot, watching her, wanting her to go faster, to wrap like the wind. With nothing else to do, I fish around in my wallet for the money. I only have a hundred-dollar bill. I pass it to her as she puts the last piece of sticky tape on.

'Oh, a hundred. I don't know if I can change that yet. I'll—'

'Don't worry about it.' I thrust the money at her. 'Keep the change. I have to go…' I race back over to the car, not giving a second thought to the lonely five cents left in my wallet.

7:03.

I'm late. Really, really late. I'll have to pick up Molly first—before my other…transaction.

I race the rest of the way to her house and find her waiting outside on the footpath.

'I was getting worried,' she says when she opens the car door. 'You're never late and it's—'

'Don't remind me.' I look at the time. 'Just get in. I've got to make one more stop.'

Molly gives me a look. 'At the hotel, I hope? We said we'd be there and making clicking noises by seven-thirty at the very latest.'

'We'll be there, we'll be there,' I say, doing a quick U-turn and heading back down the street.

'Um, you're going the wrong way.'

I ignore her and concentrate on turning the corner. Then I pull the car up again, grab my three dozen red roses from the back seat, hurl myself out of the car and sprint across the road.

'Hey!' Molly leans across the car and out of my open window. 'What are you…? Where are you…?'

I keep running. Right up to Drew's front door, where I press the buzzer. Then I press it again. Once more for luck. Then I start knocking.

Hard.

Finally I hear footsteps. And that's right about when I begin to panic. What am I going to do? What am I going to say? What if Drew tells me to go jump? Me and my mood swings.

The door creaks.

Shit. *Shit*.

I whip around and look back down the path, over to the car. Should I run? Molly gives me a questioning look.

Too late.

The door opens fully and I turn back slowly to see Drew wearing a pair of boxer shorts and a white T-shirt. His hair is standing on end; his eyes are bleary. He has looked better. But it doesn't matter.

Because suddenly, strangely, in the instant I turn around, I remember exactly why I'm here—to make up for lost time.

Drew looks at me, waiting.

And I… Well…

I take my chance. I jump in the deep end.

I step up onto the doorstep and kiss him.

And, guess what? He doesn't tell me, or my mood swings, to go jump. Instead, he kisses me back.

There's a loud wolf whistle from Molly. 'Way-hey!' I hear.

I hardly notice it I'm having such a good time. For a top-of-the-morning , seven a.m. kiss, Drew doesn't taste half bad either.

When I decide I'm done, I take a step down and hold out the roses. 'These are for you,' I say. Today, I don't care if flowers are lame. It's Valentine's Day. You're allowed to make lame gestures on Valentine's Day. In fact, it's practically compulsory.

Drew takes the huge bunch from me, staring, his mouth hanging slightly open. He looks down at the flowers, then back up at me.

'Look, I've got to go,' I tell him. 'I was supposed to be in a hotel room taking photos about—oh, five minutes ago.' I turn and start running off down the path. But I only get about halfway before I realise this just isn't going to work. Right. I swivel on the spot and run back.

Drew hasn't moved. He's still standing there, staring, his mouth hanging slightly open.

'Well?' I reach down and grab his hand. 'Are you coming or not?' I begin to pull him away from the doorstep when I remember something. 'Um, maybe you'd better get some clothes?'

'Clothes?' He glances away from me to look inside the house.

'Yep. Anything. Just make it quick. I'm late. Really, really late!'

He seems to wake up on hearing this. 'Clothes,' he repeats, and races inside, returning a minute later jumping into a pair of jeans and holding a cap and a shirt.

'Let's go!' I grab his hand again and we run towards the car without looking back.

Y Y Y Y

'Hey!' Molly's eyes are wide as I jump in the car and Drew slides into the back seat. 'You're the guy from the garbage wedding, right?'

Drew's eyes meet mine in the rear-vision mirror. 'Er, right,' he says, holding out his hand and introducing himself to Molly as I start the car and pull us out into the street.

At the end of the road I pause and turn to Molly, my mind blank. 'Where are we going again?'

'The Terraces!' She gives me a look. 'Are you all right? First you're late, and then you can't remember where we're supposed to be going. You do remember who you're photographing, don't you? Their names and everything?'

'Of course,' I lie, trying to look professional in front of Drew. Damn. What are their names? I hunt through my memory as I drive. It's not Kirsty and Shaun; I know that much. They're next in line today. It's... Oh, come on, Liv… 'Ina and Ben!' I say triumphantly. 'That's their names. Ina and Ben.'

'Well, that's a start. She's not usually like this.' Molly glances at Drew. 'It must be all the testosterone floating around that's putting her off.'

'Molly!' I give her a sideways glare and she grins.

The three of us chat as we go, every set of lights turning red to spite me, like before. Every so often Molly gives me funny little looks. I know what she's thinking—Who is this guy and what the hell are you going to do with him today? But the fact is I can't give her an answer. I don't know the answer. I've got no idea what I'm going to do with Drew today. I know what I'd like to do…

'Liv! In here!' Molly points to the car park I'm about to drive past and I pull in at the last second.

'Sorry.' I park the car and pop the boot, bolting out to flick through the couple's information sheet in case I've forgotten anything else about them.

'Liv!' Molly says, loading herself up with bags. 'We've got to *go!*' She leans her head in towards mine, using the boot as cover from Drew. 'What are you going to do with *him?*'

I shrug and keep reading. 'I'll think of something.' Ah, that's it. Wedding on terrace. Buffet breakfast. Large group photo with all the guests. Friends from high school. Molly tugs on my sleeve. 'OK!' I shove the papers in the camera bag she's holding out at me and take it from her. Drew's out of the car now and standing beside me. 'All ready?' I ask him, looking down to see he's missed a button on the shirt he's pulled on. Impulsively I reach over and do it up, only realising what I'm doing at the last second. Slowly, I pull my hands away and look up. 'Ah, um, sorry.'

There's that twinkle in his eye again. 'Don't be.'

'Feel like some breakfast?'

Drew nods. 'Sure.'

I turn to Molly. 'I've got an idea. Which room are they in?'

'Um, the bridesmaids are in 508 and the bride's in 509. They've decamped into 509 now, so they're all together.'

Perfect. Just like I thought.

The three of us head for the lifts and then, with a whirr, we're on floor five. I check the time. Seven-thirty-seven and we're here, with all limbs intact. Not bad. Not bad at all.

We hotfoot it down the carpeted corridor and I knock on door 509 and wait. Just as it begins to open I turn to Molly and grab her.

'*Ina,*' she says, pre-empting my question. 'Man, are you all right?'

I nod and glance over at Drew. 'Can you wait here?' I beg, and he nods just as the door opens and I switch into 'I'm a wedding photographer and I can deal with anything' mode. My infra-red photographer eyes locate the bride on the balcony, having her make-up done, her hair still in rollers.

Phew. Everything's going to be OK.

I move through the room, helloing the bridesmaids and the hairdressers and various other people that have been packed in the room as I head for the balcony and prepare myself to get down to business.

'Ina!' I say. The make-up artist stops make-upping. Ina looks up at me.

And my heart sinks as I realise Ina is not a happy bride.

'Don't you have any waterproof mascara?' I say to the make-up artist when I see the damage.

'It *is* waterproof mascara. But you have to let it set *some time*.' She gives me a 'this one's a mess' look over Ina's head.

Oh, God. 'One second.' I hold up a finger. I move a step inside and beckon a bridesmaid, who trots over willingly. 'Have you moved everything out of 508?' I ask her.

She nods. 'We don't have to be out till one, but we won't be around after the ceremony, so everything's in here.'

'Great.' I breathe a sigh of relief. 'Do you mind if I have the key? I might just store a few pieces of my…um…equipment in there.' I can barely look at the girl. This is sooooo not my usual professional self. But needs must, and my 'equipment' is waiting in the hall.

'Sure.' She runs over and grabs the swipe card off the dresser.

'I'll be right back,' I tell her, already most of the way to the door.

Molly gives me a 'are you ever going to tell me what's happening here?' shake of the head as I pass.

Drew's waiting patiently outside. His eyebrows raise as I open and close the door swiftly behind me, but I don't have time to say anything before he's pushed me back up against it and is kissing me. All I can think as our mouths meet is why did I let myself wait so long for this? Not that I can think of much. In fact, my knees actually start to weaken as his body moves in against mine—a very gentlemanly action, as I think otherwise I might slide to the floor.

When my brain kicks back in, and reminds me of the time, I hold up the swipe card between us. 'I got us a room,' I say, putting on my best husky voice.

Drew laughs. 'How forward of you. I'll have you know I'm not that kind of guy.' He pauses. 'No, come to think of it, I am. Exactly that kind of guy.'

I move to the door next to us and swipe away, opening it up after the little green light flashes. 'How about you order us some breakfast and I'll be back down from the ceremony as fast as I can?'

We only step inside the room for a minute and a half, but when I return to the corridor I find I have to twist my skirt a full ninety degrees to straighten it out again.

Let's just say I'm looking forward to that breakfast.

But first back to the wedding. Where, over the next half an hour, things go from bad to worse.

I photograph the bridesmaids having their hair and make-up done…and whispering about Ina.

I photograph the bridesmaids doing each other's zippers up and checking their lipstick…and comforting Ina.

I photograph the bridesmaids hanging out on the bed together, completely ready…and waiting for Ina.

We're all waiting for Ina now. Ina, the bride, who has locked herself in the bathroom.

With ten minutes to go before Ina's father is due to show up and escort her to the ceremony, Molly grabs me and steers me out onto the balcony, where no one else can hear us. 'She's really freaking out,' she says.

'Yes, I had noticed that, thanks.' My eyes swivel to the bathroom door. Everyone is looking at us.

'Can't you do something?' Molly says. 'You must've had ones like this before.'

I nod. I have. And I think it's time for The Talk. 'OK,' I say to Molly. 'She doesn't look like she's coming out of there under her own steam, so it's officially time. I'm going in.'

'In the bathroom? But she's not letting anyone in,' Molly says as I go back into the room and cross it, everyone's gaze following me.

I knock on the bathroom door. 'Ina? It's Liv. Can you let me in?'

'No. I don't want any pictures.'

'I won't bring the camera. I promise. I just want to talk to you for a moment.' To tell the truth, I hadn't even thought about taking the camera in. This isn't exactly what you'd call a Kodak moment.

There's a click as the door unlocks. I motion to Molly, and then at the bed. 'The dress,' I mouth at her. Molly grabs it and passes it to me, holding out the hanger. I take it from her, open the door, and let myself into the bathroom.

Inside, Ina looks remarkably composed for someone who's locked herself in the bathroom and won't come out fifteen minutes before her wedding ceremony.

I check out her face in the mirror's reflection. The hair's done. Great. And at least she's stopped crying. That solves the make-up problem. And what about...? Oh, good. I spot that she's wearing her fancy 'I'm the bride, so suddenly organ-displacing corsets are back in' underwear beneath the white cotton dressing gown.

I pause, watching her, thinking about The Talk. When I give it, I've usually had quite a bit of contact with the clients as a couple. I've seen how they work together and can decide whether or not I want to convince the bride to hoof it up the aisle because I've been able to gauge just how serious they are—whether it's more about the marriage than about the wedding. But Ina and Ben are a different case. Like I said, I've only met them once. I start to flounder.

But then I catch a glimpse of something out of the corner of my eye.

Something pink.

I look up, and lying on the towel rack above the shower is a hazy image—Tony. 'Love your work, babe,' he whispers, gives me a wink and the thumbs-up, then slowly disappears, Cheshire-cat-style, until all that's left to be seen is a white pink-edged carnation.

Right. OK.

Still, at least I know what I have to do now. 'Ina,' I say forcefully, and she turns away from the mirror and looks at me. 'Take a seat.' I push down the toilet lid. She sits down. Time to get down to basics. 'Ina, do you love him?' I ask her, and she nods, looking at the floor. 'Truly?'

This time, she looks me straight in the eye. 'Truly. I think… I think I'm just nervous.'

'Of course you are.' I nod. 'That's normal. But he's waiting for you, Ina. Ben's up there right now.' I think about Drew for a second, waiting for me in the next room.

Ina lifts her head and looks at the ceiling, as if somehow she'll be able to see him on the terrace.

'He's waiting for you to walk down the aisle. He can't wait to see you. I'm sure of it.'

Ina nods.

OK. This is it. Time for my trump card. 'He's waiting for you to walk down the aisle. Waiting to see you looking beautiful in your—' I take a quick glance at the dress, which is taking up half the bathroom '—stunning ivory silk gown. Waiting to marry you. You, Ina. He must really love you.'

Click.

I don't know why The Talk, in all its sappy glory, gets them, but it works every time.

She stands up. 'He's up there right now, isn't he?'

I nod.

'Waiting for me…' The thought sinks in. 'To marry me.'

'And I bet you can't wait either.'

She nods. 'I can't!'

'So—' I grab the dress now and unzip the back of it '—how about you frock up, and we'll add a touch more lipstick, and then your dad should be here.'

She nods, slips her robe off, and puts the dress on. I zip her up at the back, then I hunt around in the make-up bags on the counter until I find a pinkish lipstick. It's not the one the make-up artist used, but, really, is that the most important thing here? She applies, blots, and applies again. In the meantime I find some whitening eyedrops, and when she's done lipsticking squeeze a few into each of her eyes.

'Now look.' I take her arm and step back, making her step back with me. We look in the mirror together.

She looks gorgeous. Just like all my other brides. And then Ina smiles.

'Don't move a muscle,' I say, and open the door again. Molly's right outside. I nod at her. 'It's fine. Dad here?' She goes over and grabs him. 'Hi—Liv Hetherington, Ina's photographer,' I say, holding out my hand. He shakes it and points inside the bathroom, a worried look on his face. 'Everything's fine. Just fine,' I reassure him. 'Now, how about you come in here with Ina? I've just got to race upstairs and take a few photos of the groom. Let's say you follow me in ten minutes exactly?'

He looks at his watch.

'Good.' I let him in the bathroom and edge myself out, not wanting anyone else to think they can go in. 'I'll see you up there, Ina,' I call out as I close the door behind me.

'Let's go,' Molly says, holding the front door of the room open.

Ina sorted, I race out through the open door, dragging Molly with me. We pass rooms 508, 507 and 506 before I just can't help myself and turn back, leaving poor Molly to wait for the lift as I knock urgently on 508. When Drew appears I grab him and kiss him before he has a chance to get a word out. 'I'll be right back!' I say over my shoulder as I leave.

As the lift doors close, Molly looks at me in disbelief. 'I'd tell you guys to get a room, but I guess you already did.'

Y Y Y Y

The ceremony flows in the kind of way I wish all ceremonies flowed. And I swing into doing what I do best. I take pictures of the guests, of the family, of the groom and groomsmen. Photos of everything. Of anything. Whatever looks good. Whatever happens.

Molly follows me around, passing me things I need, swapping film, cameras and pointing out anything I might have missed.

When I'm finished, we stand halfway down the aisle as inconspicuously as you *can* stand halfway down the aisle with a ton of photographic equipment at a wedding ceremony. We wait for Ina.

And then she's there.

She and her father wait, in hiding, around a corner, while someone informs the string quartet that it's time.

'Well, she didn't call it off,' Molly whispers to me. She looks around. 'Think they've got enough gold cherubs?'

I glance around me now. She's right. There *are* a lot

of gold cherubs. I shrug. It doesn't matter. 'Whatever makes them happy,' I whisper back at Molly.

She gives me another strange look. 'What is *wrong* with you today?'

'What do you mean?'

'Well, you're not exactly your usual self. You don't even seem particularly cut up that it's Valentine's Day.'

I cough. 'Well, it's just that…I may have changed my views on some things a little. Including Valentine's Day.'

Molly pauses. 'You? You're telling me you, of all people, have changed your views on Valentine's Day? You? The defender of the single person, the—?'

'Shhh.' I put one finger up as people start turning their heads to look at us. She's getting a little loud.

'Sorry. It's just that—well, you…'

'I know. I know. Do you have to harp on about it?' I turn back and check on Ina. They should start at any moment now. When I finally get a clear glimpse of her expression I see that she looks happy. Calm. As if the bathroom incident never happened. And maybe it didn't. If I don't tell anyone what went on in there, maybe it's as if it never happened at all. I lean over to Molly, who's been silent since learning I'm no longer hating Valentine's Day. She's probably in shock. 'Want to learn something?' I whisper.

'What?' she whispers back.

'You know how you can tell if they're going to make it or not?'

'The couple?'

I nod.

'How?'

'By the look on her face when she turns down the aisle and sees him for the first time.'

Molly raises her eyebrows. I can tell she doesn't really believe me. 'How can you possibly—?' she starts, but then stops mid-sentence as the string quartet start up and Ina's father moves her forward, pausing at the top of the aisle. Because in that moment we both see it.

The real thing.

'I can probably take over from here.' Molly takes the camera from my hand as a waiter passes by, beginning to circle with a tray of hors d'oeuvres.

'Oh!' I emerge from my photographic daze.

'That is unless, of course, you'd rather stay here and help me pack up? I'd say we've got about an hour before we—'

But I'm already gone. And as the door to room 508 opens to let me inside, I'm almost shocked to find myself smiling that same smile that I saw upstairs only minutes ago. That smile that I'm always looking to photograph—not the one that's enhanced by teeth-whitening and hundred-dollar bottles of foundation, but the one that lifts up and is expelled involuntarily from right down inside, from some hidden organ they haven't discovered yet.

'You're just in time,' Drew says. 'I ordered you up some pancakes.'

I want to tell him that when I said breakfast it wasn't pancakes I was hungry for. But I can't. Because—well, this is Valentine's Day, and I'm a wedding photographer. Which means the clock's ticking.

And with the fifty-six and a half minutes I have left, I can think of much, much better things to do…

He's ambitious and cool and—
of course—extremely handsome…

THE YOUNGER MAN by Sarah Tucker

Divorce lawyer Hazel Chamberlayne is happy with
her life. Except for one thing—Hazel would like a
man. Could fellow lawyer Joe Ryan, a man ten years
younger than Hazel, be the one?

On sale January 2006.

Available wherever
trade paperbacks
are sold.

RED
DRESS
INK
™

www.RedDressInk.com

RDIST565

New from bestselling author Melissa Senate

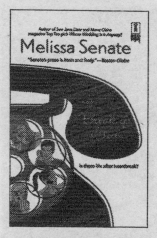

THE BREAKUP CLUB

In her most ambitious novel yet, Melissa Senate
explores life after heartbreak for four very
different yet equally memorable New Yorkers,
who have all been recently jilted and come
together to form The Breakup Club.

On sale January 2006.

Available wherever
trade paperbacks
are sold.

RED DRESS INK™

Visit us at www.reddressink.com

RDIMS558

Are you getting it at least twice a month?

Here's how: Try RED DRESS INK books on for size & receive two FREE gifts!

Bombshell
by Lynda Curnyn

As Seen on TV
by Sarah Mlynowski

YES! Send my two FREE books.
There's no risk and no purchase required—ever!

Please send me my two FREE tradesize paperback books and bill me just 99¢ for shipping and handling. I may keep the books and return the shipping statement marked "cancel." If I do not cancel, about a month later I will receive 2 additional books at the low price of just $11.00 each in the U.S. or $13.56 each in Canada, a savings of over 15% off the cover price (plus 50¢ shipping and handling per book*). I understand that accepting the two free books places me under no obligation ever to buy any books. I can always return a shipment and cancel at any time. Even if I never buy another book from Red Dress Ink, the free books are mine to keep forever.

160 HDN D367   360 HDN D37K

Name (PLEASE PRINT)		

Address		Apt. #

City	State/Prov.	Zip/Postal Code

Want to try another series? Call 1-800-873-8635
or order online at www.TryRDI.com/free.

In the U.S. mail to: 3010 Walden Ave., P.O. Box 1867, Buffalo, NY 14240-1867
In Canada mail to: P.O. Box 609, Fort Erie, ON L2A 5X3

*Terms and prices subject to change without notice. Sales tax applicable in N.Y.
**Canadian residents will be charged applicable provincial taxes and GST.

All orders subject to approval. Offer limited to one per household.
® and ™ are trademarks owned and used by the trademark owner and/or its licensee.

© 2004 Harlequin Enterprises Ltd.

RED DRESS INK™

RDI04MMP

New from the author of FAT CHANCE

Deborah Blumenthal
WHAT MEN WANT

On sale February 2006

When reporter Jenny George is sent to the Caribbean to write an exposé, she learns more about what men want and—more importantly—what she wants!

RED DRESS INK ™

*On sale wherever
trade paperbacks
are sold.*

www.RedDressInk.com

RDIDB569

New from the author of SLIGHTLY
SINGLE and SLIGHTLY SETTLED

Wendy Markham
SLIGHTLY ENGAGED

When Tracey learns that her live-in boyfriend, Jack,
has just inherited an heirloom diamond, she gets
ready for the long-awaited proposal. But just how
long she'll have to wait is the big question!

*Available wherever
paperbacks are sold.*

**RED
DRESS
INK**
™

www.RedDressInk.com

RDIWM564MMP